Mayhem
at the
Open

Also by Robert Brown

Simply Bob: Searching for the Essence
Personal Wisdom
My First Ten Days in Heaven (a novel)
Things I Learned from My Wife

The HST Model for Change
Lean Thinking 4.0
The People Side of Lean Thinking
Transparent Management
Earn Their Loyalty
Mistake-Proofing Leadership (with Rudy F. Williams, Ph.D.)
New Darwinian Laws Every Business Should Know (with Patrick Edmonds)

Invivo (a novel)
A Thousand Rounds of Golf
The Golfing Mind
Murder on the Tour (a novel)
The Way of Golf
The Golf Gods

Mayhem at the Open

Robert Brown

Denro Classics

Requests for permission to use or reproduce material from this
book should be addressed to: books@collwisdom.com

Former title: *Golf is Crazy*

This is a work of fiction. The thoughts and actions of the
characters are fictional.

Published by Denro Classics
1700 Mukilteo Speedway #201 PMB 1084
Mukilteo WA 98275
USA

ISBN-13: 978-1537558127
ISBN-10: 1537558129

To my golfing buddies, Jim Corbett and Danny Williams,
and the new friends I meet on the first tee.

Mayhem at the Open

This is a golf story that took place before the turn of the last century, when change was slower, before metal woods, before Tiger Woods, before some of the greats exited the game and before some of the more powerful antipsychotic drugs were invented.

Oscar Brown

The northeast corner of Fife is not like the rugged high cliffs of the Scottish west coast, but is mostly gently rolling farmland wandering haphazardly into the sea. Layered rocks exposed by centuries of storms rise to greet gray waves that surge in endless rows toward shore.

A blanket of clouds hung in tatters as young Oscar Brown walked along the shoreline footpath, a narrow strip of packed dirt hugging the slope between shore rocks and farm fields. He was distracted by two gulls squawking over a dead herring that bobbed in the gentle swell. Their shrill cries invited a dozen more gulls. The largest one, unblemished white with a patch of red on his yellow beak, swooped down, snatched the herring and flew toward the open sea, chased by a shrieking string of also-rans.

Oscar's wind-chapped cheeks were used to the spring chill, so too his small and calloused hands. A sweater was all he needed, but he wore a coat to conceal the revolver he had taken from his father's cabinet that morning. The thick wool absorbed the sea breeze as he abandoned the path to scramble among the rocks.

His father went to Glasgow searching for tractor parts

made scarce by preparations against the mounting threat of Hitler's Third Reich. Ordinarily, Oscar would be at work in the fields, already ploughed in long rows for an early planting of turnips and carrots. This afternoon he headed toward the Sea Bird Tavern in Cellardyke, a three-mile walk from his father's farm. He enjoyed the walk along the braes, especially at low tide when he could wander far out on the rocks looking for treasures from long forgotten shipwrecks. Since leaving school, much of Oscar's free time he spent alone. He preferred the solitary tasks of feeding the pigs and lifting the heavy rocks needed for repairing the boundary walls. Girls weren't an interest, always giggling and acting silly. The few near his age considered him small and immature, and strange, with dark eyes that made them shiver.

Oscar climbed back to the path that ran past the Anstruther Golf Course and stopped to observe the old men in white shirts, woollen vests and tweed jackets. He was angry that they wasted so much time playing such a worthless game. "Golf is daft," he would mock the boys that caddied, "hit a wee ball and chase after it." Oscar watched Mr. Mayglothling, the retired newsagent from Crail. The frantic man wiggled his large bottom from side to side like a walrus wobbling up the beach and swung violently three times before the last swing bounced the ball thirty feet along the ground. Red faced, he threw down his club and swung his fist in a wild roundhouse at the sky. He screamed for his caddie to follow as he stomped after the ball. Oscar turned away disgusted with the men. He had no patience for nonsense. Like his stern Calvinistic father, he demanded an unwavering dedication to do things that needed to be done, do them right away, and do them well. Life required hard work and allowed no time for foolishness.

Oscar's face lit up with a boyish grin, convinced he would perform his duty well.

After he reached Anstruther harbor, he sat on the stone wharf to review his plan. He had to make sure to do his task right. His father would still be gone tomorrow giving him another chance if it couldn't be perfect today. Both Nigel and his brother John had to be in the Sea Bird. Martin didn't matter. If Alan was there or any women, he wouldn't do it.

Near the harbor mouth, the open deck lobster boat Gallant Lady gunned her engine to make the starboard turn to head out to sea. At that moment, the sun burst through the clouds and turned the gray water a brilliant blue. Oscar's smile grew at this sign from God that his was a right and proper mission. He took a deep breath. His smile faded and his eyes darkened as he stood to walk the last half mile. He felt no joy in what he had to do, only the satisfaction of completing what should have been done already. He walked proud of how grown up and responsible his duty and how clearly he knew what was right.

The town boundary lay only a quarter mile away on East Shore Street, a dilapidated row of vacant storefronts. Cellardyke was an old fishing village dating from the Middle Ages, long past its glory days of clipper ships and the legendary tea races from India to London. In the eighteenth century, the sons of Cellardyke and neighboring Anstruther sailed the seas, from China to Australia, from Rio de Janeiro to San Francisco. The timid or perhaps wiser stayed closer to home, piloting the fishing boats into the rough waters of the North Sea to harvest herring and cod. But those days are as long gone as the herring. Now Cellardyke was for fishermen too old for anything but memories. Some money could be had in bottom fishing from inboard dories or for those with a piece of land to grow root crops and raise pigs and sheep. It was a quiet, peaceful place, where time had slept for a hundred years.

The town of Anstruther ends at Shore Street and the village of Cellardyke begins at James Street, marked by the eastward jog at Tollbooth Wynd. Exactly halfway between Tollbooth Wynd and Cellardyke Harbor, on the sea side of the street, sat the Sea Bird Tavern. The buildings on this street had been built in the glory years between 1705 and 1790 and except for the odd ones that had been torn down, they made a quarter mile long wandering wall of stone two and three stories high on both sides of the narrow road. Each house was painted white, the only differences being the degree of fading and the color of the door and window trim. A few doors had been lovingly lacquered deep browns or reds while most were left to chip and peel in silent, dust covered indignation.

Amongst these dwellings, the Sea Bird Tavern distinguished itself with fresh white paint and a pair of two-foot wide shiny black stripes running up the wall, one on each end. In the middle of the eye-jarring lime green door hung a brass knocker of a scowling Oriental face, a gift brought back for the third owner of the tavern fifty years earlier by a homesick sailor. Oscar paused for a moment staring at the knocker, took another deep breath, opened the door, walked in, and surveyed the dimly lit room.

Directly in front of him at the tall wooden bar Martin sat with a pint talking to the barman. To Oscar's left two small wooden tables lined the rough stone wall. Nigel and his brother shared the table nearest the wall. All were near enough, Oscar thought. The room was less than twenty feet wide and only twenty-five feet deep.

"Is Margaret here, Mr. Grayson?" Oscar asked as he walked further into the room.

"No lad," Mr. Grayson answered, barely looking up. "She's oot with her mum the noo."

Good. No women and no Alan. He could do it right now. He reached under his coat and fingered the hidden gun. Mr. Grayson looked over at him. "Did you want to leave a message?"

Oscar hesitated. "No, that's all right," he answered, unsure if the question was a sign to continue or to stop. He watched as Mr. Grayson returned to his chat with Martin. The brothers had looked up when Oscar came in, but had returned to their ales. Oscar pulled out the revolver and aimed it at the center of Martin's back.

The explosion reverberated off the walls like claps of thunder. Martin died before he hit the floor. Oscar pointed the gun at the brothers. Even before the echo of the first blast had died, he shot both of them in the chest. John spun around from the impact into a macabre dance with the wall, his face and arms smacked into the stone blocks before he fell in a heap under the table. Nigel fell straight back off the stool into the wall, then slid down along a cushion of blood to finish sitting upright on the floor, staring at his executioner.

Nigel watched wordlessly as Oscar brought up the gun once more and pointed it between his eyes. He probably could see straight down the barrel and the bullets waiting in the cylinder and the three dark empty spaces where bullets had been. Then Oscar pulled the trigger and blew apart his friend's head.

"Mr. Grayson," Oscar shouted in the eerie silence that followed.

The barman had ducked behind the bar, trapped without an exit or hope of escaping the shooting. He was on his knees. At Oscar's call, he mumbled a quick prayer and stood up to meet his fate.

"Mr. Grayson," Oscar continued. "I'd like a pint and would you be kind enough to cook us a wee banger? I know I'm under age, but do us a favor for the pint. I have the money." Oscar pulled a purse out of his pocket and counted out the coins. Grayson stared at the bodies, the blood on his walls, and the slow growing red stream winding its way toward the door. His eyes bulged when he saw Nigel and he gagged at what was left of the young fisherman's head.

"Mr. Grayson, my pint, please," Oscar insisted.

The voice brought Mr. Grayson's attention back. "Are you going to shoot me?" he asked.

"Why would I shoot you?" Oscar answered, confused by the question. Mr. Grayson composed himself enough to stop asking questions. "I'll draw you a pint," he said.

Mrs. McHendry had just finished hanging her washing on the Cellardyke laundry lines strung along the lower level of the harbor, quick at her task for there was no one there to gossip with. As she walked up the stone pathway back to her house, she heard the rare crack of gunshots. She rushed toward the excitement, her progress hampered by having to carry two wicker laundry baskets. Likely some sort of celebration. Maybe someone won the Derby or more likely Janice has finally delivered her baby to that fool Thompson and he's shooting into the sky outside the pub. She waddled up the cobblestone road as fast as her short fat legs would go.

There was no one outside the Sea Bird. She poked her head into the dim light of the pub. Oscar sat on a stool. Mr.

Grayson stood at the grill where, by the sound of it, he was frying a sausage. She turned to leave when her foot caught on a sticky substance. Her eyes followed the liquid's path from her feet to a heap of clothes at the foot of Oscar's stool. She narrowed her eyes to see better in the dim light. The crumpled pile oozed the blood that pooled at her feet.

Reflexively, she moved forward, tripped, and fell to her hands and knees, landing level with what remained of Nigel's face. She leapt like a scared cat, legs and arms straight out, screamed and staggered into the street, one hand over her mouth while the other reached forward and upward as if hanging onto an invisible trolley strap.

Constable Owens heard the echoing screams from two blocks away. He was in his third week of regular duty after two weeks training in Leven. He wanted to join His Majesty's forces like his brothers, but poor knees and deafness in his left ear ended his chances. Responding with the exuberance of a man eager to please, he dashed up the street. Like desperate lovers after months apart, Mrs. McHendry ran east as Constable Owens ran west until they met in clawing embrace in front of Mrs. Grovener's flat. "Murder, murder," she wailed when they met, "murder, murder, murder."

Mrs. Grovener and her feisty terrier Toby stuck their heads out the second story window in unison at the commotion below. "What's all this aboot?" she cried, the dog adding barks to the din. "Calm down, Missus," Constable Owens pleaded to the mad woman still tearing at his tunic. "Calm down and tell me what's happened."

"Two, five, ten dead and him calmly drinkin," she panted.

"Now, Missus." Officer Owens reached into his pocket for a notebook, took it out and licked the tip of his pencil.

"Slow down so I can understand what you're sayin."

"Go," she said, running behind him and pushing at his back. "Go. They're all dead."

"What is it, Mary?" Mrs. Grovener shouted down from her window.

"Murder. Murder," Mrs. McHendry screamed again as if reliving the memory. "Murder at the Sea Bird."

"Please, Missus, what exactly did you see?" Constable Owens asked again, his pencil at the ready.

"Willie Brown's boy drinking at the bar, like it was a never-you-mind and lying on the floor. Ohh," Mrs. McHendry held her head in her hands. "The poor man lying dead as any mackerel and lookin' like the devil had claimed him." Her voice rose into a blood curdling howl and she covered her face with her apron.

The young constable called up to Mrs. Grovener to take mind of Mrs. McHendry and went off to investigate. He strode the fifty yards to the Tavern, confident in his ability to respond to any crisis. As he reached the door, he hesitated. He had never actually seen a dead body. And though the chances were small of one lying on the other side of the door...

The inscrutable oriental face on the door mocked his hesitation. "Ach," he said out loud, shaking his head. "There's been nae murders in this wee town for over a hundred years." In that same span, he knew, there had been enough pints drawn in this one pub to float every ship of the British fleet and to drown every seaman. Someone fell down dead drunk and bumped his thick head. Mrs. McHendry has read one too many three-penny novels. He pushed past the eyes of the Chinaman.

"Morning, Mr. Grayson, what have we here?" he asked the

man behind the bar before his eyes adjusted to the smoky haze.

Grayson didn't answer, but motioned with his eyes and nods of his head to where Oscar had placed the revolver on the bar.

"Morning, Mr. Owens," Oscar said, turning to look at the young policeman. Then, responding to the uniform, he added guiltily, "I'm only having a wee pint. Only one."

Owens turned toward the lump of clothes on the floor under Oscar's stool.

"What's all this then?" he asked taking a step toward the body.

"He's dead. I shot him," Oscar told him. "And then I shot those two over there." He pointed to the dead brothers.

Owens turned and stared at the faceless body, moving toward it to make a closer examination, innocent as a lamb to slaughter. Nigel's coat. His hat. That bloody mass had once been Nigel's face. The poor constable's stomach heaved twice before he threw up over his dead friend's chest and legs, his vomit mixing with the trickle of blood that had joined the other stream and crept toward the door.

Oscar watched the scene unfold and took the opportunity to gulp down the rest of his pint before the policeman could take it away from him.

Constable Owens tottered back to the bar taking deep breaths to control his stomach. "A little water if you please, Mr. Grayson." He sipped at the water until the color return to his face. He looked at Mr. Grayson, all pretence of being in charge having evaporated, "What happened?"

Mr. Grayson, eyes again motioning toward the pistol, didn't answer, but Oscar did. "I told you. I shot them. Didn't I, Mr. Grayson? I shot them wae this." Oscar held up the gun.

"Heavens," said the policeman glancing at Mr. Grayson before looking back at Oscar. "Let me have the gun, lad, while I figure out what to do."

"Aye," Oscar said, and gave him the gun.

"Mr. Grayson, please be kind enough to run down to the call box and inform the station of the situation here."

Alone with Oscar, Constable Owens did his duty. First, he had to put the suspect in custody. "Oscar, you stay put on that stool," he told him.

"Yessir," came the immediate reply.

Then, the evidence must be inspected. He knelt by Oscar's stool to look at the body. Martin, a poor fisherman, as quiet and peaceful in death as he had been in life. Owens stood up and walked toward the front of the pub. Knowing Nigel was dead, he avoided looking at him except to note with a look of dismay where he had vomited on the man's pants. The other body faced the wall and had to be turned over to be examined. He gingerly pulled at the man's jacket until the body flopped over. Dead eyes stared at the policeman. Blood covered the body and the wall and now his hands.

Owens turned to catch Oscar pouring himself another pint from behind the bar. "Sit!" Oscar scrambled back to the stool.

"You shot these men?"

"Yes sir."

The constable had to secure the gun. Tiptoeing past Martin's body, he placed the gun on the bottom shelf of the bar. He left it there but stood next to it until help arrived.

As he waited, another problem presented itself to the young constable. Mrs. McHendry had evidently convinced Mrs. Grovener to come look. She brought her dog and every neighbor within earshot to peer into the dark pub. As the curious crowded around the door, Toby struggled from her arms and ran in to sniff the bodies.

"Now, now, the lot of you, out." Constable Owens moved to push them away when he thought better of it. He had to stay behind the bar to protect the gun. The crowd didn't move back, but pressed closer, the latecomers at the back straining to see and pushing those at the front much nearer than they wanted to be. The terrier had a field day rushing from one pool of blood to the next, sticking his nose into all manner of gore.

Oscar sat oblivious to it all. He wished he could go home and lie down; the first two pints of his life had gone to his head and made his eyes lose focus and his stomach queasy. The constable again told the crowd to step away. Oscar turned, visibly upset and yelled at them to be quiet. The group hushed and fell back, bumping into Sergeant Marsh who had been squeezing his way past the gawkers. "Make way. Make way, please. Stand back, there's nothing tae see," he kept repeating as he moved through the crowd. Mrs. Grovener dashed in to snatch her dog with one hand and cross herself with the other before running out again.

Sergeant Marsh was fifty years old with twenty-two years on the force and distinguished service in the Great War before that. He ordered the bobby who had accompanied him to take charge of the spectators, push them far out to the street, then close the door to await the doctor. The sergeant looked around and knew that an undertaker and a clean up squad were more needed than the doctor. Another look suggested that Owens would be better off returning to the station. The young constable left his post, tripping over Martin's body in his haste to escape.

The tall sergeant in his crisp black uniform leaned on the

bar to question Oscar, learning little more than the constable. Yes, Oscar admitted, I shot them. I shot them because I had to; they wanted to die and hadn't died yet. This went round and round until the sergeant realized that he and the boy were not speaking the same language.

"Son, you'll have to come down to the station with me."

"But why?" Oscar protested. He was sure the pint would be forgiven. His dad would tan his hide if he got in trouble with the police.

"Three men have died at your hand. In spite of your youth, you have committed a horrendous crime."

"I only did what was right." Now Oscar was fed up. He did his duty and then he stayed put. His head was spinning and he just wanted to go home.

"We'll straighten this out at the station lad. Come wae me." Sergeant Marsh took Oscar by the arm.

At that point, the boy's uninitiated stomach rebelled against the beer. Oscar threw up over the sergeant, the bar, the floor, and much of poor Martin.

The sergeant sighed. He had come from Glasgow to the village to get away from the memory of the gas and the trenches, from the crime of the declining city, to help a few hard working men home after a pint too many and to play a game or two of links golf. Now three men were dead and a boy too young to own a razor destined to spend the rest of his days under lock and key. "Laddie, we have tae go."

Two days later, in an early morning rain, three caskets lined up next to three graves scattered on a small hill in the churchyard. The pastor stood in front of a thin ring of dark suited mourners preaching about how God weeps at human folly.

Nigel's casket was lowered into the grave by four of his friends as the black police van passed on its way to Carwell Psychopathic Hospital. As the van bounced on the narrow stone road, Oscar sat alone in the back on a wooden bench, still trying to fathom why he was in trouble. He had done his duty as well as he could.

*   *   *

The thick leather belt lashed across Oscar's bare back. Four pairs of hands held him flat on his stomach and pressed him hard against the bare metal springs of the bed frame.

"That's five. One more to go, maggot." The thickly muscled arm rose again to strike the boy. The final blow was especially cruel, landing where the last had broken the skin. Punishment was necessary. In a spurt of adolescent bravado, he had made fun of an attendant, evoking a laugh among the patients and even the staff. The lashing was for control and to define reality. Patients could not be frivolous. The staff made the rules, set expectations, evaluated progress, and determined who could return to the light and air upstairs and who stayed below.

With a final insulting shove, the attendants swaggered back to the office for a smoke and their postponed tea. Oscar, left alone, cried to himself. He was not yet old enough or strong enough to remain stoic like the others who watched from along the walls. They showed no sign of pain, and did not wince, even when they used electricity.

He was the youngest, the one they wouldn't leave alone. Oscar tried to survive by doing what they asked, but the beatings got worse. He pleaded and begged them to stop. Over and over he promised to be good but they didn't care and they didn't stop this time until the six had been laid on.

The attendants called him "Killerboy" and made up stories about how he murdered innocent men, shooting them in the back. Oscar tried to explain, sometimes yelling, sometimes in tears. No one listened.

Oscar pulled the thin, soiled mattress back on his bed. There were no sheets or pillow, only his worn army blanket. Like he had a hundred times before, Oscar knelt next to his bed for his prayers, then curled up on the bed with the blanket pulled around his shoulders and cried himself to sleep. His entire world was his bed, the corner farthest from the staff office, and sitting alone at the long wooden table after everyone else had eaten. This is how it was for twenty years at the Carwell Psychopathic Hospital, through the entire Second World War, the death of a king, the Coronation of the Queen, a handful of Prime Ministers, and man's first flight into space. It got worse for short periods whenever new attendants needed to prove themselves.

On the upper floors of the hospital, sunlight, fresh breezes and a few primitive medicines offered the appearance of therapy, enough for seven or eight lucky souls to walk out the front door each year. Ward Nine housed criminals, those society ignored, and families forgot. It was below ground, a shallow hell with barred windows thick with dirt admitting little light and no sounds from the outside. Up a steep flight of worn stone steps was the door to civilization, a massive steel dam protecting polite society from the maniacal rages of insanity.

Eight ward attendants, some sicker than their charges, ruled this buried kingdom of five dozen subjects. A doctor descended once a week to check on conditions, always found them deplorable, and retreated up the stairs as quickly as he could. The uncrowned King was the Chief Day Attendant, his nemesis the Night Chief. Occasionally they waged war, when one of the Chiefs got bored, drunk, or mad at the other. Junior attendants, the sadistic pretenders to the throne, tormented the patients just for fun. The caretakers and inmates of Ward Nine created a society, the former by force, the later by natural selection. Neither kindly attendants nor weak patients lasted long. This was Oscar's world until Barry entered his life.

Oscar first connected with Barry in the treatment room. Every Tuesday and Friday, Oscar was wrapped head to toe like a mummy in white sheets soaked in ice-cold water laying on a raised platform of wood slates the height of a table. He was third in a row of four others wrapped the same way. An attendant leaned against the dirty gray wall of the tiny subterranean treatment room, observing the chilled bodies, waiting for his shift to be over. All of them prayed to escape upstairs to breathe fresh air, far away from this fetid atmosphere, heavy as wet wool, reeking of urine and vomit and fear.

Patients in treatment were not allowed to talk and could not move, remaining in frigid wraps for two hours. Their joints stiffen, nerves become numb and muscles cramped. The treatment, thought to purge them of the demons that haunted their minds, made them docile and was another way to teach them the difference between sane and insane.

On that day in the treatment room, on Oscar's left was Barry Hardon, the wise old man of Ward Nine. At the worst time of the treatment, after the cold had become a sharp pain and tremors shook the body, but before numbness offered relief, Barry caught Oscar's eye and winked. Barry was a stooped, small boned man of seventy with fire in his pale blue eyes and a wild thatch of pure white hair and a wilder pair of white eyebrows, sticking askew like wind blown corn stalks. He ruled over the sixty inmates being wise in the ways of handling despots, gentle when grown men were broken and lost; and with fellow patient Harvey Applebloom as his friend; six-foot six and two hundred sixty pounds of muscle and mayhem with the simple mind of a ten year old. Harvey was an imposing reality even the most sadistic guards had to accept. Barry entertained a lot of thoughts, Harvey not a one; an effective combination.

Barry was what Oscar wanted to be, dedicated to an honorable and true life. He was born in the late nineteenth century in the small harbor town of Montrose, the last of seven children. His mother supported the family by selling fish in the market while his father travelled about the country as an itinerant preacher and one of the then new breed of competing golf professionals. In most towns, his father was welcomed. But only for the first two or three days, then his strange ideas made people uneasy. Rarely did he make any money, preaching or golfing. In matches arranged by club professionals or wealthy businessmen, his drive to succeed pushed him to compete against players of the highest calibre; the likes of Horace Hutchinson, Hugh Kirkaldy and James Braid. More often than not, he lost. After a while, he had to put up his own money and sometimes couldn't pay. Matches dwindled then ceased altogether. Few towns would accept more than once his climbing their pulpit or even standing on a box in a corner of the town square. Over long and arduous years, trekking narrow dirt paths to more and more remote villages, from the windy

East Coast, to high into the rugged mountains, even to the stormy outer islands, Barry's father searched for matches to play and to tell others the message from the spirits.

Often he would be on the road for months at a time, alone with thoughts too numerous to fit into his head. Sometimes the ideas exploded and he would tremble, raise his hands to the sky and shout God's new laws into the wind. Most often, his wisdom carried into peaceful glens and deep forests, heard only by startled rabbits and disinterested deer that hardly raised their heads.

After too many villages and towns to count, he found peace in the solitude away from the people and the game that had broken his heart. Alone he could mull over the messages from the voices and begin to understand how golf made his hands shake and his heart grow weak. His ideas were precious and fragile, too wonderful for the unworthy likes of him. Someone innocent of men's sins was needed to carry on what he had begun. In mid stride one day he turned around and headed home.

Four weeks later, Barry Harden left the little stone cottage of his boyhood to follow his father to the far north, his mother wailing and crying on the doorstep, pleading with her boy not to go. His father pulled on his arm, promising him the wisdom of the ages. Barry returned at nineteen, a full year after his father had drowned in the Irish Sea. He was a man when he came back, strong spirited like his father and even more dedicated to seek the answer to the universal questions. But that was before.

In the times they were not wrapped in icy sheets and had to be silent, Oscar and Harvey spent much of the day sitting at Barry's feet listening to his stories. For long months, Barry conducted a Socratic dialogue, egging Oscar on with question after question. "How do you define the ultimate goal," he would ask, and "what is adversity?" No matter what Oscar answered, Barry had more questions. Harvey would patiently listen, sitting quietly, watching himself flex his muscles, smiling when he didn't have to answer any of the questions. One day, the prize pupil found the courage to ask a question of the master.

"Well then, Barry Hardon, just what is the meaning of life then? You have me thinking in circles."

"Aye, laddie. That's the meaning I was after. The circle."

"What?"

"The circle. That, the open sky, and all things natural. The everlasting balance between heaven and hell. That is what I mean. Triumph, tragedy, human nature and the wrath of God. That is all in the meaning too."

"How, Barry? How do I understand it? You haven't told me." The youth was an empty vessel, seeking to be filled with the wisdom of the master, or perhaps just wishing to stop the daily headache caused by Barry's ceaseless mental meanderings.

"The circle. The circle, lad, the simple hole that started it all in God's earth by the shepherds long ago and now is a steel cup thrust deep in the hallowed ground. That circle is our goal to find, to find, to fill, and to confront over and over again like the sorrows that begin at birth. We seek until we have become a circle, of life and death and our final hole in God's sweet earth and the circle is finished."

"I don't understand."

"Golf," Barry said.

"Golf?" Oohhhh, he moaned in his head. That could not be. No silly game, especially golf, could be important, certainly not as important as Sunday worship, listening to the voices, and finding salvation for all men.

"Aye, golf," Barry continued, holding out his thin, upturned arm. "An entire earth we can hold in our hand as a pure white orb. With God's gifts, we move it about. It is the search for the circle of harmony over God's green pastures. The application of wisdom, the effort of our bodies, the torment of our souls, the acceptance of our frailty and the exaltation of victory over the devil. That is the meaning of life. All of it in golf."

How could he say such a thing, Oscar wondered. Golf is such a silly game, a daft game, not good for anything except to waste good farmland, effort and time.

"Golf," Barry insisted, standing more erect and stronger than he had in years. His eyes took fire and he shouted as his father did to an assembled throng or alone into the wind from a remote hilltop. "It portrays the harmony of torment and joy, suffering and salvation, the mind and the body, the heart and the soul." He bowed his head, close to tears. "Oscar," he said, almost in a whisper, his eyes pleading for the young man to understand, "golf is a journey to hell and a taste of paradise."

Daily, Oscar sat at Barry's feet in rapt attention. He must understand this meaning of golf and what Barry said, "a beauty equal to anything found in heaven." At first, in spite of forcing his eyes tightly closed and banging his fists against his head, he could see only the scruffy nine-hole course in Anstruther and the silly men dressed in their silly clothes, taking silly swings playing a silly game. No matter what Barry told him about the spirit of golf and the magical symbiosis of human nature and God fostered by walking the links, golf was just a game, an unproductive waste of time. Righting terrible wrongs, as he did at the pub, and working hard on the land to produce nature's bounty were the ways to meaning and to honor God and man. Occasionally, Oscar had his ears boxed when he failed to pay attention to his mentor. "One day," Barry would tell him, "you mark my words, what we discuss today will bring important changes. You must be ready when called. Ready to act and do what yer told and do what's the right thing to do. Listen well, my boy."

Slowly, as time passed and he asked many questions, Oscar began to understand. "The grip," Barry would say, "is like touching a beam of light from a star. The knowledge of the universe is in the grip." He made Oscar practice the grip on his thin forearm since they were not allowed to have anything resembling a club, not even a cut down broomstick. "The swing is as powerful as the atom and as elusive as the path of a fluttering butterfly. The flight of the ball is as real and as constant as the laws of physics."

During one lesson on the swing, Oscar asked Barry a question that had been on his mind from the beginning, how he had lost the little finger on his right hand.

"I cut it off," Barry told him. "After I saw them from my window." Barry began another story. "The wee lad cried and his mum smacked him aboot. He had been playing in the puddles, not hurting a soul when she comes along and yanks him by the arm. I should have stopped her, but I didna. I was sick and couldn't get out the bed, but that was no excuse. After they left, I realized how selfish I had been. I had tae be punished. So I forced myself up, crawled into the kitchen, got down the cleaver and cut off my little finger. I kept it in a matchbox as a reminder tae do my duty and since then I have, though I've long ago lost the box and the finger. But," Barry winked, "I'm no daft. Ye ken I cut off the finger on my right hand?

Oscar nodded.

"The two left fingers are needed to pull the club down from the top of the backswing. Ye have tae do the right thing and sometimes accept the penalty for not doing so, but you've not got to be stupid about it."

"And the meaning of it all," Barry said one day while his two disciples sat on the floor in front of him, "is found in the heart of the player. It is he who adds irrefutably to the upward march of human endeavour with his every stroke. Honest, forthright, sloppy, uncaring. What is in the heart goes into the stroke, and every stroke, missing not a one, is counted on the card. Anyone who plays the game plays for us all, a symbol of man's triumph over himself and the devil. The man who cheats at golf cheats us all and the devil claims another soul. And the ignorant golfer must stand aside like the parting of the seas and let the player through who knows the importance to try, to succeed, to prevail. These gentle souls are the Keepers of the Game."

Oscar drank in everything that Barry said, encouraging the old man with how much he was learning and surprising his master with his own ideas. They talked endlessly, taking time out every once in a while when Harvey got bored and stood to mimic the full swing, going "Whoosh" at impact and putting his hand up to shade his eyes, pretending to watch the ball fly out of sight. Barry had become Oscar's guide, the man he would follow all his life. Barry knew what was right.

One day a new doctor interrupted their talk with a new tray of needles and new vials of medicine.

Ward Nine rarely had any family visitors. In the prior year, it had none. Chemical companies found it expedient to use the ward as a final test for medicines before administered to the patients upstairs. They came down the steps a lot. A handful of patients suffered grand mal seizures, a few became blind, and others developed odd assortments of tics, twitches and habitual pacing. A few died early on and a few got crazier with the medicine, but it was hard to find fault with those results since no one official complained.

Barry was one of the early failures. In the morning he was fine, in the afternoon they took him out on a stretcher never to come back. Harvey was one who got violent and hurt his caretakers before being subdued. It took a straitjacket and five men over an hour to get him under control. Then he was gone.

Oscar was a lucky one. It took a few years and a few bad times, but after many injections, they moved him upstairs onto a nicer locked ward, a place where the patients had visitors. He did not, but he could see the sky and trees and the broad expanse of lawn through the large screened windows. After they gave him different medicine later on, he moved again and they let him walk outside for the first time in thirty-five years. He liked taking his shoes off to feel the grass and to think about golf.

Every day they gave him medicine. Once a week a doctor came to talk with him. The doctor asked him about the killing at the pub. Oscar said he was sorry. He said he didn't know it was bad and that he didn't know that the men didn't want to die. They just said that, the doctor told him. They were unhappy about the village football team losing again.

"You're an intelligent man, Oscar," the doctor told him. "We've given you tests and you have done well. But you sometimes don't see things the same way most others do, and you have to remember the voices in your head are just your imagination. You listened to them years ago, and that was wrong. Don't listen to them, Mr. Brown, or you might cause a lot of trouble. And," he added, "don't stop taking your medicine." The doctor was kind and well meaning. Oscar told the doctor he understood, but the doctor didn't know Barry. Oscar knew Barry would never tell him to do anything wrong. Oscar also told the doctor that the medicine made him feel better which it did. He didn't worry about being responsible when he took the shots and the pills. They made him feel happy.

Early in the morning of Oscar's fiftieth birthday, Mrs. Donaldson, in her starched white head nurse's uniform, strode down the walkway between the two rows of beds straight for his. Gently, she shook his shoulder until he woke. "Good morning, Mr. Brown," she said. "Today is your birthday and today you're going home."

The rest of the morning he stuffed his few belongings in the small cardboard case they gave him, said goodbye to a few of the other patients, and was driven in the hospital car to the railway station. Oscar had paused at the front door thinking about the last thing Barry told him. "I will be with ye laddie. Have nae fear." All he had in his pocket was two pounds sixpence and a ticket to St. Andrews. He was to stay in a house next to the community hospital until the doctors decided he could live on his own. He needed to have his medicine every day and his family didn't want him back. To pay his room and board, the head of the house had arranged for Oscar to start work as a third class bag carrier at the St. Andrews golf courses. It was a good job for him, one that would not demand more than carrying a golf bag and learning the land, something he could do well. Oscar knew Barry approved and he silently vowed to be perfect at it.

Everyday, for more than twenty years; in the cold, in the rain, even during the blizzard of '64 that closed the roads and all the shops for an entire week, Oscar made his way to the caddie hut at dawn and sat waiting to carry a bag. For the first five months, no one asked for him and the caddie master did not send him out. Slowly, sporadically, he would carry for a tourist when everyone else had gone out. Each time he carried, he earned the standard ten shillings paid for a bag carrier, third class. Once he began making money, he mailed no less than twenty shillings a week home to the farm. He never travelled the ten miles to visit his family because they never invited him.

Oscar spent his nights in a room behind the furniture shop on South Street. Each Thursday morning he would walk to the hospital outpatient clinic for a new supply of his medicine. He had to take three pills a day to stop his mind from thinking too much. Varieties of major tranquillizers called phenothiazines were tried over the years. Every once in a while, Oscar did something bad, and spent time in jail or in the regional council hospital. After almost thirty years of working as a caddie, Oscar was one of the old men of St. Andrews, too ancient to carry a bag any more so he spent his days wandering the street, sometimes silent, sometimes shouting at the top of his lungs, sometimes to be avoided, sometimes to be humoured. It all depended on how regularly he had been taking his medicine.

1

Kevin Turner gazed out the window of the plane as it made its low approach to Glasgow International Airport. Green hills and low granite mountains shared the landscape with cozy farms criss-crossed by ancient stone walls. Clear, ice-cold streams thick with leaping trout splashed down the rocky slopes toward the River Clyde and the famous dockyards that lined its banks. Kevin couldn't see any of this. Rain pelted so hard against the window it was like looking through the glass door of a washing machine.

He had played golf in Britain before, during his year on the European Tour. But never in Scotland and never on the Old Course at St. Andrews. With hard work and a little luck, he would play the famous course in the Open, the biggest championship of all. The British national championship dated from 1860 and was the most important tournament to golfers around the world and without question attracted the premier international list of competitors.

Kevin closed his eyes as the plane taxied to the terminal. He must stay calm for the next two weeks. There was a long way to go before he competed in the championship itself. He still had to qualify at Carnoustie to earn one of the few spots remaining in the main tournament. Miss that and his trip was a bust. Bigger names than his had come over and failed to make it past the first step. Ben Crenshaw, twice winner of the Masters, was one of them a few years earlier. Other guys on the American tour didn't even bother to come over and try, the call of history sounding much fainter than the crinkling of dollar bills somewhere else. Perhaps the competition for the few spaces in the main draw was too keen for those players. They figured that some hotshot out of Siberia would have a career round and run over them like road kill. Kevin, just in case, bought an open return ticket, hoping the "open" ticket was a sign he would make it into the Open Championship.

As the plane lurched to a halt fifty yards short of the international terminal, passengers began the mad scramble to get out of the ten-hour sardine can. Kevin, as anxious as any of them, jumped into the crush. As he waited to move forward, the woman behind poked him with her umbrella every time she turned to complain to her husband about the slow exit. When he reached the door and hesitated, he was goosed one last time into the gale. To reach safety, the passengers ran a gauntlet of stinging sleet and rain sweeping in horizontal sheets across the concrete. Couples clung to one another to keep upright while young children and smaller bits of luggage flew away with the wind. Scottish golf, Kevin thought, as he flung himself headlong down the steps, through the blasts, and into the dry sanctuary of immigration.

Tired, damp bodies lugging overcoats, luggage, and odd sized packages shuffled through a maze of corridors toward a half dozen immigration booths. Some of the passengers were animated, excited to be home or anticipating adventures. Kevin tried to look like he traveled internationally every day; suave, a bit aloof. After queuing for half an hour, it was his turn.

"Good morning, sir. Passport please."

Kevin handed his travel documents to the middle-aged man in a dark blue sweater and tie sitting at the check station. His eyes followed as the man opened his passport and shifted through the pages. Before his trip, Kevin has crossed out "student" as his occupation and penciled in "professional golfer." The official did not seem to notice.

"How long will you be staying in Great Britain, Mr. Turner?"

"About two weeks, more if I'm lucky."

"And the purpose of your stay?"

Kevin wanted to say pleasure. He was in the home of golf. His spirit would soar over the hills, lochs, the glens, and the rugged cliffs and tread into the deep sweet softness of peat and bog, or, he could fail to qualify and make the whole trip an expensive disaster. "Business," he answered.

The officer's eyebrows went up. This made the process a little more complicated. "And what is your business, Mr. Turner?"

"Golf. I'm a professional golfer."

"Here for the Open?" the officer turned to the front of the passport, noticed the change and smiled. "Brilliant." He looked up at Kevin, another clone from the American tour. The official's arms become a whirl of stamp, stamp, shuffle, shuffle, stamp, shuffle, stamp. He returned Kevin's passport with permission to enter and stay six months and his wishes for good luck in the championship. He played off nine, himself, he said.

As Kevin waited at the carousel for his bags, he wondered how the Palmers, Nicklauses and Faldos of the world did their traveling. "This way, Mr. Palmer. I'll take care of that for you, Mr. Faldo." Kevin didn't mind the absence of helicopters, limousines and attendants. No matter what extras the King might enjoy, the warmth of that welcoming smile at immigration was a damn good start.

After he had his passport stamped, his luggage collected and had taken his quick walk along the green line through customs, Kevin faced the first and he hoped the worst crisis of his trip; the rental car.

On his first trip to Britain, Kevin had a devil of a time simply crossing the street. He would look left, see only taillights and step off the curb onto the front bumper of a speeding ten-ton lorry which had attacked from his right. His mind registered only that cars were going away, not that vehicles were rushing from the other direction. After a few near misses, he looked both ways three times, shut his eyes and ran. That technique would not work while driving.

Once he retrieved his car, he would have to exit the airport, traverse the Glasgow motorway through the city center, find and get over the Firth of Forth Bridge, and circle a million roundabouts along small country roads until he arrived at the small East Neuk fishing village of Cellardyke. Palmer and the other guys stayed in St. Andrews itself at places like Russacks and The Old Course Hotel or even rented an estate for the week complete with a herd of elk in the heather and salmon in the stream and maybe even a kilted bagpiper stuffed in the pantry. Kevin paid half what those guys paid a night in a hotel room for a week in a two-bedroom flat and "a view of the sea." With a little homework and one transatlantic phone call, Kevin had an affordable two-week rental away from the crowd and the tensions of a major tournament. The only inconvenience was he had to pick up the key at the Sea Bird Tavern somewhere on the same street.

The rain continued to pelt through his jacket as he pushed the trolley carrying his two suitcases, golf clubs and carry-on bag up and down the rows of cars. Head down into the wind, he pushed and pulled until his little red Ford Escort appeared. Kevin opened the boot, squeezed in the suitcases and carry-on, stuffed the golf bag onto the back seat, and then threw him into the front seat. It took only a moment to realize he was not behind the steering wheel. Rather than walk around the car, he climbed over the gearshift lever to get to the driver's side. It had been a long time since he had driven a stick shift, and now he had to do it left handed. Fitting the key into the ignition required the touch of a safe cracker, but finally he was ready to start the engine. By this time, his exertions had steamed up all the windows and the tiny engine did little to push defrosted air across the windscreen.

After five minutes of full blower with no improvement, Kevin had two choices, wait for better weather and drive with the windows open or wipe the window while driving on the wrong side of the road in unfamiliar surroundings shifting left handed. Kevin sighed. He wished his caddie Foot had made the trip with him, but that just wouldn't fit into the budget. Foot could drive on the left. His caddie's whole life was complicating simple things and simplifying complicated ones. Kevin went through the gearbox for practice then let out the clutch and lurched forward.

Roundabouts are wide multilane circles where two or more roads intersect. The idea is the motorist proceeds clockwise in a circle until the desired road appears and when it does the driver veers off to the left. If the destination is straight through, all one does is go clockwise from six o'clock to twelve o'clock, then jog left to continue on. If the road is missed, unlike the American expressway system, the traveler doesn't have to go another twenty miles to the next exit, but just go once more around until the road shows up again.

For the untutored, the system works as comfortably and smoothly as chatting with your dentist after he has climbed into your mouth, and is equally as pleasant. Kevin kept steering to the left, dreading every moment that required him to look anywhere but ahead. He circled one roundabout six times before he could spot his exit and find a big enough opening in the fast moving traffic to risk the turn. A couple of miles short of the Forth Bridge, Kevin went round twice before taking the next road that arrived, and drove along this one until the next roundabout flung him back to the first one where he found his way again. On a bit of straight road, he spotted the first sign for St. Andrews as it flashed by his desperate and bloodshot eyes.

Two hours after leaving the airport, he drove past Guardbridge and through another roundabout, up a slope past the Guardbridge Hotel and was surprised to see the vast expanse of a hog farm where he expected to catch his first view of the famed Old Course. Another few miles down the road, he took a quick glimpse left at the Strathtyrum golf course and maybe saw the Old Course and the Royal and Ancient Golf Club before traffic demanded his attention. St.

Andrews in July is a tourist Mecca. Cars, busses and walking sightseers were massing into a dizzying whirr. They came at him from every direction, most of them as confused as he was. He crept along crowded North Street, one eye on the road, one for an escape. When a parking spot appeared, he raced for it, slammed to a stop, turned off the engine, and relaxed for the first time in Scotland. The sun was shinning. It was warm. He was in St. Andrews.

He locked the car and asked the first people who walked by where he was. It turned out he had driven most of the way through town. Without knowing it, he had missed the Clubhouse by only half a block, downtown by one block, driven right by much of St. Andrews University, past the Cathedral ruins and stopped a minute's walk from the harbor.

"How far to the golf course?" he asked the couple with a map.

"Ten minutes," they said, "if you take your time and enjoy the walk." They pointed out the Scores, the street that ran along the bluff and ended at the first tee of the Old Course.

Kevin walked past the ruins of the Cathedral, where Young Tom and Old Tom Morris are buried. He made a left turn at the ruins of the castle, vowing to come back later. His heart beat faster as he walked over a rise to the view he would remember all his life. Below him on the right was the vast expanse of the West Sands and a thousand waves of the North Sea running row after row to shore, and three hundred yards in front of him were the gray sandstone walls of the most famous clubhouse in the world, and beyond that, the rolling green fairways of the first and eighteenth holes of the Old Course. His mind pictured the past champions walking up the last fairway to the echoing cheers of a thousand phantom fans. Kevin stood in the middle of the sidewalk and marveled that he was really there. A gentle breeze carried the aroma of the sea with the odd addition of the sweet smell of fish and chips.

He joined the crowd at the green crosshatched wooden fence between the walkway and the course. A few lucky golfers were playing the last rounds before the course closed for the tournament. The tourist gallery watched the tourist golfers with keen eyes, sympathetic when one hit poorly off the first tee, applauding even mediocre putts as players completed rounds that would improve during visits to the nearby pubs. Kevin. too, watched for a while, then wandered past the first fairway to the Himalayas, the Ladies Club course. For half a pound, he hired a putter and a ball, and played over the hilliest putting holes he had seen in his life. It was a humbling experience for a professional golfer to watch his ball run up to the hole, turn on a steep slope and roll forty feet away from his target. Old ladies in tweed skirts and rolled up stockings were putting the ball stony while he was lucky to keep his ball from running into groups of other players.

Every once in a while Kevin stopped and looked around. He couldn't believe he was there. He ached to hit a few putts on the first green just across the Swilcan burn and rap hard chip shots through the Valley of Sin on the eighteenth. There was plenty of daylight. It wouldn't be dark until after eleven, but it was time to find his cottage and he had vowed to play the hallowed course only if he earned his way into the championship.

The directions to Cellardyke from St. Andrews were to "follow the A 917 and hang a left at Anstruther, following that road to the harbor. Keep to your right until you're on John Street. Look to your right and you'll see the Sea Bird. Drop in for a pint and to pick up your keys." Kevin did as he was told, pulling up behind a panel truck parked halfway on the sidewalk to allow room for cars to get by on the narrow one lane street. The Sea Bird was a blue haze of cigarette smoke that obscured the few tables and chairs and the half dozen customers. It was a place for regulars; the wood floor scuffed by the same feet, seats moulded by the same bottoms, the barman ready with the same drinks. It was a place his black sheep grandfather would have liked. Kevin loved it.

All conversation stopped as he entered and all eyes were on his back as he walked to the bar.

"Hi, I'm Kevin Turner," he said to the man behind the bar drying shot glasses with a threadbare bar towel. "I'm supposed to ask for a pint and a key."

"Ah, the American golfer. I'm very pleased to meet you Mr. Turner," replied the barman offering a meaty hand. "I'm John Grayson. Welcome to the Sea Bird and to Scotland." Turning away for a moment, Mr. Grayson pulled an ale for Kevin, and with an expert flip of both wrists the beer and a cardboard coaster arrived at the same time in front of him on the bar. "This one's on the house," he said. "It's a pale ale, similar to your American beer. While you're here, we'll teach you how to enjoy a real pint. I'll be back in a jiff with your key."

Kevin leaned against the carved back of the wooden stool as the other customers went back to their talk. "You won't find many barstools like that one you're sitting on," said the barman returning from the back room. "My great grandfather was running this place when he saw stools like that in a picture from South America. He had these specially made for us. Been in here since before the Great War. Most places here have you stand or perch on regular stools. We provide all the creature comforts of home, plus all the benefits of a good pub." He placed an old-fashioned steel key ring on the bar, as large as any Old West jail key ring holding a large old brass key. "Here's your key. I hope you're not superstitious. It's number thirteen as you know. Down the way just a couple of doors."

"No, I'm not superstitious," Kevin told him. He downed the last of his ale. "I'll move my stuff in then come back here for what you call a real pint."

"Right you are. Keep your head low," cautioned Mr. Grayson.

That's funny, Kevin thought as he headed to his car, "Keep your head low." Odd way of saying "Keep your head down." Seems like everybody's a golfer in Scotland. He lugged his bags the short distance to the cottage and unlocked the door with the outsize key. He started up the steps and banged his head on the low overhang, bringing stars to his eyes and the barman's warning ringing in his ears. Leaving the luggage just inside the door, he carefully went up the three steps and turned into the sitting room. A picture window framed a wide expanse of blue-gray sea. The "open" sea. That was a good omen. He explored the rest of his temporary home with a wary eye for low ceilings and door frames. The house contained the sitting room with the view and the kitchen on the first floor, two bedrooms on the second, and the bathroom and a dining room on the basement level. All the rooms that faced south looked over the Firth of Forth whose sparkling blue waves were only a soft sand wedge from the windows. He could throw a golf ball into it, left handed, while sitting eating breakfast. Almost on the horizon was a mist shrouded island and close in, about a hundred yards offshore a small yellow boat bobbed in the waves, the fisherman leaning over to pull up a lobster pot. It was an impossibly romantic view and immediately made him lonely.

After the initial survey, he explored the details of the cottage. This second look exposed the flaws. All the downstairs ceilings were less than six feet high. The bathroom was paneled with real boards of Scotch pine including the ceiling, which lowered it even more. The bath tub/shower was the old style sitting on claw legs. He would have to double over to fit under the showerhead. He tried the water taps, first the cold, then the hot. The same frigid water flowed from both. It was the same up in the kitchen. Kevin worried. Weren't the royal princes sent to Scotland to be toughened up by living in unheated rooms and taking showers in frigid highland water? He couldn't live without a hot shower, even if he had to do the limbo to wash his chest. The icy water was not a good sign.

Another on his short list of must-haves was the bed. A golfer requires a healthy back. Soft mattresses are death to a good swing. The mattress was perfect. Last on his must have list was the speed of the carpet. The sitting room carpet had a stimpmeter reading of ten, perfect for practicing British Open putting. Kevin grabbed a glass from the kitchen and made five in a row from ten feet to earn himself a real beer at the Sea Bird.

Mr. Grayson was an encyclopedia of information about Cellardyke, Scotland, golf in Fife, the Isle of May which was the name of the island outside Kevin's window, and most importantly, that the hot water in the cottage was on a timer, turned off until he wished to use it. Mr. Grayson brought him a dark ale that tasted sour, but it grew on him the more he had.

By eight o'clock, jet lag and a couple of pints doubled the weight of his arms and eyelids. Mr. Grayson suggested staying up as late as he could and told him about the walk along the coast to Pittenweem. There was plenty of time to walk there and back along the seaside trail in the crisp evening air. Kevin fell in love with the quiet beauty of the shoreline at low tide. There were no great cliffs or pounding sea, only a gentle surge. The water and land were friends with each other here. His smile grew as he walked. This would be a glorious fortnight.

Bright sunshine rising below the clouds nudged him awake at five the next morning. Kevin sat up in bed so he could see the tide rolling over partially submerged rocks. Gulls flashed past the window. He was famished and berated himself for not buying food when he had the chance. No coffee and a cold shower made for an unhappy morning. He had to do a better job of remembering to set the timer on the water heater.

A practice round was scheduled at Carnoustie for ten. In the meantime, his stomach was empty and complaining. There was nothing else to do for the five hours but load up his gear and drive west along the coast to St. Andrews and hope he could find something open. Crail, the first town, was closed. There was nothing resembling a cafe on the ten-mile route until he reached St. Andrews. He drove the three streets that make up the commercial area and found the Pancake Place on South Street. Just American enough to serve good pancakes, just European enough for strong dark coffee, and just opened at seven.

After breakfast, Kevin made a detour at the edge of town to drive past the Royal and Ancient clubhouse and to view the course being prepared for the Open. Spectator stands were being erected to the right of the first tee and behind the eighteenth green. Kevin felt the excitement of tournament golf stirring in his gut. He was going to play in the Open. Determination lined his face as he swung the rental around and headed toward Carnoustie.

While Kevin was finding his way to Carnoustie, a familiar rotund figure was strolling along a one lane country road just outside Crieff, about thirty miles northwest of St. Andrews on the edge of the highlands. The man was dressed in a well cut, expensive, conservative, dark gray wool suit, bright, razor sharp French cuffed white shirt and a robin's egg blue tie. His shoes were shiny black Italian loafers; new and glove leather soft, best suited for a salon, not a roadway. The man looked out of place. This was the middle of nowhere. There were rolling hills peppered with scrub trees, an occasional rusted and broken down wire fence, and one cow that looked with curiosity at the stranger.

Whisper quiet, a black Rolls Royce followed discreetly three hundred yards behind him for a few minutes before swiftly coming alongside. The dark tinted passenger window slid out of sight and the head of a smiling white haired old troll stuck out to inquire in a thick Scottish brogue, "Takin' a wee morning walk are ye?"

"Yes," the walker replied. "It clears the head, strengthens

the heart, and makes a body ready to do business with a canny old Scot like yourself."

Sir Charles McMaster, the old troll in the car laughed. "Come in laddie and I'll ge ye a ride. I dinna want you complainin of fatigue while we talk." The two men contented themselves with small talk while being driven the last mile to the GlenKosta distillery. In appearance, it was a small operation, only half a dozen barn sized buildings, but it produced a Highland whisky acclaimed from London to Los Angeles. Once there, they climbed the stairs to Mr. McMaster's office just outside the visitor's dining room and across from the glass display case of rare bottles and decanters of the GlenKosta's single malt whiskies. McMaster opened the unmarked door and followed his guest to the two dark green leather chairs on opposite sides of a low table set with a silver coffee service. He poured coffee for both of them.

"Cream?"

"No thanks. I like mine black. You know that."

"So Kevin doesn't know you're here," McMaster said, ignoring the comment and leaning back into the chair with his cup.

"No. It will be quite a surprise. We talked about the expense of coming here and he decided he couldn't afford to have me come too."

"He has no idea, then, how you make your living?"

"And spoil the fun? No one does. Except you and others from the early days. We've all done pretty well, don't you think?"

"Aye. Tell me. Are you still lookin for flying saucers and little green men?"

"You're like all the rest, you little hedgehog. Unless you can see it and touch it, it doesn't exit. I won't say I told you so when a lot of what I say comes true. There's a lot about the universe we don't understand and a lot about what goes on between the ears we don't know about either."

"True enough, true enough," McMaster agreed, before returning to safer ground. "So you like carrying a golf bag up and down fairways?"

"Ah Charles. I'm at a time and station when I can do as I please and it pleases me to caddie. Plus I like projects, business ones and human ones. Kevin has come a long way and I'm real proud of him. I wouldn't miss his first Open Championship."

"Not for all the whisky in Scotland?"

"Not for all the tea in China."

"Oh. Speaking o' China. You said you're representin oriental interests?"

"Aye, as you folks say over here. I'm in partnership with Japanese distillers who want part ownership in two single malts, yours and the Laforague."

"Ah. A highland and an Islay malt. Very wise."

"Did you look over my proposal?"

"Aye. That I did."

"And...?"

"I be thinking that sometime this morning we'll be wantin a wee dram of our best to celebrate the occasion."

Both men smiled as they lifted their cups of coffee, knowing the hard bargaining was yet to come.

Kevin shook hands with Paul Wytrazek after holing out on

eighteen. Paul was the current club champion at Carnoustie and knew every square centimetre of the course. His advice had been invaluable during the practice round and Kevin wished he was available to caddie for the qualifying tournament, but Paul was following his own dream to make it into the main Championship. With a wave back to his new friend, Kevin hoisted his heavy staff bag and crunched over the concrete parking lot to his car.

"Carry your bag, sir?" Kevin turned and stared into the ruddy middle-aged face, framed by giant muttonchops and a new tartan cap, that beautiful ugly face of his ever-faithful caddie, now dressed in ragged cotton pants and a sweatshirt.

"Foot!"

"In the flesh." They hugged like newlyweds, although they had been together only three weeks earlier in Memphis.

"What…?"

"Hey, Captain, I couldn't let you play in The Open without me, even if you can't afford it."

"How…?"

"Now, officially, I can't work. I'm just a tourist, unlike you, the traveling professional golfer. But if you want me, I'm your man."

"Well of course I want you, you dumb shit. Can we do this?"

"We'll just do it." Foot picked up his player's bag. "Kev, I have a feeling about this one. This is gonna be one helluva tournament. Something you can tell your grandchildren about."

"One of your psychic predictions?"

"No. But now I'm here to help you, you have a reasonable

chance of success. I'll keep you out of trouble."

"There won't be any trouble. I've been dreaming about this ever since I knew St. Andrews existed. Nothing will stop me from doing my absolute best. I just hope my best is good enough and nothing horrendous happens."

2

Not many days in Scotland are born as this one. The summer sun was so far north that the horizon and the sea were the same deep blue hours before sunrise and the sky so cloudless that the sea blue imperceptibly became lighter and lighter until it became the nothingness of space. The Isle of May floated on the water within arm's reach. Kevin sat at the breakfast nook, a half-finished cup of coffee on the table in front of him, his mind a trillion miles away as he gazed over the quiet sea. Foot snored.

Today was the first of two days of qualifying at Carnoustie. Three or four under would be necessary to make it into the Open. It was good golf or goodbye. Kevin felt a strange calm as he looked over the Firth of Forth. He could sense the passion and the hopes of the thousands of ships that had sailed over the sea, coming home with full holds and happy seamen when she was kind, and boats high in the water carrying only tragic news when she showed her stormy temper. The five-foot high, two-foot thick rock wall that lined the back garden lent an air of permanence to the view, while the land across the firth, rolling farmland clearly visible even though twenty miles away, suggested resilience. The deep green of the root crops and bright yellow of the grains displayed the reward of man's hard work winning out over rocky soil, droughts, floods, and human folly. Kevin risked nothing more than a few thousand dollars and a small portion of his self esteem to play a simple game in the rare Scottish sunshine. What a silly thing he did for a living. He had to keep that in mind as he stood over those horrifying eight-foot character builders later in the day.

"Morning, Captain," Foot came down the stairs and into the small kitchen rubbing his eyes, his ample frame covered by a bright scarlet and blue floor length silk dressing gown. Kevin had often wondered about Foot and his clothes. On tour, Foot often looked like the winner of a high school grunge contest, but every so often he offhandedly mentioned having dinner at a place like Wolfgang Puck's trendy restaurant in Rancho Santa Fe in California or showed up like this morning in what looked like an Italian designer dressing gown.

"Foot..."

"Is there coffee?"

"Yeah, over on the counter by the window. Foot?"

"Yeah?"

Kevin noticed Foot looking for milk in their tiny refrigerator. "I thought you liked your coffee black."

"Yeah, I do. Sometimes." Foot found the milk, decided he didn't want it after all and put it back. He opened all the cupboards looking for breakfast.

"Foot?"

"Yeah?"

"How can you afford to wear a silk dressing gown on the money I pay you?"

Foot looked up after taking a deep gulp of the coffee. "I

can't. You don't pay me enough."

"So where do you get these things? I've seen you in suits that would put Donald Trump to shame. Remember the funeral for Ted's wife? When you walked in I didn't recognize you. I thought you were a diplomat or something. A lot of the guys think you have money stashed away."

Foot dismissed the idea with a wave of his hand. "The suit was a rental and even then I had to save up for the security deposit. And if I'm going to be able to continue to make payments on what I'm wearing now, you've got to play a hell of a lot better than you have been."

"Hey. I'm doing pretty damn good and you know it."

"Yes I do. That's why I'm here. I want to see your first big splash in the international scene. What you did before over here on the European tour was nothing, all B.F."

"Before Foot."

"You're catching on, young man."

By this time, Foot had assembled the makings of an American breakfast; grade one Scottish eggs, English streaky bacon and fruit scones purchased fresh last night from the newsagent down the street, Spanish orange juice and French roast coffee. Foot had purchased black pudding from the newsagent too, but hadn't yet brought it out from the back of the refrigerator.

As Foot scrambled the eggs, Kevin showered, beginning his traditional pregame routine. It took about two hours for Kevin to get ready on tournament days. He needed to be anxious and relaxed at the same time. He thought about golf or did golf tasks like picking out tees and balls while he thought about good swings to get the right frame of mind. He wanted to arrive at the first tee with his muscles warmed up, his mind relaxed, and with the confidence that his first tee shot would fly a mile down the middle. His morning routine was the first rung of the ladder to climb into that feeling. Foot knew most of the routine and did his part, which was to ignore Kevin. Foot had plenty to do himself that morning, anyway. The British tabloids, of which the newsagent had more than a dozen varieties, some with photos of well endowed and topless page three girls, others with the latest gossip on the Royal family, would keep him occupied and out of Kevin's way. He spent part of the morning filling out a coupon to join an amateur search team scheduled to cruise Loch Ness looking for Nessie the week after the Open.

Two hours before tee time, Kevin and Foot squeezed into the rental parked on the sidewalk. Foot drove because Kevin didn't want the stress. They drove past the Cellardyke harbor and onto the main road to St. Andrews. This wasn't the most direct route, but Kevin thought it would be a smart gesture to at least give a nod in passing to the Old Course on the way to Carnoustie, to make sure she knew he loved her so she wouldn't be jealous and take it out on him later.

After hitting balls on the makeshift range in calm air, the two made their way through the other pairs of ashen faced players and tight lipped caddies. Thirty or forty spectators lined the tee, which was not roped off as it would be for a professional tournament. This was old style golf and Kevin loved it. He knelt on the wet grass by his golf bag to pick out a ball while Foot cleaned the sand wedge. Foot watched with raised eyebrows as Kevin dug around the ball pocket of the bag. Kevin pulled out two balls instead of one; a number three and a number four. Kevin's smile grew as his eyes looked from one to the other. Obviously, this meant something important. Kevin looked up and smiled at Foot but said nothing. Foot smiled back, as if to a child who had held up his best drawing for approval, and didn't say anything either. Kevin put back the two balls and rolled his hand around deep in the ball pocket once more. Quickly this time he pulled out another two balls and looked at their numbers.

"A three and a four again," he beamed, looking up to Foot again.

"Yes," Foot agreed. "A three and a four once more. Aren't we the lucky ones."

"No," Kevin said rising to his feet and showing him the balls, "you don't understand. This is great. A thirty-four on the front and a thirty-four on the back. That's just perfect."

"Oh, that's what we're doing."

"Yeah. What did you think?"

"Not sure. What would you have done if you came up with two fours?"

"Par on the first two holes."

Foot laughed. "I see. Whatever you picked had a story."

"Sure. But the most important prediction would be for the entire round. And I got it. A very tidy, as they say over here, sixty-eight."

"You make sixty-eight and dinner is on me at the Grange Inn."

"Really?"

"Yup."

"And if I don't?"

"You owe me."

The sun kept shining down on the duo all day. Kevin made bogey on the long par four ninth for a thirty-four on the front nine and no-brainer birdie putt on the tough par four eighteenth for the same score on the back side. In seemed like the sun shone for everybody. Kevin's 68 was good only for a third-place tie with two others. Another round of the same score, however, and he would be in the big show.

"Did you make bogey at nine on purpose?" Foot asked as they left the course.

Kevin laughed. "It may have looked that way, but I tried my guts out. I don't want anything to screw up my chances to play St. Andrews. You saw it. A little harder it goes in, a little softer and more borrow it drops. Like that? 'Borrow?' I'm ready to play here. The language, the people, the courses, the history. This place is part of me and I want to be part of it. Just to play, to have my name on the entry list would be a dream. To make the cut would be fantastic."

"I suppose you've had dreams of being on the leader board."

"I don't want to talk about it." Kevin was well aware if you talk about dreams they don't come true.

"And, no doubt, you birdie the Road Hole everyday."

"No, I don't birdie the Road Hole everyday." Kevin was insulted. "Twice. I only birdie it twice. Once from the bunker, though."

"Do you recall the story of the Sands of Nakajema?" Foot asked with a knowing nod of his head; since both of them had viewed the videotape of the Japanese professional's putt for birdie from the front of the seventeenth green which rolled along the wrong side of the ridge and slid down into the bottom of the deep Road Hole Bunker. From there, the desperate man smacked three nearly perfect bunker shots to get out. Each one carried to the top of the lip, paused to look at the welcoming green and raise everyone's hopes, only to fall back into the sand at his feet.

"I've heard it's the best par four in the world."

"It is. At least that's what Ben Crenshaw says it's because it's really a par five."

"Say, instead of dinner at the Grange tonight," Kevin suggested, "why don't we wait until we finish play tomorrow? I'd like to have a simple dinner somewhere then a beer over at the Sea Bird. Get a little more of the atmosphere while we're here. What do you say?"

"Sure," Foot agreed.

All the omens were good, Kevin thought. His sixty-eight included only one bogey. There had been no disasters, no heroics, no three putts, no sign that this wouldn't go as he had planned and prepared for. Prior to coming over to Scotland, Kevin had taken two weeks off the tour. He hibernated in his condo in Encinitas where he read golf history books and watched video tapes of old British Opens. He didn't pick up a club for ten days.

David Joy did a particularly good tape; a St. Andrews native playing the role of Old Tom Morris reminiscing about the early days of golf and St. Andrews. Old Tom claimed to take a swim in the North Sea every day of the year, rain or shine and in Scotland, at the same latitude as Alaska, that was claiming a lot. Other tapes showed Watson hitting his two-iron long against the stone wall on the Road Hole to lose to Seve Ballesterous in '88 and Doug Sanders missing a two-foot putt on eighteen to eventually lose to Nicklaus in a playoff in 1970.

Another tape had rare footage of Carnoustie before the war when Henry Cotton skunked the entire American Ryder Cup team, leaving the likes of Byron Nelson six shots behind and sweet swinging Sam Snead ten sweet swings out of the running. The same tape showed a grim Ben Hogan as he played the last two rounds of the '53 Open in 70 and 68, supposedly playing his second shot on the par five sixth in the afternoon round from the divot his shot had made in the morning round.

Like every professional golfer, Kevin dreamed about sinking a putt to win the United States Open, yet the older British Open held a special place in his heart. Unlike most of his fellow competitors, his arrival to the game came after he had discovered girls. Although little known in the sports psychology research literature, this delayed attraction away from soft curves and toward hard hooks meant that he took a thoughtful, rather than a testosterone driven approach to golf. Kevin had no desire to punch the air with his fist, toss his putter into a lake or yell at his ball, although he has done all those things. Golfers have to or they would go crazy. But, he wanted to be the kind of player to sink a tough putt to win, shake the hand of the man he had just beaten, and buy the guy a drink. Kevin fantasized fighting and clawing his way to win the U.S. Open, then giving a promised junior golf clinic for the U.S.G.A. the next morning. He found his heroes of the game in the history books and wanted his game to include a part of their spirit. He also craved to play the Old Course the way it had always been played, with low flying run up shots. He wanted the home of golf to be his home.

During his two-week hibernation, he also broke up with his girl friend Carol. It was inevitable. She wanted a companion who would be there most of the time and would make her feel special. He hadn't exorcised enough of the golf demon to leave room for her. No matter how much he wanted her, both of them knew he was far too interested in chasing a little white ball to settle down. Over dinner at the Star of the Sea Room, with her wearing that clingy black dress with the slit up the side, she said she just wanted to be friends. Kevin listened to the message he had heard half a dozen times before, wondering if he ever would do his half. He wanted her but didn't want the relationship, wanted a relationship but didn't want to be unfair, didn't want to be hurt and didn't want to hurt her.

"Kev, why don't you want to give us a chance?" she asked while they waited to order. She toyed with her drink while he looked out the window at the harbor lights.

"Carol, you know I care about you."

"Am I special to you? That's all I need you to say."

Kevin was about to answer when she reached across the table and put her beautiful finger to his lips. He could smell her perfume. "Don't say it. I know what you're going to say. You need more time with golf before you're ready."

"Yeah," Kevin said as he took her hand. "That doesn't mean I don't enjoy you and the time we spend together."

"Yes," she said with a sad smile. "We had nice times. Like Idylewild and Ensenada and your place and my place."

"So you want to be just friends."

"Yes," she said, taking her hand away.

"That means no sex."

"Yes."

"Why don't we be good friends rather than just friends?"

"Sweetheart," she said, "as much as that is a tempting offer, it wouldn't work."

As separations go, it was a good one. They teased each other during dinner, knowing they would not get together again but very aware that the relationship had been special anyway.

Kevin had almost loved Carol, but that inner voice that drove him to be the best golfer he could wouldn't be silenced. They broke up a week before he left for Scotland. He spent his free evenings sitting in his big brown corduroy easy chair, sipping a beer, watching the videos, reading the books, and thinking. The answering machine was on, the windows open to the ocean breeze, light jazz played on the radio. He would miss her, sure, but not enough to make the great sacrifice. She was right and he knew it.

What do I want, he wondered. Kevin wasn't driven to win titles or millions of dollars. The Vardon trophy would be nice, or player of the year, but even these weren't reason enough to let Carol go. The history books? He wasn't the next Nicklaus. Avoid a day job? Kevin wondered. He had no skills other than golf, but he wasn't lazy or afraid of getting his hands dirty. Obsessed with golf? No. But wandering from town to town throughout Europe and the Nike tour looking for the secret wasn't normal. Reliving lost chances late into the night, tormented by putts running by the hole, wondering if an extra wrap of tape on his grips was the way to success wasn't normal. Letting someone wonderful like Carol go wasn't normal either. People grow up, make commitments, get regular jobs, have children, grow roots. "Eighty million Frenchmen can't be wrong," his dad always said, whatever that had to do with anything.

The week of pondering found no answers. Maybe he followed some unconscious dream, or some deep part of him that sought some higher meaning from golf than anyone else could understand, or maybe nothing else looked better yet, or he didn't know enough to make a different decision.

"What are you thinking about?" Foot asked, as he drove the two of them along the "B" road to Cellardyke.

"Life."

"Life is as good a way to pass the time as any."

Kevin smiled. "You're what, forty years older and light years wiser? Is that what you told me?"

Foot was indignant. "I said, 'Barely thirty years older and more than twenty light years wiser.'"

"Well, you are. Sometimes I haven't figured out what this life stuff is all about. There's an empty spot somewhere in there."

"Well, my son," Foot said, rubbing his chin, "as I've told you, 'life is a metaphor for golf.'"

"Yeah, and I don't know what that means either."

The car bumped up the low stone curb in front of their cottage. Foot hauled out the golf bag while Kevin unlocked the door. "Hey," Foot called up to Kevin. "They have food at the Sea Bird." He read from the signs on the window just down the street. "They've got pizza and hamburgers and a lot of other stuff. Why don't we take a shower and go there for dinner and a beer."

Kevin went into the kitchen to turn on the water heater,

which he had meant to turn on before they left. After putting away the clubs, Foot walked the six doors to the newsagent to collect the afternoon tabloids and buy a small bottle of Famous Grouse. A little nip while sitting in the back garden enjoying the crisp sea breeze would ease his tired muscles. Kevin joined him outside after his shower and traditional post-round routine. Both men sat in beach chairs, too low to see the waves crashing against the rocks on the other side of the stone wall, but they could hear them, and see the water out toward the Isle of May and the horizon in the direction of Norway. Kevin sat in his blue cotton robe, Foot still in his working outfit of gray cotton pants, yellow shirt, red socks and blue tennis shoes.

"Nice place you got here, Captain."

"Oh man, Foot. I was lucky. A guy at the University owns this, and he knew somebody who knew..."

"Yes. I'm really glad we're here rather than in town. And I'm really glad to be with you rather than that bed and breakfast over in Leuchers."

"What a surprise to see you. I..."

"You never expected me. By the way. You haven't asked, but I'm carrying only for a percentage this time."

"Pay you? You don't have a green card here. You can't legally work and I'm not..."

"Carrying for you isn't work, Kev. It's the reason I get up in the morning. The reason I live. I thought you knew that."

"Want more?" Kevin held up the small bottle of cheap Scotch, the only kind the newsagent sold. But cheap here was still good. The bottle was half empty and would be finished before Foot took his shower.

The whisky mellowed them from the inside out and the

sun warned them from the outside in. It followed its slow summer path, hanging for hours above the horizon as fishing boats chased by hoards of seagulls bounced against the swells on their way home. Boys jumped among the rocks, looking for stones to throw at invisible targets in the water. The neighbor's wash flapped in the wind.

"Does it get any better than this, pro?"

"No," Kevin answered. "It doesn't get any better than this."

Kevin popped into the Sea Bird while Foot made a few transatlantic phone calls. He sat enthralled as Mr. Grayson told the best story that Kevin had ever heard. Years ago, a murder had taken place right where he sat at the bar. A young kid came in, shot the man sitting where Kevin sat, then turned and shot dead two more. Fantastic. There is nothing like the history of Britain, he thought. People have been roaming its hills since before the Greeks carved statues and since those days it seems like few of the natives have moved away. Fifty generations grow up within a stone's throw of one another. People remember the stories because they happened to someone in their family, someone that married into their family, or the people who had been their neighbors for five hundred years. As Foot joined them, Mr. Grayson had moved on to the true story of Young Tom Morris' tragic death.

Mr. Grayson began with Old Tom, an historic figure himself. Born when Monroe was President and in the same year Napoleon Bonaparte died, he lived long enough to span the history of golf from the gray mists of the feathery to the early years of the steel shaft. His mother was from Anstruther, born only a few blocks away from the pub. He grew up in St.

Andrews on North Street just a hard niblick from the Old Course. At fourteen, Tom apprenticed to Allan Robertson, from whom he learned to make golf balls and carve hickory golf clubs, and to swing them with equal proficiency. He won the second and third Open Championships, two more later Opens and many other prize and cash competitions. He was the Royal and Ancient's first professional and died as the lifetime Honorary Greenkeeper.

Young Tom, born in Prestwick and bred for golf, was even better at the game than his father. He won the Open for the first time in 1868, the year after his father's last win, and retired the championship belt with two more consecutive wins. No contest was held the next year as the clubs couldn't decide what to do without a championship belt. When re-initiated at Prestwick in 1872 with a silver cup, he won that too. He was, by acclamation, the finest golfer of his day. Everything pointed to a career as long as his father's and one even more outstanding. What everybody knows is Young Tom was playing a challenge match with his dad as his partner when they received the telegram that his wife was in labor. Another message arrived saying she was having trouble. Young Tom hired a boat to cross the Firth but by the time he got back to St. Andrews she and the child had died. A few months later, on Christmas morning, Young Tom died, just twenty-four. People said it was a broken heart, a few said drink, for he was never the same after his wife died and was rarely seen without a glass in his hand. "Coronary aneurism," Mr. Grayson said with authority. "My great grandfather talked to the doctor who treated him. His death had nothing to do with lost love, sadness, depression, too much drinking or anything else. Just a burst artery. Purely physical, something going to happen eventually, no matter what."

Well," Foot huffed, well-known on the tour for his belief in the power of love and the power of pyramids and folk tales, medicinal herbs, copper bracelets, and tarot cards. "That's just a fancy medical term for what happened. He did die of a broken heart. How else would a heart be broken? Split into two pieces so it shows on x-ray like a broken teacup?"

"Well," said the agreeable barman, wiping the bar, "I'm just telling you what I heard. You can make up your own minds."

The night continued in similar fashion. The regulars flowed in, darts got tossed and toasts made. Most of the customers were aware of Open qualifying, and knowledgeable or not, everyone came by during the evening to wish Kevin good luck tomorrow. When the cigarette smoke got too heavy to see across the narrow room, the two visitors bid the locals goodnight and headed to the cottage with promises to come back the next evening with the results of the qualifier.

Foot headed to bed. "I'm too old to go out at night like this. You go ahead with your traditional before-the-last-day-of-an-Open-qualifier-shower and I'll do my usual get-up-in-the-middle-of-the-night-to-take-a-slow-pee."

"G'night partner." Kevin was glad to see him go. He needed alone time. The pub was a nice diversion for a while and immersed him in the atmosphere he wanted, until the smoke got too thick. Tomorrow. Just an average day was all he needed to get his ticket into the most important golf tournament on the planet. He took a shower until the hot water ran out, then, too excited to sleep, wrapped up in his robe to sit in the back garden until the sun was gone. From the Southeast facing garden, the sun rose too far north and set too far south to be visible. He sat watching as the black of deep space reclaimed the garden and the sea.

3

A lot can go wrong on the golf course. Love affairs have begun, marriages have ended, friendships damaged, character exposed, and fortunes lost, all in pursuit of hitting a little white ball as far away from yourself as possible. Through fifteen holes in the final qualifying round at Carnoustie, Kevin walked in the footsteps of saints. Tee shots soared as high as the puffy white clouds that paraded across the blue sky. His irons flew as fast and true as a rifle shot. Putts rushed toward the hole like scared rabbits. Playing companions were sure they were watching the next Open champion. With three holes remaining, Kevin was two strokes in front of the field and eight strokes above the last qualifying spot.

The eastern wind freshened with every hole. Gusts whipped the pant legs of the competitors and knocked into the heavy-laden caddies. Flagsticks bowed in the wind before snapping back to attention. Club selection on sixteen would be difficult. Kevin was up first up on the long par three, dead into the wind, just like eighteen would be.

"Two twenty to the front, two thirty to the flag," Foot told Kevin as they stood by the bag.

Kevin looked at the problem laid out in front of him; two

deep bunkers short and right. Those would come into play with his draw. The hole was cut about six feet in front of a ridge that ran across the green. Hitting long to the forty yard deep green would be safe, but make for a tough two-putt. All Kevin needed to do was bogey in and he would tee up at the Open. He wasn't going to be greedy or stupid. A three putt here was no disaster.

"One-iron," he told Foot, taking the freshening breeze into account.

"Perfect," Foot agreed and handed him the club he already had his hand on. Foot pulled away the bag.

With the confidence of a man blessed by all the gods of golf, Kevin took the club back, winding up his awesome power. At the instant he pulled the club down, the wind died. What had been a steady current of fifteen miles an hour, with gusts up to thirty and more, was, at that moment, not enough to crinkle an old lady's tea party in the back garden.

Kevin's muscles strained to slow down the swing. At full power without the wind, his ball was liable to wind up in the impregnable bushes and gorse behind the green where even Bri'er Rabbit wouldn't be able to find it. His eyes bulged and his veins pushed through his skin as he struggled to bring his body to a full stop. He slowed everything but his wrists. They came through sleek and smooth as a panther, snapping the club face closed so that the ball hugged the ground as it raced left toward more gorse and the waiting namesake of the hole, the Barry Burn.

They didn't know whether the ball made the water or remained in the thicket so it was a lost ball and back to the tee to hit what counted as his third shot on the par three hole. A smooth three-iron should get him to the green where a two putt would give him a five. Not a disaster.

Kevin, like many tall golfers hits high long irons, that can land softly on the green two hundred yards away. Kevin's three-iron climbed into the mottled sky, where it encountered all the wind that had been building behind the bubble of calm air that caused the initial problem. Like a teacup juggled by a nervous waiter, Kevin's ball hit the wall of cold air and fluttered for an optimistic moment trying to sneak it's way through. Then, succumbing to the laws of gravity, it fell straight into the front right bunker, as deep as Kevin was tall.

An explosion from the buried lie to the top portion of the green, a delicate putt that stayed above the hole, a second putt than ran over the hole and finally a tap in put a seven on Kevin's score card and propelled three players past him.

"Not to worry," Foot told his player as they walked to the next tee. Kevin wasn't worried. He was stunned. Like a cow in a slaughterhouse is stunned. Poleaxed. There was not enough awareness in his brain to worry. Worry comes when you can think ahead. Kevin's brain was in brown-out and unable to think at all. As far as he knew, he could have been strung up by his feet, his throat slit, and pulled along an overhead conveyer to be carved into rump roasts and prime rib. Another slip like that and he was hamburger ready for the barbie.

Seventeen was a tough 455 yard par four called The Island because the landing area for the tee shot was surrounded by the Barry Burn. Playing downwind, like it was, a big tee shot to the left side of the fairway carried the burn leaving a wedge to the green. Laying up meant at least a six-iron for a second shot. But. There is always a "but" in golf, especially during the last few holes of a tournament. But, the Barry Burn angled across the fairway so any long ball hit to the right was going to be wet.

Kevin's two playing companions took driver and hit downwind tee shots to the perfect landing area on the left side. Kevin stood with Foot by the golf bag. If the wind held, a three-iron would put him short of the burn down the right side but into it if he pulled it. A five-iron off the tee would be completely safe, but leave a long one-iron or three-wood to the green. A big drive would make everything simple and allow him the luxury of a bogey on the last hole. A wet ball and he may as well go home now. Foot had his hand on the three-iron while waiting for Kevin to make a decision.

Kevin's mind processed all the information, computed the probabilities and measured the strength of his muscles and his character. "Three-iron," he told his caddie.

Again the wind played footsie. One minute, gusts blew hats off spectators and the next it was so calm it almost made you drowsy. There was no point to wait. It was swing and hope the ill-wind-blew-you-good time. Kevin took his stance and looked down the island fairway. There was plenty of room for his three-iron unless he did something horrible like another snap hook into the burn. The wind stayed calm as he swung.

Unknown to Kevin however, his left foot pointed a little more toward the target than usual. And on the downswing, his left knee, which could have angled in to the right to compensate for the left foot, didn't. Instead, perhaps just to show its independence, the knee moved to the left more than usual. Meanwhile, over on Kevin's right side, at hip level, what biologists call the mitochondria of the fascia lata and the long adductor muscle cells produced a sudden burst of energy. There is no explanation why. It was simply something Kevin's body did from a surplus of adenosine triphosphate. This potent muscle fuel powered a quicker hip turn than usual. The shoulders, who were not paying attention to what was happening, blindly followed the hips in rotating much too quickly and much too far. An alert and unappreciated collection of sensory cells in the cerebellum noted this physiological fire drill, however, and attempted to put everything right before the club reached the ball. But it was too little, too late.

"Accch. He spun oot," one of the Scottish fans remarked to his friend from behind the tee. His laconic friend lifted his cap and ran his fingers through his hair. "Aye," he agreed, as they observed the ball start down the middle, then weakly fall to the right, into the only bunker on the island fairway and only one hundred and eighty yards from the tee.

Foot took the club and put it in the bag. "All we're looking for Captain is par or bogey. That's the first bad hit all day. You were due. The last hole was a fluke. You're the player. You're well in the hunt. There is nothing to worry about."

Kevin and Foot stood at the edge of the bunker and looked down at the tiny patch of white sticking out of the sand. The ball was buried.

Kevin sighed. "I have to give up another shot and hit short of the water. It would be suicide to try to fly over it." Foot agreed and handed Kevin his sand-iron. Kevin dug his feet deep into the sand, opened the blade of the sand wedge, and chopped the ball onto the fairway. He had one-ninety to the front, two-ten to the pin. The wind had returned to dance with the flagstick, dipping and swinging in a hard fought tango.

A solid three-iron left Kevin a twenty-foot uphill putt for par, which burned the lip. Four more players tip-toed past when his bogey fell into the cup. Kevin, three strokes ahead of the field half an hour ago, had climbed on the bubble.

Eighteen, back into the wind, makes strong men cry; a short par five, a birdie hole only 486 yards long. But. The Barry Burn, wandering out of play along the right side, makes a "U" turn three hundred yards out and crosses over to the follow the left edge of the fairway. This creates a cup shape of water that almost surrounds the landing area. Playing hopscotch with the burn down the left side are dozens of happy go lucky out of bounds stakes, leaning this way and that, but as deadly as a firing squad. The burn again crosses the fairway just in front of the green. This day, as yesterday, the hole played as a par four. There was no place to play safe off the tee and no safety near the green either. A five here and Kevin was out.

On normal days, with the prevailing wind, eighteen is not hard. A stern test, but not enough to weaken the spirits of a competent golfer. Kevin stood on the tee, again last in his group, knees buckling, stomach churning, eyes watering, hope floundering, with the big stick in his hands.

"This is what it's all about pro," Foot said as he pulled the bag to the side of the tee.

The clubhouse was five hundred yards away. Kevin could see people in the upstairs lounge looking down on holes one and eighteen. That's where he wanted to be. Finished, safe. But. Before he could get there, he needed a four.

Against the wind, which accentuates any spin, he had to aim at the burn and draw it back to the middle of the fairway.

If he pushed it, or if it didn't draw, there were the two burns that looped back to the fairway. Too much hook and he was a dead duck out of bounds on the other side.

"What did you say, Foot?"

Foot laughed. "This is why we're here. Don't forget that."

Kevin took dead aim at Johnny Miller's bunker, the last of the three down the right side just past the far end of the burn, and swung as hard as he could. The ball hissed through the wind directly at the burn, then turned left to the center of the fairway as if this was what it always did. Muffled applause from the gloved hands of the spectators was music to Kevin as he began breathing again.

Kevin smiled as he and Foot reached the ball. "I was watching those old tapes," he told Foot. "From just about here, Tom Watson hit a two-iron in a playoff to beat Jack Newton in '75. I think that's a good omen. Hand me the three Foot and stand back. You are going to witness the smoothest, prettiest swing you ever saw. Something to tell your children about."

"Put it within six feet and I'll buy you a beer."

Kevin pointed his finger at Foot. "You got it."

Fifteen minutes later, Foot was buying Kevin a Guinness even though the six-foot birdie putt missed on the high side. Kevin was still sitting on the bubble, tied at the moment with five players for the last spot in the Open Championship.

Players always insist that they don't root against other players. And if Kevin's mind as he watched the others finish play is any example, that statement is true. He knew which players coming in could take his spot. He watched the scores, aware of when he was in by a stroke or a stroke out of the

Open Championship. At one time, eleven players were tied for two spots. Kevin could only sit and watch as he bobbed on the bubble, sometimes on the surface, sometimes underneath. He focused only on the numbers, not on the names. He sat for two hours, fiddling with his beer, dying a hundred times. Foot clutched at the table watching approach shots land on the final green. Both leaned one way then the other as putts slid by or dropped, stomachs being twisted into a wet dishrag, then flapped and stretched and hung out to dry. The stomach churning went on until, late in the afternoon, there was one player walking up eighteen who needed birdie to knock Kevin out. An indifferent approach shot left him a nearly impossible chip over the right side bunker. The shot rolled across the green and Kevin was in.

Gaunt and wide-eyed, Kevin and Foot stumbled from the lounge. There were no obvious signs of injury, but the internal bleeding had been only seconds from becoming a mortal wound. Neither would remember how they got back to the car and into St. Andrews. Both were in shock, dazed like refugees, wishing only for it all to stop. They had intended to have their delayed celebratory dinner at the Grange Inn, but somehow had begun a series of beers at Ben's Tavern on Market street in central St. Andrews. Neither could have told you where the car was parked, or if the golf clubs were still in it, or even if this was truly a fourth beer or not.

They sat at a round table toward the front of the room and away from the bar itself. Kevin absent mindedly looked down at his half filled pint glass. Foot looked blankly at the door. No words had passed between them for almost ten minutes.

During that time, in the same tavern, Oscar Brown had

been listening to Barry Harden. Oscar knew to keep his voice down. He had been told to leave more than once from places when voices talked to him. Oscar sat at the bar, while Barry told him that this Open Championship would be like no other. "Ye've got tae make a mark," he said. "Forget the past, talk wi tha players. Be a charmer. The time is commin." Oscar listened for more, but Barry was gone. Oscar didn't like talking with strangers. If it was the right thing to do, he would do it. Without more thought, Oscar left his stool at the bar and approached the table with the two men he guessed to be Americans. He would be a charmer like Barry wanted.

"Mind if I join you lads?"

Both looked up into the well worn face of an old man. He looked eighty, maybe ninety and was dressed in multiple layers of ragged sweaters. The old man held a pint of bitters in one hand and gestured toward the empty chair at their table with the other. "Mind if I sit in the chair?" he asked again.

"No, please do," Kevin told him, motioning to the seat.

"Thank ye gentlemen," he said sitting. "The name's Brown. Oscar Brown. You here for the Open?"

"Yes," they replied in unison, neither having the energy to say any more.

"You look like a player," the old man said, nudging Kevin with his elbow. "You lookin for a caddie?"

"Yes, I play, but I'm not looking for a caddie. I have one thanks." Foot remained quiet, bordering on comatose.

"You his caddie?" the old man nudged Foot.

"Yes," Foot told him, barely opening his eyes.

"Know the Old Course do you?" the old man asked, well aware of the answer. He had never seen these two before and he knew every caddie that had carried at St. Andrews over the past three decades.

"No, but we've a few practice rounds to get a feel for it."

"A feel?" the old man mocked. "You'll need more than a feel. Yer no talking aboot some barmaid that will show you what she has. This is the Grand Old Lady. I'd be glad to offer my consulting services. For a small fee, mind you, but well worth the cost."

Kevin couldn't help but smile at the old man's enterprise. "You know the course?"

"Been here for a hundred years. Seen them all, from Snead to Faldo. Carried for the best and carried for the worst. I've walked the course in every way you could think. I could tell you what hole you were on by smelling the wind." Oscar took a deep drink of his bitters. "Have you played it at all?"

"No," Kevin admitted.

"But I take it you've qualified to play in the championship."

Kevin and Foot looked at each other. The old man had just punctured their twin funks. Yeah, they qualified. They were in the Open. Not two strokes behind, but even with everybody. In the Open.

"Sure, we've qualified Mr. Brown. Slug down the rest of that drink of yours so I can buy you another. Then tell us how you can help me win the Open."

Oscar gulped his drink and slammed the empty glass on the table. Foot got up and brought back three more pints.

"By the way, Mr. Brown, I'm Kevin Turner and this is my caddie Foot." Oscar nodded to each of them, keeping one hand around his pint. "Is the Old Course that difficult, that we'd need a consultant?"

"The course, Mr. Turner, has been here for six hundred years. No man in that time has played it enough to know it well. And tho' I no longer expect mesel to carry a bag except under exceptional circumstances, each day I walk the course and each day I see something new. The course is like a lady, always changing her mind and becoming more beautiful when she does."

"Yes. I've done a lot of reading about the course," Kevin said.

"Aachh," Oscar Brown spat. "No readin can prepare you to romance a lady and that's what you have to do. You'll no play well if you do anythin different. Do you know anythin aboot links land?"

"Well, links courses run out and back," Foot jumped. "And the ninth is farthest from the club house. Either that, or they are linked like sausages," he faltered, observing the expressions on Kevin and Oscar's faces.

"The links refers to the land," Kevin told his caddie, with a gentle nod to the old man, "not the shape of the course. Links land is land reclaimed naturally from the sea or deposits from rivers as they flowed into the sea. Rolling sand hills that have grown over with bentgrass and fescue, with hollows formed by the wind."

The old man was not impressed.

"Aye, ye ken a links course from a book well lad. And I suppose you bought yersel a yardage book to take with ye on the coourse."

Foot and Kevin laughed. They'd gone over to the bookstore up from the course on Golf Place after qualifying as their only logical act before stumbling into Ben's.

"I think it will be absolutely necessary," Kevin said.

"Oh, I've no doout aboot that, laddie. But when the wind is up, which it will be more than once, yardage means nothin. But I'll let you find out. Practice rounds begin the day after tomorrow, and if you've a mind to look for old Oscar after you've finished, I'll be here."

On the way back to the cottage, Kevin melted into the pleasure of being an Open qualifier. They had been driving in silence for ten minutes when he said, "Damn it, Foot," with irrepressible glee.

"Yeah," Foot answered.

"Geez."

"Yeah."

"Nothing can be bad now, even if I don't make the cut."

4

For a ten-year old, the week before Christmas lasts twenty years. The delay between a timid marriage proposal and the answering smile is a century. The time between pulling the bedcovers up to your chin and standing on the first tee on the Old Course at St. Andrews the next morning is more than a thousand years. Kevin had run through his night before his first-Open-practice-round routine twice and it wasn't enough. A walk down to the Anstruther Harbor and back didn't do a thing. Pulling the shades in the bedroom made it darker but brought the tee time no closer.

Kevin got out of bed once more and listened at Foot's door. The gentle snoring was unfair. So it was down the steep steps to the kitchen, banging his head on the lintel, to warm milk. He took the steaming cup to the table in the sitting room and looked out to the Isle of May and the twilight of near midnight.

I'll never get to sleep he thought, but so what. It's not like tomorrow is the tournament. A practice round is just to learn the course. But I have only a few days, part of his brain argued, and that Oscar fellow said it took more than a lifetime and a lot of the guys have the advantage of playing this place dozens of times. "Ahem," his heart coughed. "You're not worried about learning the course. You're afraid you might be disappointed by it, aren't you?"

Kevin had to admit his heart was right. When Sam Snead first saw the course, arriving by train the Friday before the tournament, he remarked to his horrified seat mate that back home they would grow cabbages on that land. Kevin worried that the Old Course would be a famous but over-revered, rough-hewn British links course way past its prime. Or worse, that he wouldn't be wise enough to appreciate its old-fashioned beauty and unique shot values. Heck, he played Cypress Point once. It was a beautiful course, but not as super fantastic as he expected. Then again, he had played Cypress Point in a hurry, with an ill tempered club member, in a cold rain, and just before he came down with the flu. But. He was afraid that St. Andrews would be no different.

Yet, once morning arrived and his feet hit the pavement of the Museum of Golf parking lot he was too giddy to walk. Foot had to tether him like a helium balloon to get him across the street, past the Royal and Ancient Clubhouse and to the starter's booth. Foot checked them in. Only then, with his spiked shoes firmly stuck in the hallowed ground of the Old Course did Kevin notice the weather.

Great Britain perches uneasily in the collision zone of three major weather systems; one flowing up from the Mediterranean, another from Canada and Greenland and the third from north of the Ural Mountains, the Barents Sea and Scandinavia. On Kevin's first day, the wind was up, roaring in from the Northeast and the regions of Arctic Norway. July in Scotland. The temperature hovered in the high forties.

Blue/black clouds waited only for a skied tee shot before emptying tons of frigid rain on thin-blooded golfers and the bag carriers burdened with extra sweaters, mittens, wool caps and various forms of body warmers, the majority of them liquid. The fierce wind blew sand in from the beach five-hundred yards away, stinging cold cheeks and noses and making the day miserable. Kevin and Foot anchored themselves on the first tee leaning into the wind as they tried to discuss the first official shot on the Old Course.

"It's gotta be a good one," bellowed Kevin even though Foot stood within a few inches.

"We'll do it fine," Foot answered in a normal tone. He was up wind. "Just take a five-iron and swing with ease down the breeze."

"Five-iron!" Kevin yelled. "This is the widest fairway in golf!"

Foot couldn't stop from laughing. This was only a practice round so nothing counted and his player wouldn't be able to swing anyway since he was wrapped like a mummy; six layers of clothing, beginning with underwear, including a T-shirt, layered with thermal underwear, a long sleeve cotton shirt, a wool sweater vest, a wool sweater and a wind breaker, not to mention a wool cap, thick corduroy slacks, and three pairs of socks. Foot was sporting a dark blue cashmere watch cap. "It's downwind, or can't you tell."

"Downwind yes, but the Swilcan burn is miles away. A three-wood wouldn't get there."

Foot wasn't going to argue. "Three-iron?"

"Sounds fine," Kevin shouted. And his first official swing at the Old Course was in the air. Kevin watched the ball with great interest. This was part of his legacy, his soon to be written part of the history books. The ball flew high and true over Grannie Clarks Wynd a hundred and fifty yards from the tee, landed parallel with the back door of the New Club, and bounced seven times before rolling the remaining sixty yards into the burn.

"Shot," Foot laughed. Once he stopped giggling, he put his hands on Kevin's shoulder and told him, "That dear sir, was a 275 yard three-iron. Too bad you pushed it a little right." They trundled off by themselves down the first fairway, his scheduled partner evidently waiting for summer to arrive.

A bump and run over the burn to six feet and a solid putting stroke put a par on Kevin's card at the first hole of the home of golf. The first chapter of his personal history was in the book, and it made good reading.

The prevailing wisdom at St. Andrews is to play the outward holes to the left. When Kevin stood on the tee at the second, he couldn't find where the fairway was to hit left of. First Foot looked at the map, then at Kevin, then both stuck their heads together to peer at the map and at the terrain in front of them. "No idea," Foot admitted. Both could make out a nearby portion of the seventeenth fairway. "Why don't you hit three-wood just this side of the seventeenth?" he suggested.

"Sure," Kevin told him, but his hitting blind produced a hacker's slice, the ball swung out over the other fairway and around the mounds that blocked their view into parts unknown. Foot hoisted the bag over his shoulder and told Kevin to "Follow me." Compared to the flat first fairway, the second was a frozen sea of grass and gorse. Up, down and around six and ten-foot swells, Kevin and Foot wandered in the direction of his ball. They were within twenty feet of it before Foot pointed out the ball past a low rise. It was dead center in the fairway, just left of what their course book told them was Cheape's bunker, a narrow and nasty deep pit, just large enough, the story has it, "for an angry man and his niblick."

"See, I told you," the caddie said to the player in the all knowing tone of relief that has been passed down generations of bag carriers. Kevin topped his six-iron and watched it pitch and run down, up, and around countless mounds and hollows until it stopped within inches of the cup.

"Shot," Foot coughed, turning so Kevin wouldn't see his face.

Hole number two shares a green with the sixteenth hole. There are seven double greens on the Old Course. The first hole, the ninth, seventeenth and last claim their own territory. Although Kevin's miss-hit made a mockery of the second green's size, like every other golfer who's played here, he stood near the hole mesmerized by the huge expanse. Laid out before him was a convoluted surface, impossible to judge the pitch and roll from off the green and unlikely to yield a straight putt from more than five feet from the hole, and more than likely to produce a three putt or worse if you were thirty feet away. And this double green was one of the smaller ones.

"My, oh my," was all he could say. He smiled. If the rest of the course was like this, he had found his spiritual home. This was true golf like the old days.

The third hole is a short par four with only the Principal's nose bunker to cause any distress, so naturally he hit his two-iron into it and took a five. Ginger Beer, the fourth hole was no different. Tee shot into a pot bunker on the right, one out, pitch, and a bad bounce off the mound in front of the green into deep rough, sand-iron out, chip to four feet and one putt for a quick double bogey.

"Have you noticed anything?" Foot asked Kevin as they stood on the sixth tee.

"Besides wearing out myself out with a million swings?"

"Yeah."

"No."

"After the first hole, the wind shifted and is coming at us now, and getting stronger."

"I've been too busy swinging a club, keeping my balance on all these mounds and holding my cap down over my ears to notice something as inconsequential as a thirty knot wind. Anyway, we'll have it with us coming in."

At the turn, the first of two which comes at the short eighth, the wind was indeed at their backs. Kevin over clubbed and took bogey. Hole nine, downwind, Kevin drove the green with his three-wood for his second birdie, finishing the outward nine as they say, in level fives.

Ten and eleven, the end of the shepherd's crook were back into the wind, but Kevin parred both, tapping in a sidehill, downhill putt on eleven that would have rolled all the way back to St. Andrews had he missed. At the twelfth tee, Foot asked, "Kev, have you noticed anything?"

"Besides that I'm playing like a professional golfer?"

"Yeah."

"No."

"We're against the wind again, and it's getting stronger."

It was true. Unknown to the two men, the tide changed

and the low-pressure cell moved further inland. They would be against the wind for the remaining six holes.

Both shrugged their shoulders. Wind or no wind, they were learning the course. Kevin looked out over the expanse of uncluttered fairway. "Finally," he said, "a target I can see."

Foot had his head in the course book. "Don't be so sure. The book says they're bunkers in that there fairway."

"Where?" Looked flat as a pancake to him.

"The book says to hit well left if the flag is on the right side of the green."

Kevin looked in the distance. The green was just past two ridges. The flagstick appeared to be on the left part of the green. "What's it say if the flag's on the left?"

"Doesn't."

"How about three-wood down the center for safety?"

Foot pulled out the club. "Sounds good," and pulled the bag out of Kevin's way. He hit a beauty that disappeared over a rise. When they got to the ball, all they could do was laugh. One shot to get out of the hidden bunker, another one too strong over the narrow green, a chip and a lucky two-putt for yet another double bogey.

A par on the road hole and a birdie on Tom Morris the finishing hole in front of an appreciative crowd saved the day and a score no higher than Old Tom's age when he took a nose dive at the New Club and died a few days later.

Foot tossed the clubs into the trunk of the rental car while Kevin changed his shoes in the front seat. Kevin had privileges in the R & A clubhouse during the tournament, but wasn't comfortable going in there. Something wasn't right about the Open, like he didn't deserve the full treatment yet. He didn't know why, but part of it was getting into the main event almost by luck.

The two men walked up Golf Place and around the corner along North Street.

"Ben's?" Foot asked.

"Ben's," Kevin answered.

"Oscar?"

"Oscar."

"You mean I'm not good enough to caddie for you any more?"

"Foot. This afternoon I hit a two hundred and seventy-five yard three-iron and a one hundred and seventy-five yard driver. I three putted three times, putted off the green once, hit one approach to the wrong flag and hit another approach to the wrong golf course. I believe Mr. Brown might have helpful advice."

"But I have this swell book, with yardages and bunkers and everything," Foot protested.

Kevin put his arm around Foot's shoulders. "Make a right turn here on Greyfriers and a left on Market. Mr. Brown has a lot to tell us. And I will hold you responsible to remember all of it."

"Cost you extra, Captain."

"You don't even have a green card. I could turn you in."

"You poor misguided boy. When it comes to blackmail, well, I'd start with what happened in Orlando with those two dancers and the..."

"Don't remind me. I'll buy you a beer."

"Done."

The two made their way through the crowded streets of St.

Andrews, past woolen shops, ice cream parlors, gift shops, a few empty restaurants and a few crowded pubs before turning into Ben's. They found this watering hole earlier when it was convenient to the only parking space they could find. Once in, they found the language was golf; old, traditional, unassuming, hit the ball low and let it run golf. Bert's Bar, just a block or two away on South Street, had been the traditional golfer's hangout, then it was The Whey Pat Tavern on Bridge Street, then Ben's, and even now, some were drifting back to Bert's.

Oscar Brown waited for them at a table with two empty chairs. He faced the door with a bemused smile on his face.

"Well, my good fellows, looked like a day to shoot an eighty or even worse," he said, scanning their faces for a reaction. He motioned to the empty chairs. "Sit doon, I want to hear all about it. Old Oscar's got an ear for a tale of woe."

Two tired bodies sagged into the chairs like half-full bags of flour. Foot spoke first.

"Mr. Brown, what are you drinking?"

"Pint of lager, please," Oscar answered.

"Same for you, Captain?" Foot asked the near comatose professional golfer. Kevin's shoulders ached from being hunched against the wind and beating the ball so many times.

"Yes."

Foot moaned as he lifted his bulk up from the chair and leaned heavily against the bar as the barman poured the drinks.

"Mr. Brown, would your knowledge made much of a difference on such a horrible day?"

"Could have saved you at least five strokes today in the bad weather, maybe two or three in good." Oscar leaned forward. "And that's each eighteen, not the tournament."

Kevin looked at the old man. Oscar looked older than he remembered, and much more grizzled. He wore a shapeless dark blue cap, an off white dress shirt with an old and dirty green plaid tie, a light brown under-sweater and over that a gray cardigan missing half the buttons. His wind-burned face was a road map of deep wrinkles and his eyes were in a perpetual squint. Probably a lonely widower, Kevin thought, spent all his life on a farm and on the golf course laboring for a tiny pension. Now all he has are his stories. Whether hearing them would help his score, Kevin had his doubts, but to pay the old man a few pounds to reminisce, how could that hurt anyone? Might be enjoyable to hear about the old days from someone who had been there and it would be nice to help the old fellow out a little at the same time.

"Here you are, Mr. Brown." Foot placed the full pint glass on the coaster in front of Oscar, gave one to Kevin, and sat down with his own. "Sorry it took so long. This place is busy."

"Aye," Oscar said, looking around the crowded room. "From April 'till past September, it's like this. Then the town is ours again."

"Mr. Brown. How can you help us? What do you know about the old course?"

"Ah. Right. Doon to business laddie. I like that. Well, first, there's the little question of my fee."

Foot coughed and glanced at Kevin. In a deep, Ted Baxter voice, he opened negotiations. "Well, Mr. Brown, in addition to carrying his bag, I'm Mr. Turner's business manager. I handle all his many engagements, offers, endorsements, TV appearances, and the like. What do you propose?"

"Fifty pounds for all the secrets and bits of local

knowledge, including a walk 'round the course with you if the weather is nae too bad."

Foot winked at Kevin. "I think we can accept that. Don't you Kevin?"

"And one other thing..." added Oscar.

Kevin was sure that now came the request to keep him in lager for the duration of the tournament.

"...I'll be wantin to be introduced to some of the other players."

"First, before we agree," cautioned Foot with a wink to Kevin, "give us an example of how you could help us."

"Aye, fair enough. You ken the Tom Morris hole, the eighteenth?"

Both shook their heads, waiting for the priceless information. Eighteen is a simple and short finishing hole, as straightforward and easy as any on the course. Eighteen held no secrets and Oscar would have had no idea Kevin had made an easy birdie there that afternoon.

"Now, tell me if I'm wrong," Oscar said. "Against the wind, as it was today, the hole is as easy as filling up an empty glass." He held up his empty glass as a visual aid. Kevin motioned that it would be filled momentarily. "But with the wind at yer back, the short hole becomes a wee devil. If you want an easy par to protect your score, your tee shot is aimed right at the chandelier of the old clubhouse great room and you come in from the left. If it's birdie you need and par is of no use, you aim at the Martyr's Monument on the hill no matter where they've put the flag and hit as hard as you can. That gives you the best bounce and roll through the valley of sin and to the green. It's what your Jack Nicklaus did in '70."

Oscar sat back and looked at his empty glass.

"I'll get it boss; you've had a tough day." Foot moaned as he struggled to his feet for a second time.

"That's interesting, Mr. Brown. What about putting on that green?" Kevin had made a ten-foot putt from the right for his three.

"They put the hole near the right center today. An easy place. Everything hit to the right will fall toward the hole and leave maybe a ten or fifteen-foot putt. Ye never want to be putting doon the hill. Poor Doug Sanders was above and three putted to lose to young Jack. Hit the approach long enough, but never to the back. Putt sidehill if you must, but never doon the slope."

Foot returned with three more glasses although both he and Kevin had more than half of theirs left.

"Are we learning something?" Foot asked, his bones cracking as he sat.

"Yeah," Kevin told him. Then turning to Oscar asked, "How did you get into this caddie business."

A glaze went over Oscar's eyes, as if he was living the long days all over again. "I was on me own and I sat waiting for the caddie master to choose me. It was months...months it was before he let me out. I had never played the game, but I knew much about it. Even today, I've never played even one hole. After a time, players began to ask me to carry, but never as much as the others. And that went on for a long time, until Tip Anderson, Palmer's caddie when he played in the Open, took me under his wing."

"When was that?" Foot asked.

"Back in the late fifties, '59 was my first full year. Carried in the '60 Open. Tip carried for Palmer for the first time and I for Eric Brown. He chose me; I'm sure, for the luck of the same name. Best break of my life. From then on, I carried for every St. Andrews Open. Never won, though, never won. Tip did, with Palmer and then with Lema when Palmer didn't come over. He deserved it. Grand man, old Tip. Gone now, you know."

Kevin and Foot nodded their heads in reverential sadness. Neither aware that Oscar was referring to Tip's frequenting another watering hole. The evening wound down, both Kevin and Foot ached in every muscle and bone. The new trio agreed to meet in front of the clubhouse, weather permitting, at noon the next day. Oscar would walk the course and make suggestions, Kevin would follow his directions and Foot would take notes. All three men slept like babies that night. Foot slept after making copious notes about his continuing business negotiations, Kevin hit shot after glorious shot on the Old Course in dreamland, while Oscar stopped taking his medicine again so his mind would be sharp for the events to come.

5

Oscar Brown pushed away the covers early the next morning and rolled his body off the warm mattress. There was much to do. He stood and arched his back, willing the aches and pains away for one more morning. Even in mid summer, and on the rare bright days, his room was dark and cold and hard on his bones. His pale, blue veined feet scampered over the wood floor as he went to pour water from the pitcher into the cracked and faded porcelain washbowl. He had found the pair years earlier behind the old bathhouse. He stood in front of the dresser that was a gift one Christmas from the Ladies Golf Union and washed his face. Out the small window to his left he saw the top of St Salvador's College and a bit of the sky over the castle ruins. Puffy high clouds promised he would walk around the course that day with the two Americans.

While drying himself, Oscar turned just in time to see his four-month old kitten Benedict crawl out from the covers and stretch to at least three times her body length. "All right princess," he called to her. She sneezed a ladylike hachew that made him laugh. "Come here ye wee urchin and old Oscar will gee ye your breakfast." Oscar twisted his opener around a can of special kitten food he bought at William Low's grocery downtown. It would be a lot cheaper to buy her food at the Safeway on the town's south edge, but that meant a long walk or a bus ride and he was getting too old for the walk on cold days and didn't like to ride the crowded bus.

He spooned half a can into her bowl, a blue one he bought just for her. Like the queen to her coronation, Benedict walked to her breakfast, sniffed, looked up at Oscar with approval, and dug in. It was his turn. First he put an immersion coil in a cup of water and added a tea bag and powdered milk. Then he opened the bread box, took out the half loaf that remained, put peanut butter on two pieces, put those on a plate, and took his breakfast to the only chair in the room, an overstuffed remnant of the forties. Once he ate, and made sure Benedict was happy, he let his mind wander again to hear his mentor.

Oscar sat motionless in his chair, his eyes closed, barely breathing. Barry was talking to him and he was concentrating hard to catch every word. Golf was becoming commercialized, he told him. The players were walking billboards, signs on every hole advertised everything from beer to pen and pencil sets. Slick magazines and books spouted bad advice to sell outlandish equipment, while players traveled with retinues of psychoanalysts, physiologists, lawyers, hairdressers and image consultants. Worse, caddies were choosing the clubs, lining up the putts, and making more money than the Prime Minister. Motorized buggies were invading from the West. Something must be done, in a most dramatic way, Barry told Oscar, to bring back the spirit of the game.

"What do I do?" mumbled Oscar, as Benedict jumped onto his lap and was ignored. Oscar didn't know she was there.

"You," Barry told him, "you who are the only one left with the wisdom, the knowledge that the road to good over evil is only for the pure in heart. The others are gone now. Cousin Shivas hasn't played in years and Angus McIrons has retired to the beaches of Florida. It is you who must stop the contamination and show the way. Only one who has been prepared, scoured in body and in spirit for the grand effort can do what must be done."

Benedict curled into a ball on Oscar's lap as Barry continued. "Oscar now is the time and none of the players is worthy. They have lost the way in the labyrinth of titles and money, Monday outings, club endorsements and even designing on computers what God must create. They can learn again if we show them how. Whoever wins the Open must be pure or we have lost. You must play and you must win."

"How? I dinna play the game. Ye ken that."

"You will remember all I taught you and take the place of a player, one who will fulfill the signs that will appear before you. Take his place and win for the great glory of golf and the human spirit. You will win to end this slide to purgatory and make the game once more God's gift and not man's monstrous abomination."

"Is that why you askd me tae meet players? So through my eyes you would ken who it should be?"

"That was only the first of your tasks," Barry told him. "But higher powers than I know the player and all you will do."

"Could it be the American Turner?"

"All is yet to be revealed. But it is known he will lead you to who it will be. It may even be him. As the bounce of the ball over rugged fairways takes many a turn, there are many things for us to learn. Only after Friday will it be certain. I will come back to you then."

After Barry left, Oscar stayed with his eyes closed, stroking the dozing Benedict and thinking about how long he had waited. He now realized that the exhaustion of carrying three rounds on the long summer days would prove worth all the pain. All the times he crawled up the hill to his room, his back in spasm, his head pounding and his arms too sore to lift were now like nothing to him. Barry told him it was important, that some day he would triumph, not for himself, but for what was right. That was important, to do what was right.

The doctors never listened. A few were nice and treated him with kindness, but so many others didn't care if he lived or died. They just wrote out his medicine and told him to go to the chemist's and not come back for a month. Even people on the street didn't stop to listen. He told them all the truth, but maybe it was too early. He had been impatient. Barry didn't tell him it would take this long. Sometimes Barry didn't talk to him for years.

Oscar opened his eyes to look at the walls of his room. He had done the right thing because Barry had told him what to do. The walls on the window side were covered with pictures of all the European golfers between five feet ten and six feet two inches tall. The photographs had been torn from old magazines and none were the same dimensions, ranging from a full newspaper page to wallet size and even smaller. Some were just tiny heads and torsos cut out of group pictures. Each was held up by a single thumb tack in the center of the picture. The wall opposite was covered with the pictures of the American players of the same height. That part of his collection wasn't finished yet, but Barry said that was okay. The wall over the bed held a black and white picture of Oscar's family taken just after the war. There was his father, mother, older brother and his sister standing in their Sunday clothes out in front of the house. The remaining wall was blank. Oscar wondered if that might be for his picture, one as Open Champion. Barry would tell him what to do.

"Ready, Foot?"

"As I'll ever be. I've got three extra sweaters, an extra hat, and a cute muff that matches your Titleist bag for your hands in case the poor dears get chilly."

"I don't think it will be that cold," Kevin told him, now almost automatically banging his head against the door frame as he came down the last step into the sitting room. "Weather report said a high of fifty-four, with rain later turning to showers after, with clear periods, whatever that means."

"That means it's going to rain sooner and it's going to rain later, with rain possible in between."

"Oh." Kevin sat at the table across from Foot. Both looked out at the view.

"This has to be the prettiest, most peaceful place I have ever seen," Foot said. He reached for the binoculars their unseen host had left for them. "And with these, you can see all the puffins and what not flying all over the island."

"Any ideas for dinner?" Kevin asked.

"Ah. Not for me. I want to run around tonight. You have to fend for yourself. I suggest you try Ziggy's for an American style burger. I know your stomach is rebelling against the sweet wine and dry roast beef from last night. A burger, fries and a shake might fool your stomach into thinking it's home."

"I don't want to fool my stomach. I just may go out and find myself some haggis. I'm in the Open. I have Scottish blood coursing through my veins. And I'm going to be true to my roots. You're off somewhere?"

"Yep. You're all by your lonesome. You can leave me in town and come back here if that's what you want to do. I'll get my own way back."

"Sure. Just don't wake me when you stumble in. I may be busy playing a quick nine with Faldo, or better yet I'll be playing a quick nine with Cindy Crawford."

"You poor boy," Foot shook his head in wonderment. "You have a dream of Cindy Crawford and you spend it playing golf."

"Hey, who said I'd be dreaming."

"Now you are dreaming. Clubs are in the car; let's go hit 'em."

There are two practice greens near the first tee at St. Andrews. One is next to the starter's booth and is tiny, with only two or three holes, just enough to try a few putts before taking the tee. The other is across the footpath from the booth and is huge, running for fifty yards along the street. If need be, four dozen players could putt here and stay out of each other's way. This was where Oscar placed himself to meet the players. He had to shake hands with as many as possible so that Barry could know who it was to be and then tell him. Both Kevin and Foot were helpful in introducing him and he had arrived early to meet some on his own. Barry told him the ones he must shake hands with had to be tall enough so their noses were above the top of his cap.

Kevin's group was called to the tee. Foot lugged the bag over, closely followed by Oscar. It was classic Stan and Ollie at golf. Oscar was as thin as a bean pole and was wearing what he had on in the pub last night; no coat even in this brisk weather. Foot had on two sweaters, a sleeveless sweater, and a wind breaker. He was bulked up almost to the point of becoming a huge sphere. Kevin was stretching to see how well he could move within his own multiple layers when his playing companion came up to introduce himself.

"Hello, I'm Murrfindingle Porgenstrudle." His playing companion's accent was too thick to decipher, but his smile was all bright white teeth set against a tanned face. A Stein Eriksen without the skis. Kevin shook the extended hand and introduced himself and his entourage. "Moe" as he asked to be called, was a young pro from the Swedish federation who was blond, serious, garrulous, and would prove to be talented. After shaking everyone's hand, Moe went back to his caddie to get ready. Kevin did the same.

"Mr. Brown," Kevin asked his consultant. "Has anyone ever driven the green on this hole?"

"Aye. But I've only seen one. That was your American Fred Couples in '84 during a practice round. And he went through the green. You ken having a go at it?"

"How far would I get?"

Oscar looked up for signs of the wind, which was slight, but behind them. "With this light wind, and a big tee shot, you might just make it... into the burn," he laughed, looking at Foot and winking. "Do you mind?" he asked Foot, gesturing to Kevin's bag. Foot shook his head "no."

"Kevin. Hit your three-wood, like you probably will each day during the championship. See if you like how that goes."

And Kevin followed Oscar Brown's lead, liking how it went.

Oscar told them on the fifth green when Kevin complained about a hundred and fifty-foot birdie putt that he was standing on the largest green in the world. He drove the tenth green and learned Snead did that three times out of four in the championship of '46. Bogey on eleven? Bob Jones tore up his score card there in '21. Oscar's advice was clear, "play boldly to all but eleven, fifteen and the last two." And his advice at times was elusive. "Play fourteen directly at the Beardies bunkers but make sure you don't go in."

Foot thought his advice on eleven was the best. "Ye ken twelve at Augusta?" Kevin told him he had seen the famous par three but had never played it. "Well, it's the same here. If you're long, you're in trouble, either in the back rough or even in the Eden estuary, or if you're puttin' from way up there you could putt it all the way doon into the deep Strath bunker in the front right and if you're short off the tee you're in the almost as deep Hill bunker. In fact," Oscar concluded, "if yer no on the green below the hole with your tee shot, you may as well pick up yer ball, put it in yer pocket and get back on the plane."

Kevin received an unexpected compliment on fourteen. "With your length lad, always go for the green in two unless Foot tells you the wind is too strong. If he says that, hit your three-wood off the tee, hit short of the green in two, and let your chipper and putter get you your four."

On sixteen he heard, "Never, never, never hit between the Principal's nose bunkers and the out of bounds. Always hit to the left of everythin." And on the famous road hole, Oscar told him, "Never, never, never hit to the green with your second. Hit your tee shot over the last "O" in the Old Course Hotel sign if you are needing a good score. The first "O" is for the faint hearted, the second if you want a good chance of par, and the third only if necessary and you are long. Then hit your second to the short right of the green. In '84," he said, "there were only eleven birdies during the championship. When Watson lost here that year, his caddie, a dear friend of mine Alfie Fyles, pleaded with him to lay up, but the courageous and foolhardy champion met his match and it wasna the Spaniard Ballesteros."

With Oscar guiding the way, and Foot scribbling notes like a freshman in physics class, Kevin played his second round on the Old Course in even par. Moe was two over and flashed his smile one more time as he wished Kevin well during the tournament. Oscar Brown pocketed his fee just off the eighteenth green and told them he could always be found at Ben's if they needed him again and thank you very much. He then went to his house to feed and pet Benedict before walking to his evening job of closing the castle ruins, sweeping up after the tourists and setting the alarm system.

"What do you think, Captain? Off to a good start?"

"Yeah. Boy, Oscar knew his stuff. Did you hear him say that his uncle was a caddie and so was his grandfather sometimes?"

"His grandfather was a friend of Old Tom Morris."

"And his uncle caddied for Jones on one of his rounds."

"Do you believe that?"

Kevin laughed. "No, but what he said about the course is true. I don't think either of us would have figured out a lot of that stuff. How about a late lunch at the Woollen Mill and we can watch the other guys finish? Couples, Price and Faldo are behind us somewhere."

One of the charming aspects of St. Andrews is how golf does not disrupt commerce. The Woollen Mill is a giant store not more than a long putt off the eighteenth green of the most famous golf course in the world. Except for its January sales, when the locals enter for once a year bargain prices, the shop is designed for the maximum and efficient flow of tourist wallets to the merchandise and the cash registers. Announcements, directions, and prices are posted in as many languages as there are currencies. Investments can be made in cashmere, highland wools and Harris tweeds. A woman from Brooklyn can buy a Tam-O-Shanter in the family tartan and a man from Osaka can be fitted for a kilt. Upstairs, in what must be a spare room waiting for the inevitable overflow of customers and merchandise is a sparsely furnished cafeteria style lunchroom with large windows overlooking the course, the West Sands and the North Sea. In New York or any modern city or town, this space would house an expensive French restaurant. In St. Andrews you pour your own coffee or tea into a plastic cup and select from plastic wrapped pieces of shortbread, sandwiches and cakes to carry to the tables by the windows; which are set high enough to make it impossible to see the course unless you stand.

Kevin and Foot sat for a while, their muscles tired and the chill of the day dissolving in the steam from the cups of tea.

"One more day, then it's the real thing. How are you feeling?" Foot asked.

Kevin shook his head in awe. "Foot, I'm happy. This feels like home. It's not an overly hard course, it's awkward more than anything. If you're in a bunker, get out. And don't expect to get fair bounces. I think he's right. A lot of playing this course well is not doing something stupid and most of all you have to be patient."

"There's Freddie," Foot pointed out a ball from the tee rolling into the bottom of the Valley of Sin, a tee shot of three hundred and thirty yards.

"Good grief."

"You could do that."

Kevin made a face. "Yeah, sure I can. He's long. I think he can hit it as long as he wants. I can't do that."

"Let's see what he does with his second."

Couples and his partner, someone they didn't recognize, walked across Grannie Clark's Wynd. The other player's ball was just on the edge of the paved road.

"I don't understand why he has to play it from the road," Foot half said to himself. Kevin jumped in to lecture about the game.

"Over here, you play it as it lies. When the railroad tracks were here, you had to play it off those. It's what makes golf so special."

The unknown player topped his shot along the ground, down and up the Valley of Sin, and over the green. Couples walked up to his ball to examine the shot. His choices were to run it up the valley slope or wedge it over to the hole. After pulling at his sweater and stretching his arms over his head, he hit a putt that popped against the flagstick and stopped an inch or two from the cup. The spectators around the green clapped.

"He's good," Kevin admired.

"You're good, too, you know."

"Is this the pep talk?"

"Yeah, part of my before-the-last-practice-round-of-Kevin's-first-international-major-tournament..."

"First major of any kind," Kevin corrected.

"Yeah," Foot continued with the title of Kevin's routine, "first-major-pre-last-practice-round routine. I dare you to say that real fast three times."

"So," Kevin took the last sip of tea. "You're leaving me this evening to do a little business?"

"Yes."

"What business do you have over here?"

"Since you don't pay me enough. I have to make money to live on somewhere. I'm talking to people about the whisky business."

"But you don't want to tell me what."

"You'd be bored," Foot said.

Two hours later, Foot was munching on delicate bits of fresh salmon piled on small crackers and sipping eighty-year old Scotch whisky in a private suite on the top floor of the Old Course Hotel. Empty, his cut crystal glass weighed a pound, full it was probably worth a thousand dollars. His host was the tiny Scot with the Rolls Royce.

"Pinky," Foot said: By this time they had regressed to schoolboys, "Does life ever get any better than this?"

"Footie, I dinna think so. There is nothing more satisfying than to make a good deal with a good friend where everybody is happy. And we both can make a lot of money."

"Pinky." Foot sat up from the deep cushions of the couch. The lowering sun turned his face to gold. "Have we missed anything? Can anything go wrong from here?"

"I dinna think so. The lawyers do all the paperwork and we sign the documents on Friday night. Nothing I can think of. I have a bit of exposure, but that's business. Would ye like a cigar?" The tiny man stretched from his chair to the center of the huge square coffee table that separated the two men. Just within his reach was a carved wooden box. He opened the lid and pulled out two massive cigars. He threw one to Foot. "Having exclusive worldwide distribution can only be good, as long as the quality is there. I see no problems for you unless the Japanese interests take up too much of your time. That and your laddie doing well and you getting distracted."

"Kevin is important..."

"I ken that."

"And he can be good. He's young. He's had his troubles; missed cuts, a dumb mistake here and there, but he's growing up. I'll stick with him until he's on the right track."

"The son you never had, eh, Footie? Going to teach him about the world of high risk international finance along the way?" The old Scot lit his cigar.

Foot smiled. "Maybe. But you canny old bugger you; I'm your equal in business. Don't you ever forget that."

"Nae fear, old man. I'll beat you when I can, but I'll never take too much advantage. This deal was perfect for the both of us and that's why we're celebratin.' How about dinner doonstairs? On you."

"Pinky, Pinky. I'll let you think you've won this little one, like I have all the others."

Kevin stopped to say hello and have a half pint at the Sea Bird, but he was too restless to sit for long. A walk along the streets of Cellardyke to Anstruther was just the cure for the Open nerves that toggled deep within his muscles. He wanted just that right amount of tension to be at his peak, too much or too little and he would not play well. A walk, with the feel of Scotland under his feet and the sight of the North Sea for his eyes and the sound of gulls for his ears would be just the tonic he needed.

He strolled along John Street between the walls of flats on either side of a road built for horse-drawn carts. In places the sidewalk stopped, either to make room for steps up to a door or the road narrowed too much to allow a sidewalk. In fifteen minutes, he had walked to Anstruther Harbour, where the dull red North Carr Lightship museum rested at anchor and where a line of shops faced the sea. There was a lot of noisy conversation carried on the smell of beer and cigarettes from the four pubs along the way and a long double queue waiting outside the Fish Bar, where the sweet aroma of fish and chips and vinegar filled the air. Kevin continued to wander up and down the streets, past the road to St. Andrews and onto the road to Pittenweem. Along this road, away from the water, his eyes spotted the Dreel Tavern at the same time his stomach registered empty. "Bar lunches and suppers," the sign said, and added, "good food since the 16th century." The worn stone walls laid claim to venerable age, the low ceiling inside proved it. Like their rented cottage, any sudden move without paying attention resulted in a painful knock on the head.

The bar was straight in front of him and on either side were almost identical dining rooms. One was for bar suppers, the other for regular dinner. He hadn't yet figured out the difference since you could eat the same food in either place. He chose the room to the right and found a corner table. Of the other tables, two were empty, one had a family of five, one a couple, and the last held four local fishermen. By the looks of their clothes and the sweet aroma of seaweed, they were just in from the sea. Kevin sat and looked around.

This was the oldest restaurant he had ever been in. According to an old notice on a nearby wall, a king or two had stopped here back in the 1700s, even before the United States existed. He closed his eyes for a moment envisioning the King's finely dressed retinue arriving in carriages, colorful flags and banners flapping in the breeze and the innkeeper dashing about worried that his head might be chopped off at the slightest miscue.

"May I help you, sir?"

The voice was sweeter than the perfume of the heather, softer than the lightest breeze through the glens and purer than the sunshine of the highlands. Kevin opened his eyes to look into the deepest pools of liquid green in the universe.

"Sorry to disturb you. Would you like something?" she smiled, warming the room and everything in it.

Her skin was baby smooth with just a touch of sunburn on

her cheeks to set off her long auburn hair.

"Ah," Kevin's tongue was in spasm, his mind on holiday, his senses on overload. Say something. Say something. "Ah..." Kevin stammered.

"Something to drink?" she asked.

"Ah..."

She left to retrieve a menu. He watched her come back from the bar lost in the bounce of her hair, the white blouse, the black skirt, the dark stockings and the sensible shoes. Her return enveloped his whole world.

She handed him the menu and told him she'd be back to take his order.

The most beautiful, wonderful, sweetest woman in the world, he thought. A waitress in a small town pub ten miles outside St. Andrews and of all the places she could be, I'm here too.

When she came back again, he asked if she had any recommendations just to hear her voice and because he hadn't taken his eyes off of her long enough to look at the menu. Her Scottish accent was light and airy, not like the guttural snort and spit of most he had heard.

"The lasagne is good. That and a glass of one of our premium red wines would make an excellent supper."

Of course, she would know what was best. She would know everything. She was an angel. He handed her the menu and told her that's what he would have. He prayed to the chief of all angels that his smile would make her wonder about him. It must have. She turned back just as she was about to leave and asked him if he was an American.

"Yeah," he said. "I'm here for the Open."

"Ah yes, crowds of tourists here for the Open." She smiled and turned away before he could decide if it was uncool to tell her he was a player. She brought the glass of wine first. Kevin tried to thank her so it would be a meaningful moment, something they would someday tell their children. When she brought the lasagne he thanked her and asked her if she had made it herself. He tried to chat with her when she brought a second glass of wine but the tables were occupied now and she was scurrying from one to the other. He noticed that she was not good at her job. She mixed up orders and had to backtrack to bring items that should have been automatic. He couldn't decide between ordering more or leaving her alone.

A crash reverberated off the walls. This angel had dropped a full tray of empty dishes. The bartender glared and told her, "That will come off your wages." She looked at her scowling boss and bent over to pick up the smashed dishes and the silverware that had bounced all over the floor. Kevin got up to help.

"Oh, no, no," she tried to shoo him away with her hands, with a growing blush that a customer had come over and was picking up pieces of dirty plates and was on his knees reaching for errant knives and forks among the legs of the tables and customers. He insisted. The bartender came out from behind the bar to help. Once finished, he gave Kevin a wet towel to clean his hands, a clean dry one to dry them and an offer of the best whisky in the house as thanks.

Ten minutes later, Kevin sat at the bar, nursing his drink, hoping she would have time to stop and thank him again. She rushed to the cash register behind the bar, squinted at the bill and the machine before pushing at the buttons with one hand while the other held the bill as if it were a dead fish. It took four tries to ring up the sale. Once done, she turned to Kevin.

"Thank you again for helping me. That was quite a mess."

"You're welcome. It doesn't seem like you've been doing waitressing for long."

She smiled that smile again. The one that made him want to smile too and take her in his arms.

"You can tell."

"First week?"

"First two hours. My brother, the barman, owns the tavern. I'm helping out until his waitress can come. She rang up saying she'd be late. I'm just subbing. I guess it showed."

"Your accent is beautiful." She blushed. "You're not from here are you?"

"No. I'm from way north, a small town called Dornoch, on the East Coast off the Dornoch Firth."

"Dornoch." Kevin nodded his head as if he was as familiar with Dornoch as he was Los Angeles.

"You've heard of it?"

"Yes. It's a famous place. The home of Donald Ross, one of my heroes and a great golf course, designed by Old Tom Morris himself."

"Aye, that's right. Not many people know that, even up there. We don't see the golf as anything special."

"Ah..." Kevin didn't want to rush things, but he didn't want to lose the chance either. She could be leaving tomorrow. "I don't want to be forward, but if you're not married or engaged or going with someone, may I buy you a drink?"

She laughed. "The bartender is my brother you know."

"Would he mind if I bought his sister a drink in his bar?"

"He's a Scot. He'd be delighted if you bought me a drink, and so would his sister."

6

nd you probably told her that didn't you, you sweet talker you."

Kevin didn't pause to acknowledge the teasing, or even inhale.

"Man, she is something. Beautiful, intelligent, great personality..."

"Are we playing today?"

Kevin looked startled. "Of course. Why?"

"I thought you might be leaving me. For this new woman. And after all we meant to each other."

"Foot. I just met her. I don't even know her. Hardly." Then his eyes glazed over again. "Oh, man."

Foot laughed. "You do know that the British Open is this week."

Kevin blushed. "I guess I am blathering on."

"Blathering?"

"Yeah. Blathering."

Foot got up and started collecting the breakfast dishes.

"Kev, go take a shower, a cold one, then a hot one to wash, then another cold one so you can play some golf. We've got a lot of work to do before tomorrow."

Kevin was suddenly serious. "Tomorrow. That's so soon. Tomorrow." His eyes wandered off, his mind followed to the pageantry, the history, the excitement of the British Open. Prestwick, 1860, Willie Park, first Open Champion, three times around the twelve-hole course in a day. The champions who had won at St. Andrews; Faldo, Ballesteros, Nicklaus, Locke, Snead, Jones, and way back to J.H. Taylor. All the greats had competed at St. Andrews. Bob Jones, a member of the R & A was given Freedom of the City, only the second American after Ben Franklin; and Jack Nicklaus an honorary doctorate from the university and Gary Player, too. This was the place where everything happened. Even in practice rounds, walking over the stone bridge spanning the Swilcan Burn at eighteen had given him goosebumps. The first tee shakes tomorrow just might knock him out.

The practice round was mostly uneventful. On the par three eleventh, Kevin put his tee shot into the right greenside bunker. Foot quickly consulted the notes he had taken from Oscar's tutorial. "That's the Strath bunker. Oscar says you don't want to be in there."

Kevin shrugged his shoulders. "Let's see how bad it can be."

The two walked down from the elevated tee the hundred and fifty yards to the bunker and waited a couple of minutes as Chip Beck and Davis Love played seven. This was the very top of the shepherd's crook where eleven and seven shared a green and the shots criss-crossed. Love and Beck had the right of way.

Once to the bunker, they understood why Foot had underlined "do not be in the Strath," in his notes. Kevin's ball was nestled against the near vertical face of the bunker. He couldn't advance the ball. Even hitting it sideways would be a problem. Kevin looked at Foot. "Any suggestions?"

"You're not going to be able to get it out in one shot. I think what you have to do is hit it well enough so you might be able to get it out with your next shot."

Kevin took his pitching wedge and climbed down to the sand. The problem he faced was compounded by being on the left side. If he were left handed, he could have hit toward the flat part of the bunker. Right handed, he was limited to hoping the ball would bounce against the side of the bunker and far enough back so he could have a good swing with his second bunker shot. That didn't happen. He swung as hard as he could, and moved the ball only an inch. One more swing pushed the ball out toward the right lip. This gave him just enough room to gouge the ball out of the bunker and back toward the tee. "Nice shot," Love told him from high up the green. Kevin turned to see both he and Beck standing above him on the eighth green and giving him a little wave.

Foot stood by the ball. Screwing his eyes tight in concentration and holding up fingers as he counted, he said, "Now let's see, one off the tee, one against the face, another one against the face, and one to get out. We lie four," he said proudly, opening his eyes.

On eighteen, Kevin had a tap in for par. As is his nature, he mused on how this was his very last-golf-shot-before-hitting-for-real-in-the-Open-Championship. And as is the nature of golf, he repeated his musings after he missed the tap in and had to hit his very-last-shot-before-the-Open a second time.

"Gloria, is it?" Foot asked as Kevin handed him his putter. Foot had been waiting with the golf bag just off the green and near the steps up to the public walkway. Two or three hundred spectators wandered around. Kevin was oblivious to them all.

"Yeah," he smiled. "She's going to meet me back at the Dreel Tavern and we're going to take a walk along the coast."

"Okay," Foot said. "I'm going to hang around here for a while. Later, I'm going to take a look at the old castle up the street." He looked sternly at Kevin. "Don't do ANYTHING that will throw off your tempo. You are playing ace's high right now and we want to keep it that way. DON'T we?" he asked his nose against Kevin's.

Kevin paused for a moment. "I guess so," he said, scratching his head. "You know. I haven't even kissed her yet. Didn't seem right. She's just something so special. I'll be in early." His fist smacked Foot on the shoulder. "I promise."

Two hours later, Foot was trudging up the hill of Bow Butts, above the Royal and Ancient Clubhouse toward the castle ruins. Foot was well travelled and well versed in the small details of history, fact or fable. He loved the stories of Lancelot and the round table, the behind the scenes intrigue of church and state, and all of the pomp and circumstance of Kings, Queens and beautiful princesses. A visit to the medieval castle ruins in St. Andrews was a bit of reminiscence. He had first seen them in the late forties, when his father brought the family over for a holiday.

The castle itself was set back on a lawn of deep green grass and behind a fence whose gate led to the entrance of a modern gift shop and museum. He gave the woman behind the glass counter a pound note and took back a green ticket. Foot raced through the displays of torture and grief to the walkway that led to the actual castle ruins. He had told Kevin that he wanted to feel the stone under his hands and see if the famous Bottle Dungeon that had scared him out of his wits as a child was still as frightening. The dungeon's name was from its shape, narrow at the top and ballooning out like a bottle at the bottom. Most prisoners were thrown roughly through the narrow opening to tumble fifteen feet to the bottom. The majority suffered severe bruises and broken bones from the fall, and in the blackness of their lonely hours, many prayed for death to free them from their agony and hopelessness.

It was still scary. The dungeon itself was in a small room with a stone ceiling even lower than their cottage. Foot shivered as he entered. A placard noted a few of the infamous events of the castle. Especially poor Cardinal Beaton, who sat with his cronies and enjoyed the spectacle of George Wishart, a Protestant reformer, being burned at the stake outside the castle; only to become, a few months later, a ritually tortured corpse floating in a pickle solution at the bottom of this same Bottle Dungeon.

Foot bent over to get under the sill of the entrance to the Dungeon room. As he straightened up he saw Oscar Brown raking some leaves on the other side of the inner courtyard.

"Mr. Brown," Foot called and waved.

Oscar looked up. "Hello," he waved back.

Foot went over to him. "Mr. Brown, those tips you gave us really helped. I think Kevin is as well prepared as he can be for tomorrow's start.

"Aye, I though I could be of some service. The old woman takes a bit of getting used to." Oscar suddenly stopped and looked distracted. He nodded his head for a moment, and then suggested to Foot, "If your player does all right and is playing on Saturday, tell him to come by and see me Friday night. I may be able to help a wee bit more."

"Sure, I'll do that. I'm pretty sure Kevin will play well enough to make the cut. I wouldn't tell him, but I think he has a chance to win it. Not many have, first time over, but he has the skill and the desire. We just have to stay out of the bunkers." Foot told Oscar about the Strath experience earlier.

"Aye. That's all you can do."

"You work here too?" Foot asked.

"Aye. A wee bit of cleaning and sweeping and most nights I close up after the tourists and staff have gone." He winked. "It pays a few bob so they let me in Ben's where I spend all I make."

Foot moved to go. "Well, Mr. Brown, think of us tomorrow."

Oscar agreed. "That I will, laddie," he said softly, "that I will."

The touch of her hand in his was like holding a cupful of rainbow. They walked together down to the harbor from the Dreel Tavern and hopped like nine-year olds across the stepping stones where the stream that separated Anstruther Easter from Anstruther Wester meets the small sandy beach. They walked down the dirt path that ran along the low cliff top to Pittenweem, Kevin leading, until he took her hand to help her up a steep portion, slippery with mud.

She suggested they rest a while on the nearby bench. They

sat close, not touching, but wanting to. The sun was way to the right, still high although it was early evening. Gloria pointed out the cormorants, gulls, and oystercatchers. "There are lots of puffins on the Isle of May," she said, "but few fly over here."

Her every word was as golden as the sunlight that reflected off her hair. He sensed her sweet heather fragrance in the gentle breeze that came off the sea. Without looking, he knew she was smiling and it made him smile too. He felt his heart pounding like a bass drum.

She rose first and led the way into Pittenweem. "This is where all the local restaurants get their fish," she told him when they reached the harbor. "There was a market yesterday morning as there is every morning except Mondays. They also sell on Monday and Friday afternoons. The fishermen go out late Sunday or early Monday for the fish we sell on Monday night. The fish we cook is so fresh; you almost have to catch it again at the table."

Kevin laughed. He would have laughed at anything. He was giddy. "Gloria, I've never met anyone like you," he said, squirming like a hungry puppy.

She sat them down on the bench outside the antique store with the two giant Japanese vases in the window. "And I have never been so smitten in my life either, Mr. Kevin Turner. It's like magic, isn't it?"

They sat facing each other, knees closer and almost touching.

"I think it is magic. You coming down for a little holiday, not going out in order to help your brother, my wandering in, you spilling the tray."

She laughed. "You still think that was an accident, do you? I had my eye on you the whole time."

"You did?"

"The truth?"

"Yes."

"No."

"Oh."

She laughed that way again. "I'm not going to put you off your game, am I?"

"Golf? Oh no, not at all," he told her without conviction.

"I wouldn't want to do that. But if you don't mind, I'd like to stay the weekend and watch you play."

Kevin began to realize, again, that there was this golf tournament beginning tomorrow that he hoped would continue for him over the weekend. "Well, even if you were a distraction, which you are not," he lied to her. "I'm a professional and that makes a big difference," he lied to himself. Kevin looked into her deep green eyes again. "Who am I kidding?" he told her. "You are the most beautiful distraction I have ever known and I have no idea how I'm going to be able to play tomorrow."

Gloria reached over and took his hand in hers. Kevin melted into a pile of glop. "I'll make you a deal, Mr. Turner. You play your best tomorrow and I'll make us dinner. And you have to tell me true. You play your best, every shot, no matter what the score. Deal?"

"Every shot the best I can do. No matter what I score and I have to tell you if I've done that or not."

"Aye. You do that and I'll make a wonderful dinner."

"How will you know if I tell you the truth?"

"Two ways, Mr. Turner." She got up, took his hand and started leading him back to Anstruther. "I can tell by your eyes and, there is nothing unless there is trust. I know that and you know that. Now let's get back, I have a wee bit of work to do and you need your rest." She held his hand all the way back, mostly to stop him from floating off.

Kevin didn't want the evening to end. Instead of turning into the cottage, he went the few extra steps to the Sea Bird. Mr. Grayson called out a hello and pointed to an empty seat at the bar. The place held the usual crowd accented with the usual heavy smoke and a touch of haddock and cod.

"A pint of our best British ale, Mr. Turner?"

"Half pint, please, Mr. Grayson. I have a big day tomorrow."

"That's right. The Open starts tomorrow. Do you know when you're playing?"

"No. Foot was going to find out. It could be any time. I think the first tee time is something like seven in the morning and the last around four in the afternoon. But I wasn't planning to sleep much anyway."

"You're off at three o'clock on the nose. Foot was in earlier and told us."

"Three."

"Yes. Is that good or bad?"

"I don't know. I've never started that late, and this is my first major tournament. I guess it's bad. There's a lot of time to wait and think too much."

"Aye," Mr. Grayson said, putting the half pint glass on a coaster. He left for other chores while Kevin wondered what he was going to do all day. Waiting would drive him crazy, yet he had to keep his edge all afternoon. He could see Gloria but that probably would be exactly the wrong thing to do. But he couldn't just hang around and he couldn't go to the course early and watch. That would drive him crazy too. He sipped his beer wondering, then wisely left most of it, and the problem, for tomorrow. He had some dreaming to do.

Oscar was deep under the covers. Benedict had squirmed down to his feet and was tickling him every time she moved, which was often. Barry had come by again while he was heating a can of noodle soup on the hot plate. The player was going to shoot even par. That was the first sign. He could read the list of players in the Friday morning paper if he wished to guess which one it might be. Only after Friday would he know who it was going to be for sure.

"Make your move?" Kevin was sneaking up the steep stairs of the cottage when Foot's booming voice startled him.

"What?"

The voice behind the bedroom door continued, "It's past midnight. You're not much of a drinker. You don't gamble. You don't do drugs. The place is too small to get lost. You didn't take the car. Need I go on? Has to be the woman. But..." The bed groaned as Foot made a show of rustling the covers and pounding the pillow. "Tell me tomorrow. I'm asleep."

Foot regretted the invitation the next morning as he lounged in front of the sitting-room window. Neglected cereal bowls were still on the table, corn flakes drying into cement on the bottom. Kevin came in from the kitchen and sat opposite. And continued where he had left off before making more toast. "I can't believe she plays golf. She is the first woman who has really understood my love of the game. She loves it too. Isn't that fantastic? And to be from the highlands. How Scottish can you get? She says it's beautiful. But she is beautiful. Take her out of the highlands and they wouldn't be as beautiful without her..."

7

"What are you so nervous about?" Foot asked.

By five minutes to three, spectators had jammed the stands to the right of the first tee and the stands behind the eighteenth green. Royal and Ancient members, all of them in coats and ties, peered out the windows of the clubhouse and down from the balcony outside the Secretary's office. Kevin was paired with Bernhard Langer, a major tournament winner, and Devon Buxley, an Englishman who played on the European Tour. Both had already wished him well and were preparing themselves for play. Kevin had run back to the locker room once to make sure he didn't have to go to the bathroom any more, but he was sure he had to go again. There was no feeling in his hands. His eyes kept going out of focus. He was sweating in the sixty degree weather and about to throw up on his shoes. The history weighed heavy on his warm yet shaking shoulders.

"I'm nervous Foot. Very nervous."

"What do you have to be nervous about?" Foot asked again. "You're a golfer about to play a round of golf, not a neurosurgeon about to cut into somebody's brains. What's the big deal?"

"Foot, this is the frigging British Open." He clinched his teeth, finishing the sentence in a partial Dirty Harry growl.

"Kev," Foot put his hand on the deluded boy's shoulder, "I hate to point this out to you, but the tournament is famous and a big deal. You're not. You are not the big deal here. You are a nobody. So lighten up." Foot pushed Kevin's shoulder as he finished his mini lecture.

Kevin relaxed. "You're right." He managed a small smile. "The tournament is the big deal. I'm not." Then he thought about Gloria. She had given him her scarf to carry. It nestled in his pocket and he planned to touch it as part of his routine before every shot. "All I have to do is play golf one shot at a time," he confirmed their earlier discussion. "How hard could that be?"

Now Foot relaxed too. "That's right. You know the course. A little anyway. I have Oscar's thoughts written all over the course map. And we know the whereabouts of the Strath Bunker. We're ready." Foot mulled over whether to bring something up. "Remember Gamez?"

Kevin remembered. Robert Gamez was in the same situation then as Kevin was now; new on the Tour, first British Open, nervous as all get out. On the first tee, first day, in front of twenty zillion people, sunshine and still air, he dead topped his drive. Barely made it past Grannie Clark's Wynd. Grannie Clark could have done it better. Even Grannie's grandmother. Gamez was expressionless. He walked the short distance to his ball, pulled out a long iron and screamed his second to the green. Some say he sank the putt for birdie. Kevin didn't know if he made it or not, but whatever Gamez did, he did it right.

They watched Bernhard hit. A smooth, veteran's swing

with driver put the ball down the middle. Kevin rolled Gloria's scarf around in his pocket. Buxley was next, also with a driver and got underneath it, skying the ball only a couple of hundred yards.

"Smooth it," Foot told Kevin as the starter announced his name. Kevin had a three-wood. He planned on aiming right of the stone bridge and cutting it back to the fairway. Pretending to be Lee Trevino, he did just that. He watched his ball fly high and arc back to the middle. He was playing in the British Open.

Four and a half hours later, with only minor disasters here and there, the three o'clock group putted out on eighteen. Langer made a ten-foot birdie putt for a 69, Buxley made a five-foot putt for par and a one over 73, and Kevin tapped in for a four, and an even par round of 72. Kevin had one confession for Gloria, but was pretty sure she would forgive him.

On the seventh hole, running along at two under, Kevin hit his approach to the green short and left, into the familiar Strath Bunker. He got fancy trying to turn the ball right to left into the wind and pull hooked it. Dumb. Dumb. Dumb. The ball sat tight against the wall again and he hacked it out to the green, way over on the eleventh hole side leaving a sixty yard par putt. Three putts later, he was back to even par.

But that was then and this was now. Foot took the clubs to the car and left for the cottage. Kevin finished the formalities of signing his score card and proceeded into the Royal and Ancient clubhouse and down the steps to the locker room. He loved it that his assigned locker was that of Baron Lawrence T. Tindel. A real Baron. He wandered through the narrow aisles reading other names. There were lots of generals, a few Field Marshals, a smattering of various kinds of royalty, famous business magnates and even a few TV and movie stars including Sean Connery. There were also a lot of golfers in various stages of undress and the sounds of at least half a dozen languages other than English. Guys laughed, kidded one another, retold disaster stories. A few, three or four, were quiet, going through the business of showering and getting out of there. They were the ones that would be at the bottom of the list in the newspaper with scores like 85 or so. One or two disaster holes adding an eight or nine to the scorecard. Playing the Old Course was like walking a mine field. One false step and it's over.

There are only a few shower stalls in the basement locker room. As unobtrusively as he could, Kevin took a shower in each one. He started in the one at the far left, not getting his hair wet and drying off afterward so it looked as if he was waiting to take one. Once, because other guys waited, he left the shower room, wandered around for a while, then came back when they were gone. Finally, he reached the last one, washed his hair, and completed his first-round shower-in-the-same-shower-that-both-Nicklaus-and-Jones-had-used-after-their-first-round-on-the-Old-Course routine

Gloria waited for him outside the entrance to the R & A. She was dressed in a long dark blue wool coat that was almost down to her ankles and wore heels, the first time he had seen her out of sensible shoes. He smiled when he saw her. She smiled back.

"How did you do?"

"Pretty good. One mistake cost me two strokes, but I had

three birdies, one double bogey and a bogey. Not bad for a start."

Gloria took his arm and led him up toward North Street. "Did you earn your dinner?"

Kevin proceeded to tell her about his mistake and provided a blow by blow description of his round. She actually listened. "But you didn't play your best on each shot, did you?" she asked.

"No," Kevin admitted, surprised at how strict she was.

"Well then," Gloria told him, "You are now to take me to dinner." She looked at him a little worried. "If that's okay, of course."

Kevin tightened his grip on her arm. "I couldn't be happier. Where would you like to go?"

"We have reservations at a Chinese restaurant on South Street. I made them just in case. I hope you don't mind. Do you like Chinese?"

Kevin loved everything she said and everything she did.

He fell in love again when he helped her with her coat at the restaurant. She wore a knee length knitted wool dress with buttons down the front that his mother would have said was pretty and his father would have been holding his chest, trying to breathe. It wasn't tight or revealing. It was pretty. But it moved, it flowed, it slid around corners. It draped, it cupped, it caressed, it made Kevin stop breathing too. "I'm glad you like it," she said.

"Gloria," a familiar voice called from the dining room.

They turned toward the voice. "Hi, Arnold," Gloria waved.

Arnold Palmer. Arnold waved his arm for them to come

over. Gloria had to grab Kevin's arm and pull.

Arnold Palmer stood up and hugged Gloria. Arnold Palmer held out his hand to Kevin and said, "Hi Kevin, I'm Arnold Palmer," with that infectious Palmer grin.

"Mr. Palmer. Arnold Palmer. This is unbelievable." Kevin pumped the poor man's hand like he was milking a cow. "Arnold Palmer. I'm Kevin Turner, Mr. Palmer. My God. Arnold Palmer," Kevin repeated, with all the style and grace of an amphetamine addict.

"I know," Palmer smiled. "I've been looking forward to meeting you. Sit down," he motioned to one of the empty chairs. Kevin plopped down and turned to Gloria.

"Arnold Palmer. Pinch me," he told her, "and make it hurt. I don't want this to be a dream."

"Shhh," she told him. "It's no dream. The Palmers and Kinlochs go back a long time. My grandfather knew Deacon Palmer, my dad was friends with Arnold and I am still."

"Gloria is like a daughter to me," Arnold said. "Or maybe I should make that a granddaughter," he added with a shake of his head.

Gloria touched Kevin's hand on the table. "I didn't think you would mind the surprise. I knew he was coming and planned to see him. That was before I met you. It seemed a good idea to bring you along."

"I can't believe it. Here I am, sitting with the King. Wow."

"What about me?" Gloria asked.

"And the princess," he added quickly.

During dinner, Arnold asked Kevin how he liked the Open so far.

"I love it. I hope I make the cut and go on from there."

"Me too," Arnold said.

Kevin was surprised. He hadn't realized Palmer was playing. Arnie noticed.

"They always invite me to play in the Open. And since it was St. Andrews, I told them I'd play one last time. I sure thought my time was over, but I'm hitting the ball pretty well and they wanted me to come. They're starting a ceremonial thing like what's done at the Master's. I confirmed only a week ago, so few people knew I was coming. I wanted to avoid all the press hoopla. I'm not taking anyone's place so it's just a little trip down memory lane. You beat me by seven shots, and believe me, I was glad to break eighty."

"That's pretty good."

"Ahhghh. It's always the same story, a little bit better driving, a few better approaches, a few more putts. It doesn't seem like so much, but that's the difference. You get older; you can't hit the shots as well or as often. But the games been great to me and I still love playing."

"Mr. Palmer," Kevin asked, "any advice for me?"

"Patience. The Old Course will break you if you push too hard. Take your lumps, and there will be plenty of them. Don't panic and don't press. Accept the rub of the green like a gentleman, but never give up. And please, it's Arnie."

"Sounds like good advice," Gloria interjected.

In the presence of the King, Kevin asked a million questions about playing in the Open.

"What else? Anything specific?" he asked once again, twenty minutes later.

"Well, Kevin, I had Tip as my caddie, helping me every step of the way."

"I have Foot."

"I know Foot. He's a terrific guy. Has he been over here before?"

"No, but we both walked the course with this guy named Oscar."

"Oscar." Palmer gave the name some thought. "Oscar. Brown? Is his last name Brown? Old guy? Always wears dumpy clothes?"

"Yeah," Kevin told him, pleased that Arnold Palmer knew of their consultant Oscar.

"He's a strange guy."

"Why?"

"Oh. Just stories I've heard. If I remember correctly, somebody said he had murdered somebody or something like that."

"Oh, I don't think so. Oscar has caddied here for thirty years. He doesn't seem the type to have murdered anybody. Must be whoever you talked to had the wrong guy. Brown is a common name."

"Maybe so. But the Oscar Brown I heard about knew the course frontwards and backwards. Tip took him under his wing and taught him a few things, so whatever he told you, you can trust and I suggest you do whatever he said to do. That's what I did with Tip and that's what Tony Lema did and won. The best I did here was second to Kel Nagle in '60. Seventeen killed me that year," the King drifted back remembering the details, "and that same year the Valley of Sin flooded from a huge rainstorm on Friday. That was really something." Palmer shook his head at the memory.

"But you won the next year," Kevin reminded the King.

"Yes, I did, Kevin and thank you for remembering. But take my advice this time, patience and do whatever Oscar Brown told you to do. Local knowledge is critical on the Old Course."

The evening continued like a fairy tale for Kevin; stories of the early days on the Tour, intimate personality profiles of all the greats back to Walter Hagan, and stories from Gloria about the old pro himself. Arnold insisted both on paying for dinner and inviting Kevin and Gloria to dinner on Saturday night. Kevin was wise enough to recognize he had ignored the love of his life for a hoary old golf pro. As they walked down South Street to where she had parked her car, he started to explain.

"Gloria, I'm sorry for tonight. I was so awe struck. I'm afraid I ignored you and I certainly didn't mean to."

Gloria smiled. "I would have been surprised if you hadn't focused so much on Arnold. He's quite a guy."

"He sure is, but you're quite somebody too, you know."

"Kevin, you're embarrassing me."

Kevin stopped in the middle of the road. "I mean it. I've never felt this way before." He moved to kiss her but she turned away.

"Kevin, don't. Not now. Please."

"I'm sorry. I didn't mean anything."

They walked together to the car, the silence between them awkward. On the drive, the conversation remained Arnold Palmer. At her door he thanked her again for the fantastic surprise. She said "you're welcome," smiled what seemed like a sad smile, turned, and went into her brother's flat.

Oscar tossed and turned, making Benedict scurry for her life as his legs whipped back and forth under the covers. Barry had told him more of the plan and it scared him. He didn't want to go back to the hospital, to people who hurt him. Barry kept insisting it had to be done his way and Oscar argued right back he couldn't do it. Then Barry said he had to do what was right, without fail, even if it was hard. Oscar feared pain, the police, and being locked up. He liked his job at the castle and he liked drinking at Ben's. They didn't bother him there like other places.

He once tried living back in Pittenweem and even in Cellardyke. By the time they let him move away from the hospital, his father and mother had died. His brother told him he wasn't needed on the farm and his sister had moved to Glasgow and nobody would tell him where she lived. He stayed for a while in a room in Pittenweem until the time the police had to come. They told him he couldn't stop the children to lecture them in the street any more. Oscar tried to explain the importance of school work and doing the right thing. The police told him to leave the kids alone but the landlady told him to get out.

It was worse in Cellardyke. One day as he walked past the Sea Bird three young fishermen came out. They taunted him, yelling, "Crazy man" and "thriller killer" and said they would fix his busted brain. They chased him all the way to the dirt path to Crail that ran through pig farms and rocky hillsides. There, away from the houses, they pounced. They pushed him back and forth in the tall grass for a while to warm up. He kept pleading with them to stop. The youngest one, Fred, punched him in the stomach, doubling him over. Steve, the thinnest and most vicious of the three, kicked him in the head. The sight of blood spurting from his nose spurred them on. They took turns hitting him in the face and body until their arms ached. They left Oscar crying in the dirt while they went back to the Sea Bird. Dirty, bloodied, scared out of his mind, Oscar stumbled to the precinct police office. There, he was cleaned up, and told that it might be better if he went back to St. Andrews.

The fear woke him. Wide-eyed he sat up, trembling as if he were freezing but the room was no colder than usual. Barry told him that if he did his duty well, he would never be cold or hurt or be alone again. "I'm scared," Oscar cried out loud, rubbing his eyes with his fists, trying to make Barry go away. He loved Barry but he was afraid of him too. Benedict crawled out from the covers to nuzzle his neck. She pressed her face against his and purred. That made him less afraid. Benedict always made him feel better.

Oscar climbed out of bed and poured her a small saucer of milk. He lay next to her on the floor running his hand softly back and forth from her head to her tail while she drank. "I dinna want to hurt naebody," he said. "I dinna want to go back to the hospital. I want to do my duty. I dinna want to hurt naebody. I want to do what's right. I dinna want to hurt naebody." He said these words over and over until he went back to sleep, Benedict curled up next to Oscar's belly. After a while, his arm wrapped around his kitten and they both slept, until Barry woke him up after midnight. "Today is the day," Barry said.

8

Kevin broke his rule and read the sports section of the Scotsman to see where he stood. Thirty-three players shot even par on the Old Course Thursday. Six shot over eighty and nine scored under seventy. A complete unknown, Irish professional Terry O'Donald led the field with a 66. Normally Kevin would look at the comic section, drink coffee, and eat a roll with cheese and fruit. Foot had run to the newsagent for fresh morning rolls, the paper and cheese and brought back homemade fruit scones.

As soon as he saw the scores, he regretted it. Beyond his control, his brain calculated what he must shoot to make the cut. It was the same in high school. After each test, he would figure how many "A's" he would need to get his average to a "B" or sometimes to pass the course. In golf, he looked at how many were ahead and how many of those might score poorly, usually not too many. Often he folded and went down the road empty handed. This morning, he found Oscar's words comforting. "Nae bother with scores," he said. "The old beauty cannae be measured in numbers. She'll measure your heart. Your score will folla." It also helped that Oscar said that the numbers on the scorecard meant nothing. The weather could change from one hole to the next, the morning players finding one course, midday players another, late players a third. Kevin had an early time and faced, "Morning wind and rain, turning to showers, then clearing with rainy periods."

"That means," Foot explained, "that it's going to rain, it will rain more, less, more, not at all for a while, it will rain again, but maybe less or more."

"Man, I just want a chance. It wouldn't be fair if the afternoon guys got the break." Kevin hit himself on the forehead. "What am I saying? It won't be fair. It's not supposed to be fair! But boy, the difficulty of St. Andrews depends so much on the wind. I sure hope it doesn't blow too much." He looked at Foot. "But if it does," he repeated his catechism, "I will be patient. I will be patient. I will be patient."

"Got a game plan for today," Foot announced as he spread a thick coat of butter in between the halves of a fruit scone.

"And..."

"Remember how we played that one round in Vegas? You listened to me and didn't over process. If things get rough out there, either weather-wise or any other reason..."

"Like I made six sixes or something?"

"I didn't want to put it like that. But what I'm saying is that if you lose concentration on that course, we could be in deep shit. So, if it's getting tough, I'll tell you and you have to agree to listen, take the club I give you and swing. Concentration is first to go when frustration gets you."

"So you want me to play like a robot?"

"Yeah."

Kevin pretended to mull over the proposal. They had this

conversation often. Kevin considered that Foot had his own pre-game routine, one that included giving him a lobotomy. "I don't think. You decide the club and I hit it?"

"Yeah," They had done this too before important tournaments as a way to tell each other they would be okay no matter what. They were a team.

"Drop dead."

"I beg your pardon."

"You read from your notes what Oscar says and I'll do whatever that is. You don't know anything about this golf course either and in the wind last time you helped me to an eighty something."

"How are you feeling?" Foot asked seriously.

"About as good as a man could feel. I had a great night with Gloria last night. She is super. She is the best woman I have ever known, by far. I mean, it's like I never knew anyone before her. I feel energized, alive..."

"I meant golf."

"Oh. I'm okay."

The small sitting room above the Dreel looked out over the street. On the opposite side a row of flats blocked any direct view of the harbor and the North Sea. Gloria sat in an overstuffed chair on one side of the window, her sister-in-law sat in an identical one on the other side. The wind rattled the window, but the rain hadn't yet begun. Both held mugs of coffee in their laps. The fire in the fireplace behind Gloria popped and fizzed. She appeared to be hypnotized.

"He must be awfully special. I wish I had been here to

meet him."

"Tonight you can. I'll bring him."

"And this might be the real thing."

"Oh, Lil. It must be. I can't eat, I can't sleep, I ache for him. I have never felt this way and I never imagined I'd feel this way about a man."

"I feel that way about your brother."

Gloria looked up. "Yes, I never understood that. My brother of all people. But I guess anything's possible."

"Gloria, if this is serious and I don't believe you can tell so early, but if it is, what are you going to do?"

"You mean..."

"Of course."

"No idea."

"He has a career in America, and you have a big job here."

"I've thought of those things."

"What did you tell him?"

"Nothing's come up. We talk about how happy we are together and what an amazing thing that is."

"Are you going to tell him?"

"Yes, but not right now. There's no point in telling him everything all at once."

Oscar huddled under the covers of his bed, clutching Benedict to his chest, afraid to move. Barry was angry. Barry had given him all the signs. Their target was to be the player who had improved on his first day 72 with a 69 today. He will birdie the last hole, be wearing white shoes and a hat; not a visor. Once he knew the player, Oscar was to act and not worry about consequences. Barry said it was too important to falter or to take chances. There will be no mistakes, Barry warned. When he first came, Oscar said he was sacred about going back to the hospital. That's when Barry yelled.

Oscar didn't argue when Barry came back a second time. He had given more thought to what Barry was asking him to do. Barry wasn't always right. Oscar had to do his duty, but Barry didn't know everything. He didn't carry heavy golf bags everyday. The Caddie Master didn't tell him what a fine job he did and no one gave him ten shilling tips. Barry didn't tell the players where to aim and to watch out for the wind.

Barry said it was Oscar's privilege and duty to save the game. Golf would become a natural game again, a walk on God's good earth, a test of human spirit, a reward for intelligence and bravery. No one would ride in little powered cars that sped along miniature paved motorways. Equipment would be simple. Indulgence, hyper-technology, uniformity, and predictability would all end at the first tee. Bags would be small again and carried by the player or a young caddie. People would talk as they walked together down the fairways. They would smell the flowers and touch the trees. The eye would judge the distance and par would be irrelevant. Oscar would make it happen. When he won the championship, people would listen and he would tell them what was right.

Yet Oscar was afraid to disagree with Barry. Barry had ordered him to do what was right; his duty to the spirit of golf and to help players rediscover the essential values of the game. The game had changed. Greens are pitted by unrepaired ball marks. Divots litter the fairways. Few players walk. Even fewer play by the rules. Barry said Oscar was the last chance to return to the times when golf meant honesty and fair play. If golf continued the same way, it would be corrupted like everything else. Oscar pulled Benedict closer to him. If only he could talk to someone. But no one cared. No one ever did, except Barry. He would not upset Barry.

Oscar cuddled Benedict for a while longer before he got up. Barry had ordered him to sit in the stands all day and record everyone who made birdie on eighteen, note who shot a 72 on Thursday and followed that with a 69. It had to be in that order. The one that did and fit the other signs he would eliminate and take his place.

The town hall had free tickets for old age pensioners. He would pick one up as soon as they opened at nine and walk over to the course. It would be a long day. Late finishers would come in at eight o'clock or even later, a lot to ask of an old man. But he would always do his duty. It was too bad his mother and father would not be there to see him walk down the last fairway to the cheers of the crowd. No one had ever cheered him. Oscar began to cry. For once he would do something glorious. The fans would wave and cheer as he walked up the eighteenth. His triumphant walk on Sunday would mean they liked him. He would never be lonely again.

"Morning, Bernhard. Morning, Devon." Kevin peeked out from under his red and white umbrella and shook the hands of both men on the first tee then retreated under cover as did they. The rain fell in sheets, sometimes blown sideways in the wind, like the morning he flew into Glasgow. Only this time he stood outside waiting to play in a golf tournament. Kevin wondered about the conditions for the players on the course.

As suddenly as it began, the squall disappeared, replaced by a light drizzle; light enough so that the manmade bouquet of umbrellas that appeared in the stands also disappeared. Most of the spectators were well prepared for the elements. British fans are both knowledgeable and sensible. A few prepared for the elements by bringing extra bottles rather than extra rain gear. These men in shirt-sleeves primed themselves to stay warm from the inside and would be shirtless by mid-afternoon.

Kevin was less anxious today, but equally excited as yesterday. That seemed a year ago. Gloria made all the difference. She was so caring and so wise and so starched shirt proper. Kevin obsessed undoing the buttons on the blouse she had on the first night at the tavern. Wanting her was driving him crazy. Foot offered to come back late that night and Kevin took him up on his offer. He was sure the sexual revolution had reached Britain. She liked him and he liked her. It was only natural they would make it physical. But he would respect her needs if it killed him. He thought more about her buttons and how...

"Stop!" he yelled at himself. His blood was rushing elsewhere than his brain and golf was impossible when that happened.

"You okay?" Foot asked. He seemed to sense the problem; Kevin's flushed cheeks and his constant squirming all the clues he needed.

"Yeah,"

"Kevin, I am in the middle of a significant business deal over here with an old friend of mine. I am standing in a cold rain. And I am about to shepherd a love-sick puppy around the most famous course in the world in the biggest tournament of the young pup's life. Can you help me out a little here? Do you want me to take over now, like we agreed?"

"No. But I'll tell you, my concentration is terrible. All I can think about is Gloria."

"Can you see her in your mind's eye?"

Kevin smiled. "Every sweet wonderful inch of her."

"Sounds like good concentration. All you need to do now is apply it to golf."

Kevin pursed his lips. "Easier said than done."

"Tell you what, Captain. You have three jobs today. I want you to think about her in between shots all you want. That's fine. You remember *The Golfing Mind* book, the one that said you had to be fully prepared before each swing? That's the second thing I want you to do, be fully prepared. And last, I want you to swing the golf club as well as you can. So, think of her, be prepared before you swing, and swing as good as you got. I'll handle the rest. Can you do that?"

Kevin distrusted his feelings. "You mean you want me to let my mind wander to Gloria?"

"Yeah. It's going to anyway. We may as well let it."

"Sounds good. How will we tell if it's working?"

"Easy. If the weather stays somewhat consistent, the odd holes going out are the easier ones, and the loop from seven to ten is especially good for scoring. Your play on them will tell us how we're doing. If the weather changes, we'll have to play it by ear."

"Okay."

"Now the deal is to listen to me." Foot continued, "I have

Oscar's notes so I'll suggest the club and the direction. If you're okay with that, just get prepared and put a good swing on it. We'll go find it and start over again from there. Deal?"

"Absolutely."

The drizzle had stopped by this time, and Langer walked to the tee. Foot handed Kevin his driver.

"Three-wood," Kevin whispered, handing the club back to his caddie.

"No," Foot hissed. "The ground is wet. Driver is the right club. See where Langer's went?"

"Yeah, but I'm a lot longer than him and it feels like a three to me."

"Kevin!" Foot growled.

"What?"

"I'm letting you moon over Gloria all afternoon. Hit the damn driver."

Kevin took the driver.

Through the first eight holes, Kevin scored four on each of them. On nine, a three hundred and seven yard par four, Foot handed him driver again, although they had always planned on playing a three-wood. Foot noticed Kevin's hesitation. "Shut up and hit it," he told him. The tee shot rolled to within fifteen feet of the hole.

"Shot," Foot said, raising his eyebrows to add "I told you so." Kevin went out in a one under 35.

By the seventeenth hole, Kevin had undressed Gloria twenty different ways, and had made love to her in every way he knew. Kevin was supposed to be keeping Bernhard Langer's score, but Foot had to tell him on every green what he had shot. On seventeen, Kevin asked Foot his own score.

"Three under partner. We are cruising along. Par in for a 69.

Seventeen, the Road Hole, a tough par four called the "easiest par five in the world," played against a freshening wind. "Hit over the middle 'O,'" Foot told him. "Let's get out of here with a four."

Kevin aimed his driver over the middle "O" of the reconstructed railroad sheds straight out from the tee. The ball, flew straight over the "d" of "Old" and hooked even further left, leaving Kevin with two hundred yards to the green out of the light, but wet, left hand rough. Foot handed Kevin his six-iron.

"Six!"

"Six."

"You're nuts. I can't get a six to the front."

"Kev, imagine Gloria for a moment. Then I'm quite sure you can do anything you want with a six-iron, including getting to the front of the green."

"Give me the five," Kevin insisted.

"Kevin." Foot sounded like a stern schoolmaster.

Old memories flooded Kevin's unconscious. The bad teachers who ridiculed his spelling, the vice-principals who lied about being his friend, the counselors who never understood his interest in things other than homework, all the evils of adolescence rose up as one and shook a collective finger in front of his nose. He would not back down.

"Dammit. Five-iron, Foot."

Foot the caddie handed Kevin the player the five-iron. Kevin got fully prepared, focused on the ball and swung hard The ball leapt out of the thin rough and sailed high. The ball hit short of the green, bounced up to the green, rolled across the hole, rolled on toward the edge of the green, over the edge of the green, down the slope on the other side, and came to rest in the middle of the dreaded road. Foot didn't say anything. Neither did Kevin.

Langer and Buxley waited on the front edge as Kevin surveyed his shot. From the road, his ball had to go up a three-foot slope and another thirty feet to the hole. Only a nearly impossible-to-perform swing with a wedge to pick the ball off the asphalt would save par. His bump and run stuck in the grassy slope. Kevin waved over to Devon to play his shot from the sand while he decided what to do next. The road hole had done it again.

Foot handed Kevin his nine-iron. A closed face run up the slope with a little extra roll and a wobbly seven-foot putt produced a bogey. Not a bad outcome for a dumb mistake on the Road Hole.

A sky ball off the eighteenth tee left Kevin on another road, Grannie Clark's Wynd, the road across the first and eighteenth fairways. At only two hundred and forty yards off the tee, this road doesn't come into play at the professional level. But against the wind it's possible, as Kevin learned, to leave yourself only one route to the green, a bump and run through the Valley of Sin.

The flagstick stood in the center of the green, which made Kevin's shot a lot easier. Thanking God for little favors, Kevin took a seven-iron for this hundred yard shot, played it well back in his stance, took a half swing back and through, and punched the ball so it hit fifty yards in front of him, bounced up and over three or four mounds, rolled down into the Valley of Sin and up to the green, stopping about twenty feet above the hole. Spectators along Links road and in the stands behind the green applauded the fine shot.

One of the spectators applauding with mitten covered hands was William David, an unemployed coal miner from the English midland town of Wolverhampton. His wife remained at home worried how the bills would get paid if her husband insisted in taking trains all over Great Britain. For much of the day, Mr. David loved the golf and the course, this being his first visit to Scotland, and was amused by the man sitting to his right, to whom he had not introduced himself. While Langer looked over his birdie putt, Mr. David listened.

"Let's see," the man next to him said, looking down the list of yesterday's scores. "Langer. Ach, no. He shot a 69 yesterday Barry, so he will nae be the one, will he? Barry do I have tae wait for everybody? It's cold oot here. Okay, if that's how we have tae do it, I'll dae it. Whatever you say, Barry."

From this monologue, it appeared only the American Lee Jansen had done what he was supposed to do, according to this invisible Barry fellow anyway.

Langer tapped in for par. Buxley came up short with his birdie effort and tapped in for par too. Kevin allowed for three feet of break, left to right. The ball reached the hole and spun around as if afraid of the dark, and dropped.

"Kevin? Barry, do you ken it's Kevin? He's over my cap brim and he's got white shoes and everythin. You said somebody not like the old players like Robertson or Braid. Jansen or Turner? Jansen or Turner? Can it be?" Oscar looked at his sheet. He never expected more than one. "How am I to know, Barry? Are you going to tell me? Oh," Oscar said, realizing what Barry tried to say. "Of course, Barry. I ken what yer sayin."

Although naturally curious to see who else might fit the standard, Mr. David had promised to explore the tent village for his wife. She was fond of tiny souvenir teaspoons. As he squeezed his way past the others of his row, Oscar asked this Barry a long string of questions. Mr. David would have to remember the names of the players mentioned to see how they finished. The old man might have a link to the guy upstairs and a leg up on the betting agents. He had five pounds on Norman himself.

As Mr. David descended the last metal step of the spectator stand, Kevin handed Foot his putter. Foot would take the bag to the car and meet Kevin back at the cottage "very, very late" as Kevin reminded him. Gloria had planned to meet Kevin outside the clubhouse in about an hour. Unlike other venues, at St. Andrews wives, girlfriends, even mothers were not allowed in the clubhouse. They have a few lady employees, and on only one or two days a year, like on St. Andrews day, are women allowed in the lobby and the trophy room, but that's about it. Once a woman stayed all night, but only because the entire town was snowed in. She volunteered to help keep the fires burning, and she couldn't have gotten home no matter what. Rumor has it that four members resigned in disgust.

Kevin showered, using only one stall this time, changed into a new deep blue sweater he bought across the street at the Woollen Mill, and dashed up the steps to meet Gloria. She looked like an angel. The sun was shining and the air warming as they hugged by the front door.

"I saw your score posted," she said. "I'm glad you played well. Is there a plan for tonight?"

Kevin took her hand. "Yes. We'll have an early dinner, beginning in about fifteen minutes, pop over to Ben's Tavern where I want to talk with this guy I'll tell you about while we eat, then we'll drive back to Cellardyke where I have a small bottle of Champagne, a few crackers, and cheese waiting for us."

"And you expect this girl to follow you and do whatever you wish?"

"Yes."

Dinner was at the Golf Hotel, up the hill on the Scores only a few yards from the clubhouse. The maitre d' asked if they had reservations and with a shrug of his shoulders Kevin admitted they didn't. They were led to the hallway outside the dining room and given menus. Within five minutes, a waitress came out and asked for their dinner selection. They ordered dinner as if nothing was unusual and appetizers and glasses of wine were brought out.

Kevin turned to Gloria with an alarmed expression. "They're not going to make us eat out here in the waiting room are they?"

Gloria smiled.

"Oh." Kevin said, his face wind blown face becoming beet red. "I get it. We order out here, have a glass of wine, and then go into the dining room like civilized people for dinner." He laughed. So did Gloria. He grabbed for her hand. She let him hold it for a while before having to search for something in her purse.

Clarence McFee missed a five-foot putt that would have given him a birdie three and a hard-earned 69. That was it. Only Jansen and Turner met the signs. All that time waiting in the stands and he could have finished two hours earlier. As all the others climbed down the steps, Oscar waited for a word from Barry as to what he should do now. Barry didn't say anything. Oscar shook his head. When Barry didn't tell him what to do, he knew well enough to go about his business. When he least expected it, Barry would tell him.

Oscar reached into his pocket and fingered his bottle of medicine. He hadn't had any pills for a few days. If he took any now, Barry might not let him do what was right. He pushed the bottle deeper into his pocket and headed towards Ben's. A drink or two before he went to the castle was just the ticket and maybe Kevin Turner would show up and Barry would tell him what to do.

9

Where did you say the car was?" Kevin asked as they walked along Market Street.

"Back by the ruins of the cathedral. Parking was a real problem."

"Ah, well, Ben's is on the way. We won't spend too much time there."

"Kevin, let's not hurry. Let's enjoy each thing we do. No rush. We have a lot of time. Please."

"What do you mean?"

"I've heard about you American boys, especially the ones from California. 'Love 'em and leave 'em,' that's your motto. We're different over here. More serious." Gloria's tone was light, but with an edge.

"I may be a guy, but I have been catching the signals."

"Now I've offended you."

"No offense," Kevin said, raising his hands in surrender. "I have been a gentleman so far, but now it looks like I've stepped over an imaginary line."

"I'm sorry. You haven't stepped over any line. It's just me. Please understand. Kevin, I'm sorry." She took his hand. "Come on. Let's get to the pub and I'll buy you a pint."

Ben's was packed. They found Oscar sitting at a small table against the wall near the back. Gloria's breath caught in her throat when Kevin pointed him out. He was not a charming old man, like an older version of the caddies on television or at least someone like Foot. Oscar looked like a demented Mick Jagger, his eyes rolling and darting as if seeing monsters everywhere. They fixed on her. She drew back for a moment and held tighter to Kevin's arm.

"Mr. Turner," Oscar called out. "Ye brought yer wee lassie we ye." He stood and offered Gloria his chair as Kevin went to find two more in the crowded room. "Sit doon. Please sit doon," he insisted. Kevin returned lugging two chairs and made the introductions. Oscar didn't look any different than usual to Kevin. He was wearing a shapeless cap and three layers of sweaters and wrinkled and baggy old wool trousers. Kevin never paid attention to his missing teeth, his unnerving stare, and the way his head seemed to snap around rather than swing smoothly.

After Oscar downed two pints and during his quick exit to "unload the weight of my sins," Gloria asked Kevin if Oscar was okay.

"Sure he is. You haven't met any of the old school. They're not like the new caddies, professionals who tour with the players like Foot. This guy is from the days of yore. They stay at the same course, don't make any money and wind up sick and drunk. That's one reason why I hired him. He can use the money. The other reason is that he knows his stuff. He's helped me. And what he told me tonight has helped too."

"You're sure he's okay?"

"He's great." Both watched him weave through the crowd

to get back to their table. "I'll buy him one more pint, give him twenty pounds for tonight and we'll be off."

Unknown to Kevin and Gloria, Barry paid a visit to Oscar while he was standing at the urinal. Barry said it was Kevin. Oscar told him it couldn't be Kevin because Kevin cared about the history and the spirit of the game and shouldn't Jansen or one of the other players be taken? Barry told him no. It was Kevin who had to be eliminated and whose place Oscar must take tomorrow. Oscar wondered about the lassie. He never wanted to get involved with any lassies.

Her too, Barry told him. There is no reason to complicate things. They were together, eliminate them together. Oscar told him he would and Barry said "good" and went away.

Oscar didn't tell Barry he wasn't going to kill them. He had an idea that did the right thing but wouldn't make him go back to the hospital. Barry reminded him how important the mission was and Oscar understood it was more important than his life, but not more important than going back to the hospital. His plan was well formed by the time he returned to the table.

"Ahhh," Oscar sighed, leaning back in his chair. "That's better. Ach, I'm sorry. My apologies," he said looking at Gloria, "I dinna mean to offend the wee lassie."

"No offense, Mr. Brown. We lassies have bladders too."

"Oscar, we have to be leaving." Kevin took some bills out of his wallet. "This will cover the drinks and I want you to have another twenty pounds for your consulting efforts tonight."

Oscar paused, holding his hand to his mouth. "There's more to tell you before you play tomorrow. Would you care to walk with me a wee bit? I'm needing to get to my evening's work."

"That's right. You work at the castle, don't you?"

"Aye. Just oop the Scores. Two blocks is all."

Kevin looked at Gloria. "It's on the way," he said. "Do you mind?"

"Oh, no. I'm the one that suggested slow. May as well go by the castle and go really slow," Gloria told him, with a touch of irony. "No, really. I'd like to take a peek at the castle anyway."

"Acchh. It's settled." Oscar led the way out of the tavern. On the way, he described the castle ruins and the brutal history of the castle but added some of the more charming history of the cathedral ruins and the town. When they got to the gate, Oscar asked, "Would you like a quick personal tour, the Bottle Dungeon as naebody else gets tae see it? If ye promise to be careful, I can show you how they used to lower the prisoners, the ones they didn't throw down. Ye ken we canna do that for the general public."

The receptionist was closing the ticket counter as the three came into the gift shop. "Hello, Oscar. Cheerio, Oscar," she said as she put on her coat and went out the door. Oscar locked the door behind her and led them through the eerie shadows of the museum hallways. The route during the day is along narrow, well-lit corridors guiding the tourist through a circuit of life-sized, bas-relief figures depicting historic events. In the dim illumination from widely spaced security lights, the figures jumped out from around corners and even the most peaceful scene took on the atmosphere of a hanging. Gloria said it was scary and Oscar told her, "Aye, it's a wee bit unnerving 'til ye get used tae it," and led them out the door that took them to the castle itself. On the way, he picked up a flashlight from the little office off the main hallway.

Gloria and Kevin walked behind Oscar, who gallantly lit their path. It was more a gesture than a necessity. Once outside again, there was still plenty of daylight. As they went through the main entrance, Oscar pointed out the various features of defense and where the castle had suffered artillery damage five hundred years ago. He had them wait inside the walls while he went over to a locked wooden storage cabinet. He returned carrying a long length of thick rope. "We canna do this with most of the tourists, but by yoursel we can have a good peek at the dungeon."

"What's that?" Kevin asked.

"From the bottom. I can lower ye doon, laddie and ye can see what the prisoners faced."

"Oh, I don't know," Kevin and Gloria moaned in unison.

"Ah, weel, suit yersels. I dinna care. But ye can if ye want."

"Well, let's go look at it anyway," Kevin told him.

The dungeon room itself is across the inner courtyard from the main entrance. It's up a few steps and through a low passageway. The three of them stood looking at the opening from behind the thin metal rod fence that kept the public from falling in.

"Wow. That opening is not very big. I'm not sure if Foot could even fit in there," Kevin observed.

"Would you like to have a go?" Oscar asked Kevin, motioning to the hole and holding up the rope.

Gloria held tighter onto Kevin's arm. "Oh, I'm not sure, Oscar," Kevin answered.

"What we do is lower you on the rope looped around the metal support. Once you're doon, you walk a wee bit to get a feel of the place, then we'll use the torch tae really see it."

Kevin turned to Gloria. "What to you think?"

"I don't know. Did you ever want to see a dungeon from the bottom up?"

Kevin shrugged his shoulders. "Never occurred to me."

"Well, ye can dae it the noo, or no, I'm nae saying one way or the other."

"You can support me by yourself?"

"Oh, aye. Wrap the rope twice aroon the support. It's nae bother. Ye'd be as safe as a baby in a swing."

"Oh, hell, why not?" Kevin took the rope from Oscar and began winding it around his waist."

"Nae lad. Under yer arms. No aroon yer waist. You'd go doon folded like an empty wallet if ye did it like that."

Gloria watched as Kevin prepared to descend into the pitch black of the dungeon. Oscar wrapped the rope around the nearest fence post while Kevin stepped over the railing and walked up the slight stone slope to the opening of the dungeon.

"Now crawl to the edge and put yer feet doon the hole. I'll support ye from here," Oscar directed. Kevin got on his hands and knees and crawled backwards toward the hole. Once there, he put his feet over the empty space. "I'm there now, hold on." Gloria grabbed the end of the rope with Oscar to make sure they could hold him. Kevin laid flat on his belly at the edge of the opening as Oscar and Gloria let out the rope inch by inch. Kevin disappeared down the hole.

"How far down is it?" his voice asked.

"Aboot ten feet. A way to go yet laddie."

"I forgot the flashlight." the voice said again.

"We'll get it to you, laddie. Dinna worry."

"Will he be okay?"

"Ach, aye. We'll lower him doon all the way, then flash the torch or even drop it to him. Nae bother."

They kept lowering the rope, inch by inch. There was no noise from the hole. Finally, a muffled, "I touched bottom!" Gloria's face sagged with relief. It could have been a bottomless dungeon, her new man never to return. She glanced at the strange old man who held the rope.

Oscar loosened the rope from around the pole. "Why did you do that?"

"So he can walk aroond doon there. We canna have him tethered to the post."

"Oh."

"Now, lassie. My bones won't take crawling to the hole with the torch. Would you take it and shine it doon? See if he wants it dropped."

"Sure." Gloria took the flashlight and bent under the railing and on hands and knees, crawled the short distance to the dark opening. "Kevin," she yelled, "are you all right?"

"Yes," came out of the blackness. "It is so dark down here. If I move away from the opening, I can't see up at all. Can you see me?"

"I'm not that close. I don't want to fall in thank you," she shouted back. "I have the torch. Do you want me to drop it down?"

"Shine it down first. I want to see what it looks like."

"Wait, lassie," Oscar told her. "Have Kevin untie the rope

and I'll put the rope around you for safety. I dinna want ye fallin in."

"Kevin," she shouted. Untie the rope and we'll pull it up so it can go around me."

"Are you coming down?"

"No. I don't want to fall in."

Untying the rope was not a pleasant idea for Kevin. The pit was so black, letting go of the rope was like drifting into deep space. The little umbilicus was all he had to connect him to the real world. But untie it he did, and he heard it snake up the cold stone walls of the dungeon. He was alone. This was only a part of what those guys thrown down here suffered. Kevin was glad he was here for another five minutes then it was back to the cottage, champagne and Gloria.

In the meantime, she had backed away from the edge and Oscar was tying the rope around her waist. With a deep breath, and feeling much more secure, Gloria crawled back to the opening. "I'm back," she called.

"Great," Kevin answered, tethered by her voice.

"Do you want me to shine the light down now?"

Kevin was never so glad for a little light. This little adventure was becoming scary. A quick look when she dropped the flashlight to him, and he wanted out.

"Yes. Shine it down. When I tell you to, drop it and I'll catch it." Kevin stood back from the opening and waited. Suddenly screams echoed off the walls. There was a flash of light and a body came hurtling down in the darkness. Kevin rushed forward and bumped into Gloria, legs and arms dangling as she hung by the waist five feet off the ground.

"Kevin," she screamed, "help me." He had to lift her

flailing body to loosen the rope.

"Relax, Relax. I got you, I got you," he yelled back.

"I'm relaxing, I'm relaxing," she screamed in his ear. Before he got it undone, the rope dropped on them and they both fell to the floor.

Above, Oscar called down. "I hope you're both all right doon there. I'm verra sorry but I must play in the championship tomorrow Mr. Turner. I very much hope ye understand."

"Hey!" Kevin yelled; the sound echoing as the footsteps died away. There was no answer. He felt Gloria shiver. "You okay?" Kevin asked, holding her close.

Gloria buried herself deep in his arms. "Yes, I think so. What do we do now?"

"You had the flashlight, didn't you?"

"Yes."

"Then it's down here somewhere. We have to find it."

"Don't leave me yet." She clung tighter. Kevin didn't relish leaving her to crawl around in the dark anyway. "Why would he throw us down here?"

"I don't know what the hell he's doing."

"Oh, Kevin, what are..."

"Glo, I have no idea. This...oh man." Kevin's heart started pounding at the vivid memory.

"What?"

"This... what's going on ... this... oh man. Something like this happened to me last year."

"You were tossed into a dungeon?"

"No." Kevin had to smile in spite of his pounding heart and quick breathing. "Last year in Las Vegas I got shot at. It was before the last round of the tournament, well, actually I got shot at after the tournament too, sort of."

"Kevin, is there something you haven't been telling me I should know about?"

He laughed. "Hey, we're going to be okay," he said, as much to himself as her. "You stay here and I'll look for the flashlight."

"Where would I go?"

"No, I mean stay where you are so I can use you as a reference point to know where I've looked already."

"So now all I am to you is a reference point?"

"I'll be back." Kevin went down on his hands and knees and crawled in a small circle, keeping his toes touching Gloria's feet. All he could feel were old candy wrappers and unknown disgusting things. He kept going in wider and wider circles around her until he was at the bottom edge of the cavern itself. Crawling around the perimeter finally paid off. Kevin found the flashlight and pushed it on.

The dungeon was about twelve feet across, hollowed out of solid rock. Kevin pointed the light up the opening. They were at least twenty feet below the surface. The opening was impossibly far away.

"Oh Kevin, what are we going to do?" Gloria wrapped her arms around him and held tight.

"I guess we wait until they open in the morning." Kevin looked up at the tiny opening. "At least now I know why a golf ball sometimes doesn't want to drop into the hole. This is scary."

"Kevin, a sign said they weren't going to be open this weekend."

"That's crazy. This is Open week; everything should be open for all the tourists during Open week. Heck, that's why they call it Open week."

"Honey, this is Scotland. We don't do things the same way you do. If it's time for routine maintenance or whatever, that's what we do. Making money from the tourists is not the main idea."

"Even if lots of people would come?"

"Doesn't matter. We're used to things being closed when they're closed and open when they're open. If something is closed, you come back when they're open. Pretty simple."

"So what Oscar said about playing in the tournament meant that we're stuck here until Monday and he, somehow or other, thinks he's going to take my place? That's crazy."

"That sounds like what he plans to do."

"Hmmm. Well, in the meantime, let's poke around here."

Holding hands they explored the dungeon. It was high enough for Kevin to stand upright. Thank God for little favors. The floor was smooth rock as were the walls. And it looked like someone came down and cleaned on occasion, although probably not for a while since the floor was littered with paper candy wrappers, tissues and a few less desirable items whose passage and arrival were hard to explain. But as dungeons go, it wasn't bad. They found a comfortable spot against the wall and sat down together.

"Are you cold?" he asked.

"A little."

Kevin put his arm around her and they huddled together, the flashlight sitting between their feet shining up to the opening high above and the darkening sky they couldn't see.

"You comfy, Footie?"

"Pinky, I couldn't be more comfortable if I were lying on a cloud."

The two men were neck deep in the Old Course Hotel spa. The hot water bubbled around them while both men allowed their feet to float to the surface. Relaxation after signing the papers was total. Charles McMaster had one of his own single malt whiskies in a glass next to him, while Foot was enjoying a sampling of the number two whisky from the Royal and Ancient Club.

"Your laddie played well today, Foot."

"Yes he did. Being only five back, with the bad weather coming in tomorrow is not a bad position to be in. There aren't a lot of bodies in front of him. I'm real proud of the guy."

"And yoursel. I understand that you are learnin' to caddie like a Scot."

"That's right. I tell my player what club to hit and what cloud to aim at."

"And make sure he concentrates."

"Aye," Foot sighed. "The young Kevin Turner, I fear, has been bitten by the bug of love, a beautiful young lady from Dornoch. I can understand why he's fallen head over heels."

"Dornoch. Away up there? Hmm. So you had tae lead him by the hand aroond the coourse."

"We make a good team. He trusts me and I trust him. That plus a lot of useful information from an old caddie, Oscar Brown."

"Oscar Brown. Seems that name is familiar. You may have stumbled across one of the famous links caddies, like one who caddied for Palmer or somebody."

"He didn't name anyone I knew, but he was full of stories, so maybe he did."

"How's your drink?"

"Fine."

"Are ye keen on a massage later? They have the most wonderful masseuses here."

"Are they men?"

"Ach, no. Ye dinna think I would enjoy some brute pushing away on me de ye?"

"Well you guys go around wearing skirts all the time."

"Laddie, the kilt is not a skirt. And it has its advantages."

"Like what?"

"Well, ye ken highland sheep have great ears and they can hear the sound of a zipper from miles away."

"Pinky, that's sick."

"Laddie, it's lonely sometimes up in the highlands."

Foot took another sip from his drink. "How long have we been soaking in here?" Both men were turning a light pink and fingers and toes were wrinkling like prunes.

"Oh, I'd say ten minutes. They'll come and tell us when to get oot. Then off to the massage."

"If it's women, that's okay with me."

McMaster reached for his drink, took a sip, then submerged his arm back under the hot water. "How is Kevin in bad weather? Forecast is for a bad day."

"Only fair. Coming from California he doesn't have a lot of experience, but he did play in Europe for a year."

"Aye, that's right. So he's not bad in the wet."

"Well, you'd never find him in here. He's hates water. That's not quite true. It's worse than that. He almost drowned surfing one time. Got himself caught in kelp off the California coast. Now he's terrified around anything deeper than a puddle. I've seen him turn white as a sheet looking at an empty bathtub, just imagining it was full of water."

"We all have those fears. What's yours?"

"I don't like the dark, and I'm a little claustrophobic, but I really hate squishy things."

"Well," McMaster held up his glass. "Here's to light and space, hot bubbling water, excellent whisky, deep massage, good business, and good friends."

Foot held up his glass. "Cheers."

Gloria and Kevin sat side by side. Kevin was holding Gloria's hand in her lap. "This sure wasn't what I wanted to be doing tonight."

"Kevin?"

"What?"

"Turn off the torch."

"Why?"

"Two reasons. One of them is that I can't stand looking at these walls any more. I have them pretty much memorized. The other is to save the batteries."

"Good thinking."

With a loud click the hole became pitch black. They sat in silence for a minute or two.

"I can't stand this," Gloria said.

"Me either. Shall I turn the light back on?"

"Better not. Would you hold me?"

"You won't mind?"

"Kevin, we're trapped at the bottom of a dungeon. It's getting cold. I believe we're both scared. I am anyway. We may be here for two or three days."

"Okay. Sorry. I don't want to screw things up"

Gloria laughed. "Kevin, as I said, we're in a dungeon. Help is two or three days away…"

"I get the picture. I could always figure a way out of here and be a hero."

"Kevin, just hold me."

Kevin put his arms around her and she snuggled against his chest.

"Why do you suppose he wants to take your place in the golf tournament?"

"Glo, I have no idea. How can take my place is beyond me and why he would do such a thing is even stranger."

"I thought he was weird when I met him. But I hoped it was a harmless weird."

"It seemed like he made sure you weren't going to be hurt when he tossed you down here."

"Boy was that smooth. He let us walk into the trap didn't he?"

"Like lambs to the slaughter."

"What about tomorrow? What if I'm right and this place is closed?"

"Glo, there's not much we can do. All we have is the flashlight and rope."

They cuddled together against the air that they both

noticed was getting damp and cold.

Oscar was snoring deep under his thick pile of blankets, resting for his big day tomorrow. Benedict was warm and cozy down by his toes.

Foot slept as if he had no bones.

10

D o you smell something?" Gloria sat up. Kevin moaned awake. He had been sleeping against the wall while Gloria sat between his legs and leaned her back against his chest, his arms around her and her arms tight against his.

"What?" he groaned, stretching his back and feeling awful.

"There's an odor. See if you can smell it."

Kevin sniffed. "Nope."

Gloria got to her feet and circled in the darkness, sniffing the air. "There's something. I can't tell what it is."

Kevin stood up and turned on the flashlight to find the opening. He craned his neck to get his nose as high as possible, he sniffed again. "I can't smell anything."

"Maybe I was dreaming," Gloria said. "But something made me think of breakfast. What time is it?"

"Six-thirty."

"So, we slept for four hours down here?"

"Doesn't seem possible, does it? What time would this place open, if it does?"

"I would guess nine or ten. We have at least three or four hours to wait. Or, maybe a lot more than that. But there is no way to climb out of here."

"We have a rope, that's something, but without a way to get it up there and hooked onto something, there's nothing we can do. How about tying the flashlight to it and throwing it up like James Bond would shoot with a crossbow? Whatever you call those things with the prongs at the end."

"A grapple."

"A grapple," he repeated.

"That wouldn't work. All we can do is throw it straight up."

"Want to try anyway?" he asked.

"Sure," she told him. "After all, 'Dum spiro spero.'"

"What?"

"We're in St. Andrews and that's the town motto, 'While I breathe, I hope.'"

Half an hour later after making twenty tosses each with no success, they sat down in the dark to rest. "I still smell something, like bacon. Do you smell it yet?"

Kevin gave it another try. He stood up and pointed his nose to the opening. "Nothing. I think you're hallucinating."

"No, I'm sure it's something. Come down here and try."

Kevin sat next to her and sniffed her neck. "Kevin, I'm serious."

"Okay." He sniffed the air then put his nose almost on the floor. "Got it!" He followed the scent along the stone floor. "It isn't coming from up above. It's coming from over here somewhere."

Gloria joined the hunt, both on hands and knees sniffing like bloodhounds, weaving from one end of the pit to the other, bumping into one another in the dark.

"You know," she said, "there may be a tunnel."

"What?"

"If I remember right, the castle had a lot of shafts and countershafts."

"I don't get it."

"The Catholics conquered this place, and then Protestants overran it; the Catholics stormed back, then the English, the Scots, and then the Spanish and the Russians for all I know. If I ever overran this place and had the chance to stay a while, I'd make darn sure to construct a new secret exit for myself in case I ran into trouble, especially after what happened to the Bishop."

"What happened to him?"

"Oh God, you don't want to know. But tunnels have been discovered. One went all the way to a building across the street."

"From here?"

"I don't know. But, again, if I were in charge, I'd make sure I had a way out. That poor Bishop didn't."

"So the smell might be from a secret passage?"

"It's as good an idea as any we've had."

"So let's keep sniffing and see if we can find where this is coming from," Kevin suggested.

They were only fair as bloodhounds, but they agreed the aroma was bacon and seemed to come from an area of rough rock on the south side of the pit, the side toward town. Kevin shined the light on every edge while they both scraped and pulled to loosen any rock that might hide an exit. After they failed to find anything, they decided to out-think the trap they had fallen into.

"If you were thrown in here four hundred years ago, where

would you look?" Gloria asked.

"The only thing is hunt along the floor and the edges. Ahhh. If someone put in a safety route, they would put it up high where no one else would look."

"Exactly. There doesn't seem to be anything along the floor and we have the advantage of a torch. Makes sense that we have to examine the wall where the smell is coming from."

Twenty minutes of inch-by-inch examination revealed nothing. It would be easier and much less frustrating to wait for rescue.

"Any more ideas?" Kevin asked, not yet ready to give up.

"It's up high if it's anywhere. Let's keep looking."

"Hold it. Hold on a second. What are we looking for? I was looking for a secret passage, like a loose stone or something. That's not what it would be. Who ever put in a secret passage would have to make it feel the same as everywhere else, right?"

"I suppose that's right."

"But, if it's here, it might sound different. Not many prisoners four hundred years ago would have a metal flashlight. I can tap each rock to see if one sounds different than the others, or even take it apart and use it like a stethoscope."

"Great idea," Gloria agreed. "Give it a try, Dr. Watson."

"Hey, more like Sherlock Holmesish."

"Okay, Sherlock, have at it."

Kevin tapped at each rock until he had five contenders for the hidden entrance to the secret tunnel. He removed the back of the flashlight and the bulb casing. Putting the large end to the rock, he put his ear to the other and listened, his ears keen in the darkness.

"There's air or wind or something behind this one."

Gloria touched the rock that Kevin had found. "Five feet off the ground. That's clever."

"Think we may have something?"

"I'm sure hoping. Dig around the top edge of the rock. If the tunnel is behind it, I imagine we would have to go in from the top like climbing into the top drawer of a high chest of drawers."

Kevin poked and prodded at the wall. "The rock is coming loose. This may be it."

He kept digging at the rock with the edge of the flashlight. Dirt and small rocks tumbled away. Soon larger stones came free. Gloria threw them behind her.

"Oh, man. This is going great."

"Air," he said. Moments later he shouted, "I'm through! You were right. The passage way is over a big rock. You have to pull yourself up over it and then down to the tunnel." He put together the flashlight and lit up what he had found.

"Pretty narrow," she told him, looking at a hole not much more in diameter than a front loading washing machine.

"Yeah. You're okay. It'll be a tight squeeze for me."

"Maybe it gets bigger further in."

They decided that he should go first just in case more digging had to be done. It would be easier for him to dig and for her to transfer the dirt behind them.

Kevin climbed up over the rock and squeezed himself into the tunnel of stone. It was like putting on a wetsuit in a phone booth. Gloria had promised she could manage without his help and struggled without complaint to pull herself high enough to crawl into the opening. At the last second, she remembered the rope. That might be useful for something. She fumbled around until she found it and clambered head first back into the tunnel entrance. As her feet wiggled out of the dungeon and disappeared into the narrow space, the rain that had been threatening all morning began to fall on the old gray town.

"You okay?" Kevin called back, hearing her grunts and groans.

"Fine," she panted. "How is it up there?"

Kevin had the flashlight pointed into a tube, dark at the far end where it twisted to the right. "It doesn't get any bigger, but it sure looks like an escape tunnel."

At this point, about ten feet in from the Bottle Dungeon, the tunnel was not much higher than Kevin's shoes were long, and not much wider than his shoulders. The sensation was like crawling through an inner tube. Kevin had to keep his arms in front of him and wiggle with his elbows and knees to move forward. He prayed that when they reached dirt, the tunnel would give him more room to move his arms and chest. Each time he scraped his head, which was every time he inhaled, the walls of the tunnel pressed tighter around him. He paused to catch his breath for a moment, resting his face against the hard rock. Gloria grunted and moaned behind him. "Are you doing okay?" he yelled back.

"What?" Gloria yelled behind him.

"Are you okay?"

"Yes," she grunted. "Keep going."

"Okay. Carry on," he yelled back, inching forward again.

After crawling another five or six feet he stopped to sniff the air. "I can smell bacon again," he yelled back.

"Me, too," Gloria told him, her face squished against his

leather-soled shoes. The only light reflected off the rocks in front of Kevin. Behind her was nothing but black. A blackness where ugly potbellied spiders crawled on long hairy legs, toads hopped and millipedes scurried. And a large black snake or three or four squirmed together, invisible in the dark, slithered up behind them.

Kevin worried about the twenty feet and thousands of tons of dirt and rock above them and the chance of it all sagging in on them and crushing them. He also worried about coming to a block in the tunnel and having to crawl backwards back to the pit. His breathing was shallow and quick, and his pulse beat hard. Every breath pushed his chest against the bottom and his back against the top of the tunnel. Panic churned in his stomach. He was about to stop when he reached lots of air. He pointed the flashlight.

The tunnel dropped into a dirt cavern about the size of a large dog house, big enough for them to sit together if they both hunched over. Kevin crawled down and aimed the flashlight to illuminate the space next to him. She squirmed first into his lap, then twisted and turned so her bottom squeezed next to his on the dirt floor. Both had to pull their knees up to their chins into upright twin fetal positions in a tiny cavern thirty feet underground, like resting in a wet wool sock. Kevin freed one arm to point the light at where they had to go. It was a dirt hole, larger than the one they had just exited.

"You still okay?" Kevin twisted his head against the dirt roof to look at Gloria. Bits of it fell into his hair and down his neck.

"Yes. A little claustrophobic, but I'm trying to ignore it."

"Yeah, me too. But we're on our way out. Who ever did this finished the job well enough to work."

"I hope so. Right now, that big dungeon looks pretty good."

"You want to go back?"

"Heavens no. Lead on, McDuff."

"What's that thing about breathing again? While I breathe, I hope?"

"Something like that," Gloria told him. Kevin poked his head and arm into the new passage and prayed to keep breathing and hoping.

It was dirty going. His head constantly brushed against the dirt and brought down grit and dust that got into his eyes and nose. Poor Gloria inhaled what Kevin kicked up and suffered her own knocking against the ceiling and sides. But she pushed on. Then she heard a timid "Uh, oh."

"What is it?"

"Water. The tunnel goes into water."

"What do you mean?"

"There's water. We have to go through water."

From Kevin's vantage point, the tunnel was flooded, leaving only five or six inches of air space between the water and the ceiling.

"How deep?"

"I don't know."

"How far?"

"I don't know."

There were only two options. They could crawl backward to the kennel-sized cavern, then twist around to crawl frontwards back to the dungeon and await rescue or Kevin could continue forward and see what happened. He was afraid to go ahead and with all his heart did not want to go back.

"I'm going for it." He handed the flashlight behind him to Gloria. Kevin stretched his hands into the water and crawled forward until his face was just short of it. Then, pulling with his elbows and keeping his hands as high as possible, he crawled into the water, holding his face above it praying that his hands would continue to feel an air space in front of him. He would have to crawl through the water rubbing his face sideways along the dirt ceiling in order to breath.

Sometimes there were only two inches of air space above the cold dirty water and he gulped it in, sucking in dirt and water too. Then the space with air ran out. The tunnel had angled down.

"Honey," he said into the dirt ceiling, afraid of water getting into his mouth. He hoped she heard for he couldn't turn his face toward her and if he inhaled much, he would breathe water. Panic and choking to death, were only seconds away. "Honey?"

"Yes?"

"There's more water. It goes all the way to the top. The tunnel is filled up with water."

"Oh." She was silent for a moment. "What do you want to do?"

"I don't know. How far have we've come?"

"Thirty feet, maybe forty feet. It's been a long time since I've crawled out of a dungeon and through an escape tunnel so I'm not real sure."

"I was hoping you would have said forty or fifty yards." Kevin reached as far forward as possible. Water. At best, he could hold his breath and crawl eight feet or so. He would have to judge how far to go before he needed to squirm his way back. A misjudgement and he would drown. Kevin began to sweat. He remembered the near drowning in the Pacific surf. The choking, the gasping for air once again grabbed around his throat. The waving kelp pulled him deeper as the waves washed over his head. He needed fresh air and room to move. Kevin was desperate to run, to scream, to fling his arms into the air and get out of this trap. But he remained trapped under the surface beneath tons of rock and dirt, in a black crawl space with his face pressed against dirt, his mouth inches above the water, blocked by the water forward and by Gloria behind. He swallowed hard to keep his composure. "Honey, when we get out of this, will you give me a kiss?"

"I will give you a wonderful kiss. My guess is that I'll be giving you an especially nice kiss in about fifteen minutes."

That helped. "I'm going forward to see how far the water goes. Reach as far ahead as you can to hold onto my foot, but don't come too far forward. If I kick my right foot, pull once on it as hard as you can, then go backwards as fast as possible. I'm holding my breath and going for it. If I don't come back, then the water is lower and it's okay for you to hold your breath and come through too."

Neither of them mentioned the other reason why he might not come back. And there was the possibility he would find an air pocket, but that it would be small and would not lead to a dry tunnel. He would then have to take another chance going forward or maybe collide with Gloria under the water when he crawled backwards or if she came forward too soon. He was almost sick to his stomach with dread.

Kevin blew her a kiss and turned toward the water. He rubbed his cheek forward along the dirt roof until the water rose to the level of his mouth. He stretched his arm in front hoping for another air space. None. Taking deep breaths, he filled his lungs one last time and put his face under the surface. He pushed with his knees and elbows, two feet, four, five, his shoulders rubbed against the sides and his head banged on the ceiling. His right hand thrust ahead grasping for a pocket of air. Nothing, nothing. His lungs burned. He jerked his right foot, felt the quick pull and pushed himself backwards with all his might. Back he pushed. His lungs cried for air. Kevin's head was down as he forced his arms against the dirt. Hold it, he screamed, hold it. Keep pushing, keep pushing. Down, keep down, push. An eternity later he heard a yell.

"Stop! You're okay."

Kevin twisted his face upward and gasped for air. He made it back. Gloria had pulled, and then scurried backwards. Not so fast that he didn't kick her arms and force a lot of water and dirt into her mouth and eyes.

"No air," he panted.

"Should we go back?" Gloria asked.

"I don't see how we can get out of here."

They lay in the tunnel collecting their thoughts.

"Kevin, that bacon smell had to be coming from somewhere."

"It couldn't go through the water."

"There might be air holes somewhere."

"Or maybe there's just enough air in the tunnel above the water to let it through and I didn't go far enough. I'm going to give it another try. Can you get the rope to me?"

"You're going to hang yourself if you don't make it?"

"No. If I get to air, I'll yank on the rope. If I don't yank on it after a minute, you pull me back. I'm going to use all my air going forward, you'll have to pull me back 'cause I won't be able to do anything."

"Kevin."

"It's our best chance."

"Going back is an option."

"I don't want to go back. Can you pass me one end of the rope?"

Kevin rolled on his back and tied the rope around his waist. He reached back to touch her outstretched hand. Kevin almost told her he loved her, but didn't. Instead he told her he would see her in a minute. Heart pounding, he crawled to the water's edge again. This time he would fight his way forward until he lost consciousness or he found air. Kevin pushed his cheek hard against the dirt ceiling as he again took a series of deep breaths. He filled his lungs, ducked his head and raced forward. Five feet, seven, ten. Head down and ploughing, elbows thrusting, feet kicking in a frenzy against time. His head hurt; his lungs ached to draw in a breath. Kevin had vowed to go as far as he could, lift his head and suck in air… or water.

Forward he pushed. His eyes were popping out of their sockets. His head squeezed by a steel band. He was blanking out. At the last possible moment he lifted his head and sucked. Air. Stale, damp, glorious air. He lifted higher. Lots of air. He gulped it in and remembered just in time to tug at the rope.

Kevin sat in a little cavern, a wonderful heaven of a little cavern, large enough for him to sit in water up to his chest and not have to bend his head. He sat facing back to Gloria and tugged the rope twice, the signal for her to get ready for him to pull. She tugged three times. He had told her not to use her arms or feet but to keep them as straight as possible.

Kevin pulled as if his life depended on it. Gloria popped up to the surface hardly out of breath.

"Hi, Kev," she said, as if they had just met on the street. He wordlessly grabbed her and held her close. Kevin was in tears. She held tight. "Honey," she said, "I'm okay, I'm okay. We're all okay."

He took a deep breath. "I don't ever want to do that again."

Gloria took his face in her hands, closed her eyes and touched her lips to his. It was the softest, sweetest kiss Kevin had ever experienced.

They sat in the water holding hands, recovering, gaining strength from each other. Kevin tried the flashlight, but it wouldn't work. They would have to go the rest of the way in complete darkness.

"Do you want me to lead?" Gloria asked.

Kevin told her no, this was men's work. She punched him in the arm. They still faced the unknowns of the rest of the tunnel—that is, once they found it. It might be below them and flooded and they would face returning through the water to the dungeon. They ran their hands along the smooth walls at water level and found nothing. Then, just to find out sooner rather than later, they explored under the water's surface. Nothing there either.

"It's got to be above water," Kevin said.

On a hunch, Kevin prodded under the surface with his foot until he found the tunnel they had just escaped. In a direct diagonal, he reached to the other side and poked his hand into empty space. Rolling his arm in it, he discovered a bigger hole than the one they had already negotiated. This time he kissed her before moving into the next tunnel, big enough for him to crawl on hands and knees and as wonderful and easy as a big wide expressway.

Foot was upset, eight o'clock and no Kevin. At seven, the alarm had gone off and Foot expected to find Kevin and Gloria at the sitting room window when he went down to the shower. When he came back upstairs, he listened at Kevin's door. All was quiet inside. Foot couldn't expect a call or a note, but he didn't like this one bit. Tee time was at twelve fifteen. Kevin's pre-third-round-of-the-British-Open routine would take him at least two hours if not more, since he hadn't ever done this routine.

But there might not be play. Foot looked out the sitting room window barely making out the gray North Sea through the downpour. It had come down in buckets since he'd gotten up and had formed pools of standing water in the back garden. The greens at St. Andrews were probably getting close to the same condition, the players out there now having a tough time of it.

A quick call to the course confirmed his suspicions. At any moment the tournament director would halt play until the greens were playable. The rest of the course could be almost submerged, but too much water on the greens made the game impossible. They told him to call back in half an hour.

In the meantime, Foot was dressed and ready to go. A few

doors down the street, the newsagent had still warm fruit scones and Danish and fresh squeezed orange juice. A quick dash under Kevin's oversized golf umbrella and Foot made the trip without suffering a drop of rain or even wetting his shoes above the soles.

Foot would start the pre-third-round routine without Kevin and in his own way. Which entailed sitting in the easy chair with two fruit scones crammed with butter and a Danish on a plate balanced on the arm, a glass of orange juice and a cup of coffee on the floor, and four of the worst examples of British tabloid press on the cushion next to him. Foot would feast on fat, gore, scandal, sex and French roast coffee and Kevin would have to be content with whatever he was doing.

One person getting ready to play in the third round of the Open Championship at that moment was Mr. Oscar Brown of South Street, St. Andrews, Scotland. That was how he wanted to be announced on the first tee. Oscar had planed out everything. He couldn't be sure if Kevin's clubs would be available so he borrowed a ragtag set from the man across the way. They waited for him in a light, oil stained canvas bag which leaned against the wall by the door. It wasn't a full set and one of the woods had cracked and the whipping around the hosel was unraveled, but as Oscar told himself, "Beggars can't be choosers." He was very pleased the bag had contained a few balls, some so old they were yellow. He was happy that he didn't have to spend the money to buy a plastic bag of used ones at one of the resale shops.

Wardrobe worried him. He had nothing that looked right

for the golf course. He didn't want to resemble the young players, the walking billboards, nor did he like or even have the old style plus-fours that Americans called knickers. Gladly, he would dress like they did long ago, in a vest and a coat. Oscar pulled down clothes he hadn't worn in years and laid them on the bed. Benedict found them just right for a snooze. Oscar sat next to her and petted her for a while as he imagined the day to come. He would make the message clear to the world that this prostituting of golf had to stop. He would show them a pure and simple game. And if he did his duty well, they would learn and he would have done the right thing.

Oscar would hit the ball well and par every hole. He would never be angry. The only emotion they would see was contentment. Oscar wondered if he should hit one or two bad shots just to show them how to handle adversity; maybe a bogey or two balanced with birdies. Scoring an eagle might take away from the message he wanted them to receive. Nowadays, everything's bigger and better. They wanted a spectacle. That was all they understood. Hit the ball a mile and you were a hero. Score ten under par and you were the next superstar. And they liked numbers, the number of putts, yards off the tee to the nearest tenth, percentage of sand saves to three decimal places. Oscar held his head in his hands. Stadium courses; playing the game in a bloody stadium. Next they'll put a roof over them and pump the place full of conditioned air. The player's will get a massage before every round and talk to a psychiatrist afterwards to help cope with bogeys and unfair lies. He had to stop it. Soon match play would be gone, the Ryder Cup become competition between management companies. With new computer applications, Oscar wouldn't be surprised to see style points count toward victory. His head shook in sadness. "They've nae heart any more," he told the sleeping Benedict, "They've nae heart."

Kevin was miserable. He spat out dirt and what may have been a burrowing beetle. It was hard to breathe though his stuffed up nose so he kept his mouth open and his eyes shut. The tunnel had closed in again. He could barely expand his chest to breathe and he had to keep his arms outstretched ahead and push with his knees and toes. It was slow going. His wet clothes clung heavily and rubbed him raw. He thought about Gloria in her dress and high heels. "Hey," he called back, "I don't smell bacon any more."

"Kevin, I don't think we made a wrong turn anywhere."

"Very funny."

"They probably finished cooking it. It has been served and consumed while we've been fooling around down here."

"I hope you're right. You okay?"

"Yeah. Doing just fine." She had to be as miserable as he, more so since she had his dirt and mud wake to contend with too.

"Water," he called back.

"Oh, no," Gloria groaned.

"Water is running somewhere up ahead," he added. Kevin moved his knees and elbows faster, like a horse to the barn. This is either very good news or very bad. Be positive. It can't be worse than what they'd already been through. The trickling grew into a rushing stream, an echoing rushing stream.

"Light," he shouted. "I can see a little light, maybe."

Gloria was in darkness. Kevin blocked everything. There was the dirt, and the wet, and the cold, but no light, and Kevin existed only because he made noise and regularly kicked her.

"Yes, I'm sure it's getting lighter."

Kevin's hand touched the edge of the tunnel. He crawled to the edge and reached below, feeling only the vertical face of dirt. He heard the water running below him, but it wasn't light enough to see the other side or in either direction, or how far the water was below him, but it did seem lighter.

"Gloria," he shouted behind him. "I've got to stop. We've come to a big tunnel or sewer or something. I can't see how big or how far down it is. I also can't see where it goes."

"So what are you saying?"

"Well, I'm going to have to drop, head first unfortunately, and I don't know how far. I guess I'm asking if you still want to have the rope connecting us. It might be a big fall and I could drag you with me."

"Or I could stop your fall," she replied.

"You couldn't, actually, but it's a nice thought."

"We'll stay tied. We've come this far. Break a leg."

"Thanks, sweetheart."

Kevin reached with his now free arms, up and across the open space. Empty air. He squeezed out further, his arms braced against the dirt wall below him until his hips slipped out of the tunnel.

"Here I go," he yelled and threw his arms out to break his fall, just in time to slap against the concrete bottom of a drainage pipe containing no more than four inches of fast flowing rainwater. He was doing a hand stand, his legs still in the tunnel. He lowered his body into the water. "I'm okay," he laughed with relief. "Come on in, the water's fine." Gloria joined him right away.

It was an easy decision to walk bent over and upstream to find the bacon. They slogged along the bottom of the pipe and around two corners, gaining a little elevation and a lot of light with each step. "Look," Kevin said. They both saw the shaft of light, the end of the drain, the rain falling through the grate and the rusty metal rungs that led up to the street. It proved a simple matter for Kevin to stand on the middle rung and push on the metal grate until he shoved it aside. He climbed up into the pouring rain and onto North Castle Street, just outside the Wilson Restaurant, "open for breakfast, lunch, suppers and dinner, fully licensed." He reached to pull Gloria out.

"Care for breakfast?" he asked.

11

Foot shouted into the phone. "Did you call the police?...Why not?...Okay. I'll be there in twenty minutes."

Thirty minutes later, after driving ten miles through an intermittent downpour, Foot parked the car in front of Wilson's Restaurant. He spotted the couple sitting way in back, separated from the other diners by an empty table, looking like they had just spent most of the night crawling through mud. Each had obviously washed hands and face. Gloria's beautiful, long, auburn hair looked like it had been replace by a wig made of layers of week old green pasta, her dress frayed and stretched to double its original size. Pounds of mud caked on their clothes. Their shoes unrecognizable under even more mud and dirt. Both wore bright smiles as if they had just won the football pools. Plates of bacon and eggs, complete with black pudding and boiled tomatoes sat unfinished in front of them. Kevin and Gloria relaxed, sitting back in their chairs, contentedly drinking coffee.

Kevin motioned Foot to join them. "Want some breakfast?" he asked.

"Are you two okay?"

Gloria patted his hand. "We're fine."

They were dazed. "I should take you over to the hospital for a check up, one of those 'examined and released' deals? Okay? A quick check to see if you're both really 'fine?'"

They both shook their heads. "We're okay, Foot. A little tired and sore. That's all. I have golf to play. Have they delayed the tournament?"

"Yeah, at least an hour. You've got plenty of time. You two should see a doctor."

"Foot, we're all right," Gloria said. "I'd be the first to say if we weren't. All I need is a bath. A shower and then a bath."

While Foot insisted on a visit to the hospital and Kevin and Gloria remained stoic, erstwhile professional golfer Mr. Oscar Brown of St. Andrews had unhappily returned from the course and was unlocking the door to the Castle Gift Shop. His attempt at playing in the British Open had failed even though he had done everything right. With the bag of clubs thrown over his shoulder and wearing his best shirt, favorite tie, vest and jacket, Oscar fought his way through the rain to the entry gate nearest the bleachers by the eighteenth green. The stands were empty. Only a few diehard fans stood inside the gate, huddled under umbrellas and a lone guard hidden under black rain gear.

"Where are you going, then?" the guard asked the old man carrying the golf clubs.

"I'm substituting for Kevin Turner," Oscar told him.

"Substituting for Kevin Turner," the guard repeated.

"Aye, and I'll need tae find a caddie, preferably a young boy needin a few bob."

"Kevin Turner is one of the competitors?"

"Aye, and today I'm taking his place. Where do I sign in?"

The guard narrowed his eyes. There were a few ways to handle this; play along for a while to make standing in the rain a bit more fun, allow the old man through and let somebody else handle it, or have someone take the fellow away. "What's your name, sir?"

"Brown," Oscar answered proudly. "Oscar Brown of South Street, St. Andrews."

"Well, Mr. Brown, without a player's pass, you can't come through the gate."

"A player's pass?"

"That's right. To be allowed in as a player, you have to have a player's pass. Without a pass, you can't be allowed in."

Oscar's heart sank. The logic was irrefutable. Players had passes and you needed a pass to play. He didn't have a pass, so he couldn't play. Nothing could be more simple or clear. Oscar thanked the guard and returned through the rain to his room.

Barry came while Oscar put on a dry shirt. He said that Oscar had done a good job so far and it was too bad about the passes. But rules had to be obeyed. Oscar asked him what they should do now. Barry told him he didn't know for sure. But, if Oscar couldn't play for Kevin, then it was only right that Kevin be saved so he could continue in the tournament. To prevent him from playing now would be unfair. Oscar quickly agreed, relieved Barry didn't notice Oscar didn't kill Kevin as he instructed.

Once inside the room containing the Bottle Dungeon, Oscar called out. "Mr. Turner, Mr. Turner." Getting no answer, Oscar pointed his torch into the pit. No one. "Mr.

Turner? Miss Kinloch?" Oscar was afraid. Maybe they died. Maybe they escaped and told the police what he had done. They would make him go back to the hospital. Barry told him to quit whining, go back to his room and not to worry.

All the way back to the cottage, Foot kept asking if they were okay. They kept answering yes. Foot dropped Gloria off at the Dreel, where she kissed Kevin, told him she had a marvelous time and dashed into the building. With just the two of them, Foot pushed for answers.

"Why'd he do that to you?"

"Foot, I have no idea. It doesn't make sense. We would have been found in two days at the worst. It seemed like he wanted us out of the way at least overnight if not the entire weekend."

"Any idea if it has to do with the tournament?"

"He wanted to play in it. It's weird. I mean, he helped us figure out the course. It makes no sense and I had a lot of time down there to figure it out."

"I hope you don't add this kind of activity to your usual pre-third-round-of-the-British-Open routine."

"No. Oh, God. I want a long hot shower. Did you adjust the heater timer?"

"Taken care of, Captain. You can shower as long as the water holds out, which may be as long as ten minutes."

The water lasted fifteen minutes, just long enough to clean Kevin's encrusted pores and revitalize his spirits. Thanks to the rain delay, now replaced by bright sunshine, Kevin had three hours to relax and get himself prepared for the third round. He had a two o'clock tee time paired with Greg Norman whom he had not yet met. It should be a fun afternoon. Kevin lay down for an hour's nap, dreaming for a while about lovemaking in a dark cavern which somehow turned into a struggle for his life as he was jammed into an underwater mailbox, water gushing into his mouth and nose. He woke already sitting up in a cold sweat. He tried sleeping again and lasted long enough for the heater to supply another ten minutes of hot water. Once it ran cold again, he chose the clothes appropriate for the third round of the Open. They had to be traditional, as much as his Ashworth wardrobe allowed, a bit British while still Yankish, comfortable wet or dry, warm, and although he didn't admit it, lucky.

He presented himself to Foot who gazed out the sitting room window. "How's this for the third round?" Kevin wore dark blue slacks, dark so they wouldn't show the mud and dirt, a green shirt, green for British racing green, and a green and blue sweater.

"Perfect," Foot told him. "Looks like you'll break par in that. Especially if you wear the present I got you."

Kevin was touched. He and Foot were men; tough competitors, manly men who punched each other on the arm and set up practical jokes of questionable taste. But they were also attached to one another, sentimental types to the degree that women would say they loved each other. This, of course, they would deny.

Foot went over to the hutch in a corner of the sitting room and brought out a gray paper bag. He reached in and pulled out a Scottish cap, similar to what Ben Hogan wore, but in a muted plaid, with greens and blues.

"Foot, it's perfect," Kevin told him, trying it on. "But what about my Titleist cap?"

"The contract says you can't wear any other hat but theirs. They can't complain if you're just wearing a plain one over here."

"You sure?"

"Yep."

Outfitted like a bride, and equally as nervous, Kevin rode to the Old Course at St. Andrews, Scotland for the third round of the British Open Championship, just hours after clawing his way through a pitch black, tight as a straitjacket, water filled tunnel. Kevin didn't realize it, but his positive frame of mind was fuelled only by fumes of adrenaline that were quickly evaporating from his body.

Greg Norman was attired in yellow, yellow everything. "Bringing a bit of Aussie sunshine," he explained, pumping Kevin's hand. Greg had seen Kevin warming up at the driving range and came over to introduce himself. "Good luck," he said, flashing that famous broad smile.

"I feel light," Kevin told Foot. "As if my feet weren't touching the ground. Not sure if that's good or bad."

"You're hitting them super," Foot said. "So it must be good."

Good lasted as far as the eleventh hole and that diabolical Strath Bunker. Greg Norman had played well up to this point, five under for the day. Kevin had played better, six under so far. At the eleventh hole, the sun was shining, the wind behind, and all the world thought birdie. At the professional level and under normal conditions, the Strath Bunker should not come into play. These were better than normal conditions. Kevin's condition had deteriorated. The adrenaline fumes were gone and he ran on empty. He hit his five-iron thin. The ball was a line drive that burrowed deep into the sand.

Kevin collapsed. His energy tanks filled with fatigue and dread. A blast out the bunker sapped his strength. He stabbed his first putt ten feet past. His flinched next putt wobbled into the hole. He pared the next hole, the short "Heathery," with a lucky four and did the same at thirteen with a chip in. On the long fourteenth, he heeled his drive into the hopeless Beardies, put his third shot into the Grave Bunker short of the green, chipped out and managed a six. Kevin was exhausted and miserable. Perhaps God wanted everybody to be miserable. Just as Kevin putted out for his second bogey, the skies opened and the wind howled. Not enough rain to flood the greens again or enough wind to bend the flagsticks, but enough rain and wind to run down the backs of necks and to remind everybody that this was true, cold and miserable Scottish links golf.

On the tee at fifteen, Kevin had just enough presence of mind to tell Foot he was finished.

"Not to worry," Foot yelled at Kevin through the wind. "We'll go back to plan B. Do what I tell you. Pretend you're Ken Venturi playing in the Open, when he went thirty six holes, the last eighteen of them while unconscious."

Fifteen, called "Cartgate" played against the wind. The principal problem, the Sutherland Bunker, wouldn't come in to play if Kevin hit an iron. Foot gave him his two. Without questions, Kevin took the two-iron and aimed it at the bunker. He smacked it hard and watched it land short of the bunker, rolling no more than a yard.

"Perfect," Foot said. "Let's go get it and hit it again. This worked all the way to the last hole.

On eighteen, Foot allowed him to hit driver again. Even a Kevin running on empty could hit this fairway if he aimed far enough left. Standing against the blast of cold rain, Kevin aimed at the first tee and swung away. He ended up so far left that the Valley of Sin wasn't in play. A bump and run to the green and a two putt par was on the card.

"Kevin?" Foot pushed at Kevin's elbow. "Do you have Greg's scorecard?" Kevin fished it out of his pocket. There were no scores from twelve onward. Foot read off the card he kept while Kevin wrote them down.

"Sixty-six. Nice round, Kevin," Norman said, holding out the scorecard he recorded for his playing companion. "Sure will be nice to sit with your feet up somewhere with a fireplace and have a beer, won't it?"

"Yes," Kevin agreed, handing him the now completed card. They shook hands again and wished each other well for tomorrow. Kevin finished the official duties of signing his card before he and Foot rushed to the car and home. Kevin wanted his warm, comfortable bed. He didn't care where he stood in the field or even if play would be finished. He had nothing left.

There is something about being bone tired. The tired that is miles beyond fatigue or muscle soreness. Bone tired is when the ache is from the inside out and the muscles encapsulate the pain, keeping it deep down in the bones and seeping like a caustic drip into the lungs and the bowels. It is the angst of weariness that comes from a lifetime of defeat when you can't fight any more or walk another step. Or, like with Kevin, it comes after you have never been more afraid in your life and you continued to do things that scared you even more and you're afraid the next thing you have to face will be worse.

Bed was a sanctuary, a fleeing from any more stimuli, good or bad. Kevin sagged under the covers like a raw egg onto bread, his body oozing to the contours of the mattress. His head sank into the pillow and his mouth fell open. His eyes closed with the finality of a casket. Way off in the distance, much too far away to be in this world, a phone rang.

"Kevin," came the shout from the other side of the door. "It's Gloria."

There are two treatments for bone tired. One is a long period of rest. This treats the symptoms until enough of the clouds go away. The other, love, cures it completely and instantaneously.

"Be right there," Kevin called back.

Gloria, sweet wonderful Gloria, told him she had called Arnold and gotten a rain check, planned dinner for just the two of them and how did he play today anyway. Kevin went bounding down the stairs, banging his head on the bottom arch before turning into the sitting room.

Foot held up his hand. "Stop. I have already changed the timer on the water heater so you can take another shower as soon as you like. I have no dinner plans, and certainly no plans to eat with you tonight. I won't expect you to return until tomorrow and I will not be concerned unless you tell me you plan to visit the castle in St. Andrews. I will not ask what you will do tonight nor how you expect to have the energy to do anything, including playing golf tomorrow. By the way, you're tied for the lead and go off last tomorrow with Tom Duggin, the other surprise of the tournament. You're also tied with

David Duval. Norman, as usual, is right there too."

There is one other cure for bone weary, leading the British Open going into the last round. Kevin floated the mile to the Dreel Tavern, leaving Foot the rental car to enjoy his own version of a great Saturday night.

Gloria opened the door to the private living area of the Dreel looking a lot different than he remembered from the morning. She wore a satin gown that came down to the floor and pushed out at her feet when she walked. She brought him a whisky and sat next to him on the couch, bringing up her legs underneath herself.

"Are you hungry?" she asked.

"No," Kevin admitted.

"Me neither. I can fix something. I told you I had planned dinner. I didn't make anything, but I looked in the fridge and there are things we can have."

"Are you okay?"

"Now you sound like Foot. Kevin, I was never more scared in my life, and never felt so well taken care of and secure in my life either. You were terrific."

"You kept me calm. I don't know what I'd have done if I was alone."

"I called up the tourist centre today," she said. "They said the castle is closed all weekend. We would have been there until Monday."

Kevin put his arm around her. "Doesn't sound so bad."

She leaned away. "Does any of this make sense to you?"

"No. I'd like to grab that Oscar Brown and wring his neck. He went nuts or something. But it sure seemed like he had it planned, even to the rope so you wouldn't get hurt when he pushed you."

"Lil and I went back for my car this afternoon when the rain stopped. She thinks he snapped again. She said he's done horrible things."

"What horrible things?"

Gloria told him.

"Mr. Grayson, I'll have a pint, please." Foot began his wild single man's Saturday night down the street at the Sea Bird. "Mr. Grayson, you're a student of human nature. Why do people do what they do?"

The barman was an experienced observer of human nature and aware Foot didn't want an answer, only conversation and mostly conversation from himself. So he replied, "Lots of reasons I guess."

Foot took the opening. "Well, for instance, this fellow Kevin and I met. Old caddie in St. Andrews. We paid him for information about the course. Last night, he tricked Kevin and his girlfriend into going with him to the St. Andrews Castle and he dumped them into the Bottle Dungeon. Now can you make sense of that?"

Mr Grayson stopped wiping the glass he had been polishing. "Were they hurt?"

"Luckily, no. A little beat up. Kevin still played in the tournament and even, by God, shares the lead."

"That's amazing. And you say he was in the Bottle Dungeon last night?"

"Yeah. He found a tunnel and crawled out. What I don't understand is why this happened in the first place. You got any crazies like that around here?"

"Oh, aye. You can bet your life we do, and more all the time. My great uncle had one in here years ago that would put your dungeon pusher to shame. He was tending the bar, just like I am now and this lad, hardly out of short pants comes in and shoots three men dead, one of them at the very spot where you're sitting."

"Interesting. Kevin mentioned something like that a couple of days ago."

"And back then, before the war, people just didn't have guns. Even today, there's been no other murder around here except for a few years ago in St. Andrews somebody was killed over drugs. Nothing closer than that. From what I heard, this place was swimming in blood."

"Why'd he do it?"

"Never found out. Something like the people he killed wanted to die and he helped them do it or a voice told him what to do."

"So a psychotic."

"Aye. So young too, just eleven or twelve. I'm sure he had no idea of his crime. They put him in hospital. He came back around here once, but wasn't made welcome. Brown was his name. I heard he lived in St. Andrews for a time, but I would guess he's long dead by now."

"'Brown' you say?"

"Aye. Brown."

Foot hesitated. "First name Oscar?"

"Aye," Mr. Grayson said, surprised Foot would have known about their small town murderer. "Oh, oh. That's not..."

"Oh, boy," Foot said.

"You called the police?"

"No," Foot admitted. "I worried about the tabloids. They would have made life miserable for Kevin. We were going to wait until after the tournament tomorrow."

"You're right about that. But you're dealing with a crazy and dangerous man."

12

Foot looked around for what he should take. His pockets already stuffed with pins to use as lock picks if he was handcuffed or locked up somewhere, gum for any sticky needs, a small coil of twine, matches, coins for emergency phone calls, a notepad and pencil, a small bar of soap, a screwdriver and a small kitchen knife (since he forgot to bring his twenty blade Swiss army knife), a penlight, one of Kevin's golf balls, and a candy bar. Satisfied with his tool kit, he hunched over the bathroom sink to check himself in the mirror.

His uncombed gray mutton chops looked like the paws of a French Poodle struggling to escape from under his cap, producing just the offbeat appearance he sought. When you go looking for the bizarre, you must be bizarre. Like everyone, Foot had an element or two of his personality that mocked his upbringing. Foot had benefited from a top-rank education. His parents, well educated themselves and from the best of families, provided him with everything that money, privilege, position, and love offered. Something in his background, either a hiccough in his gene pool or perhaps one too many Saturday afternoon serials at the local movie house, had caused him to become fixated on melodrama and adventure. Foot's Achilles heel was a damsel in distress or a bad guy on the run. Tonight's expedition would hunt down and eliminate the most dangerous game, a man gone bad.

Mr. Grayson had been a fountain of information, at least until up to the last fifteen or twenty years. Oscar was a sick man, a dangerous man when the mood struck, unable to control his impulses, unconcerned about the damage to others' lives and unfit to walk the streets with decent law abiding citizens.

Yet another case of national health insurance not doing their job, Mr. Grayson complained before going off on a tangent about taxes being too high and the price he had to pay for inventory ruining his business. He drifted away from Foot mumbling about emigrating to Australia.

Before Foot lost him, Mr. Grayson had listed the places in St. Andrews where somebody like Oscar might hang out. The plan: chat up the people who knew him, track him down, confront him, and haul him to the police for safe keeping. Mental illness was a sad condition, but nonetheless, Oscar must be caught and stopped. Foot was the man for the job.

Foot squeezed behind the wheel of the rental car and sped along the "B" road to St. Andrews. First stop would be Ben's Tavern where he and Kevin first met this madman, and where the trail might still be warm.

Kevin and Gloria sat on either side of the fireplace. Wrapped in a blue afghan, she sat with her feet tucked under. Kevin sprawled all over his overstuffed chair. Gloria smiled. "If I had any wish in the world, I would want the energy to lift my arms to give you a hug, or maybe just enough energy to open my eyes to look at you."

"I look the same as I did fifteen minutes ago. Your usual man in love. All starry eyed and like that."

Gloria opened her eyes and turned a little to face him. "You did say you loved me."

"Yes. I said I loved you and I do love you."

Gloria closed her eyes and sighed.

It wasn't high noon or the dark of midnight; only dusk in downtown St. Andrews. Foot stood outside the door of Ben's Tavern ready to charge in and save the innocent women and children of the town. This part of Market Street, just past the fountain, is like the shopping district of any small town. On one side of Ben's Tavern a restaurant boasted of a large selection of prime highland beef and the best salmon in the district. On the other side a pet store remained open late on this summer evening. Two roly-poly basset hound puppies wrestled in the window.

Foot ignored it all and pushed through the door like a sheriff at high noon. His steely eyes examined the room. At the bar, with his back to the door, sat a familiar figure with an open stool next to him. Foot didn't take it right away. Despite his extensive preparations, he had not counted on finding Oscar so quickly. And he did not plan on finding him in a crowded bar. Foot wanted privacy to give Oscar the third degree like they did in the back room of all those black and white movies he grew up watching.

While Foot stood near the door, Oscar turned and spotted

his new friend. "Foot," he called out. "Come over here. Have a seat." He patted the bar stool next to him.

Foot went over and sat at the bar next to Oscar. The beer in Oscar's pint glass near the bottom. "Can I buy you a pint?" Foot asked his unsuspecting quarry.

"Aye, that's mighty kind," Oscar replied.

The barman came over and Foot ordered two pints of lager. Oscar opened the conversation.

"I understand yer player did quite well today."

"Yes, he did. He played well."

"Is he keen on tomorrow?"

"Yes, he is keen on tomorrow."

"Weel, I wish ye both the best of luck," Oscar hoisted his glass for the toast. Foot raised his and they both took a drink. Oscar went back to toying with his drink as if the conversation had reached its obvious conclusion.

Foot rubbed his forehead in puzzlement. "Ah, Oscar," he began, "Did you see any of the tournament?"

Oscar turned back to the man who bought him his drink. "Aye, laddie, that I did. I stayed oot the rain part of the time, but I saw your man finish with Greg Norman. They both hit smashing drives at the last hole."

"Ah. Hmmm. Were you surprised to see him play?"

"Oh, no laddie. I'm sure he had a player's pass. They had tae let him play."

"Yeah. Of course he had a player's pass. But I'm wondering about you being surprised. Like him being stuck somewhere else?"

"Oh, I ken now what yer sayin. Aye. Surprised. I thought he and the lassie would be stuck doon the dungeon."

Foot sat silently.

Oscar continued. "Barry thought it was the right thing to do, to get rid of Kevin, but since I couldna play, I'm glad that Kevin played and did so well."

"Barry?"

"Aye."

"Barry," Foot repeated.

"Aye," Oscar nodded.

Both were silent. Foot ordered another couple of pints. With two filled glasses in front of them, Foot admitted defeat.

"Oscar, who is Barry?"

"Ach. He's a grand man in the hospital with me long ago. He talks with me sometimes."

"Does he live around here?"

"I dinna think so. I've havenae seen him in donkey's years. He's probably deed ba noo."

"Dead?"

"Aye."

"So this Barry told you to get rid of Kevin?"

"Aye. He said it was the right thing. What had tae be doon."

"Why? What made it the right thing for what?"

"Ye ken the game's no the same as before. Barry wanted to change it back. Bring back the spirit, ye ken. Teach the players and the spectators the beauty before it's tae late."

"Why get rid of Kevin?"

"He fit the signs."

"Oh, of course. What then?"

"I was to take his place, but I'd no pass. So I wasna allowed tae play."

"Oh. So you got rid of Kevin so you could take his place but they wouldn't let you play because you didn't have a player's pass?"

"Aye. So I went hame tae wait for Barry."

"Did he show up?"

"Telt me tae rescue Kevin and the lassie."

"Oscar, do you have anything against Kevin?"

Oscar looked shocked and hurt that Foot would ask such a question.

"Ach, no lad. What makes ye ask such a question?"

"You threw him into a dungeon."

"I had tae. It was what had tae be done. I already telt ye that."

"Would you ever hurt Kevin or anybody?"

"Ach, no," he shook his head.

"Okay Oscar, that's fine. I trust what you're saying. It actually makes sense. I need to go to the loo, but I'd like to clear up things a bit more when I get back."

Barry came while Foot was in the men's room. "Oscar," he said. "We can still dae it. You have tae take Foot's place tomorrow. He doesnae need a player's pass and you're still strong enough to caddy for one round. You can be oot there and help Kevin tae do the right thing, tae show all the people aboot golf as it should be."

"Aye, that's a right good idea," Oscar said out loud.

"Order a pint for Foot and put some of your medicine in it," Barry told him. "Put a lot in. Then take him home wae you and hide him there."

"Aye. A right fine idea," Oscar said. He did what Barry suggested; ordered two pints, took the capsules out of his pocket, and opened them. He poured granules from ten of the pills into the glass before Foot returned.

"What's this?" Foot was pleased there were no hard feelings.

"Ye bought me one, I'll return the favor. Drink up laddie and tell me how Kevin is going tae play the coourse on the final round."

"How are you going to be able to play tomorrow?" Gloria asked. "It's half ten and you're like in a coma." Neither had moved from the side of the fire.

"There is no way someone competing in the Open can't find the reserves to play no matter what. I'm sure guys have played with the flu, pneumonia, heart conditions and even a broken leg or arm. It is bigger than life. When you're on the first tee, there is nothing else."

"How do you like it, anyway, to be leading the British Open?"

"Tied," he said, pushing back against her. "I'm tied for the lead."

"Yes but how is it?"

"Exciting," he answered, raising his hand then letting it fall back on the arm of the chair.

"I've had enough excitement lately to last me many a fortnight, Mr. Kevin Turner, but I wouldn't miss tomorrow's play for anything."

Kevin stirred in his chair. "Glo, I think I will take you up on your offer of using your shower. I need to get my blood moving even to make it home tonight."

Gloria sat up. "I'm sorry I can't let you stay."

"I still don't understand what you're afraid of. We're attracted to each other. That's obvious. You want to have a physical relationship. I don't understand the difference between 'can't' and 'don't want to.' You do want to. Right?"

"Kevin, it's not that simple. It's something I have to deal with. It has nothing to do with you. I promise. Thank you for being so patient."

Kevin struggled out of the chair and knelt in front of hers. "I don't know why, but being patient with you is easy. I wish I could be as patient on the course."

Gloria patted his hands. "Go shower. After, we'll talk about how you can be patient on the course and win the Open."

The hot water reminded his muscles of cramped spaces and crawling inches at a time through cold mud in the dark. He had to keep his mind on golf. By the first tee tomorrow, nothing must exist for him except the shot; not Gloria, not Oscar, not the tournament, just one shot at a time, add them up at the end, and see what happened.

So much depended on his ability to concentrate, especially on the Old Course. One bad bounce and one bad reaction could mean the whole tournament. Kevin smiled. His mental game guru had been preaching to avoid defining shots as good or bad. They just were, he said. Like the universe isn't good or bad, it just is. Tomorrow, he would have the advantage of an extra mental club in his bag with a lot of odd, not good or bad, bounces.

The water poured over him. Unlike the shower in the cottage, Kevin stood tall in this one and he enjoyed enough hot water to run as long as he wished. Gloria being at the course would be a problem. Seeing her there, the smooth narrowing curve of her waist and the girlish hips and the long legs, and the thick shoulder length hair and her deep green eyes. How the hell was he going to concentrate tomorrow?

When Kevin returned to the sitting room, the fire was ablaze, Gloria sat on the couch, and a pot of tea waited on the table.

"I've been thinking," she said. "Is it a good idea for me to walk along with you tomorrow? I'd like to."

Kevin sat next to her. "I thought about that in the shower. I have to concentrate and I have to define you as a distraction. A nice distraction," he added with a smile. "But a distraction, nevertheless."

"Can good distractions be helpful?"

"Yeah. Some distractions can be good, if they distract you from something bad."

Gloria poured them both a cup of tea. "That sounds like you're making it up as you go."

"But good distractions can be bad if they're distracting you from something good," he added.

"Who's on first?" she asked.

Kevin ignored the reference. "What we need to do is figure out a way for you to add to my concentration, not make it harder."

"And how do we do that?"

"We, my darling, must figure out how to make you part of my preshot routine."

"How romantic. We just met and already you're taking me for granted."

"Gloria, I'm serious."

"I'm sorry. Yes. I will become part of your preshot routine, whatever that is."

"If you plan to follow me around the course, how about if I look for you before every shot? That way when I see you, it will be a nice thing for Kevin the guy who's madly in love, and be part of the routine for Kevin the world class golfer about to win the British Open."

"Do you want me to wave or anything?"

"No, just be there. I need to keep everything simple tomorrow. If we do it this way, I have to see you. If you got lost in the crowd, I'd have a breakdown or something."

"I'd never let something like that happen."

Foot sat on Oscar's bed staring at the wall as if it was the big screen television he had in his den back in California. The rough patterns of the plaster walls undulated, calling his eyes to pay close attention to what they would do next. So far he had seen horses racing across vast Siberian plains, crashing through deep snowdrifts, and leaping over rushing streams. He had watched in awe the birth of a killer whale and laughed until his stomach hurt at an undiscovered Laurel and Hardy short. The best thing was seeing Kevin win the British Open. Foot cried like a baby when he saw that. He dried his tears. "I love you, Oscar," he called over to his mate.

Oscar sat in the old chair near the foot of the bed that was his only other furniture. "Yes, Foot. You told me that ten times if you've told me once."

"Well you can't tell someone you love them too much."

"Aye, that's true enough."

"And I love you too, Benedict." Foot cuddled the cat and pushed his face into her face and kissed her on the nose.

Oscar held the note Foot had written earlier. It said Foot had taken ill and that Oscar was a good man and should be Kevin's substitute caddie for the last round. Not that it would be needed, Oscar said, but we should make sure of every eventuality, shouldn't we Foot? Foot agreed to everything. Heck, he could break a leg driving home. You never knew. Stranger things have happened. May as well have a note telling Kevin what a great guy Oscar was and how he would help if Foot broke his leg or something. It was a real good idea to have a note.

Periodically, Foot fell into a trance. He wouldn't fall off the bed, but Oscar could talk to him and he wouldn't answer. Oscar could turn him one way or another like a child's doll and Foot would stay that way. He lifted Foot's arm once and it stayed up a long time before slowing coming back down. Other times, Foot wouldn't stop talking. But those times were less frequent. He was quieter now, like he would fall asleep soon. Oscar hoped he would. Barry had told him to take good care of the professional caddie. Foot was from the old school. One of them, always putting his player first. He must not be hurt.

"Would you like tae go to bed Foot?" Oscar asked.

"Yeah," Foot answered, as happy as if he was going to the circus. "I'd like to go to bed."

"You can use mine. You're sitting on it noo. And you can sleep wae Benedict, too. She likes you a lot."

13

On the doorstep of the back door of the Dreel Tavern, in the Saturday twilight, Gloria reached her arms around Kevin's neck and kissed him on the mouth, her mouth open, her body pressed against his. Kevin returned the kiss softly at first. As soon as he pressed against her, she withdrew.

"That was nice," Gloria smiled.

"You do that well, 'though we might need a little more practice to get it perfect."

She pushed at his chest. "I'll no start being a distraction the night. You have a long day tomorrow and so do I if I'm going to be part of your routine. Go home, young man. Confer with your trusty caddie and I, dear sir, will see you on the first tee."

"Ah, but ye're a crueell woman," Kevin said, in his best imitation Scots accent.

"Go on. Go on, away with you," she said, then turned and closed the door behind her.

Kevin walked back to the cottage along the wharf. Surrounding him were the muted sounds of a village readying to end the day. Fishing boats chugged into the harbor. The line in front of the fish bar was down to only three teenagers.

Families scattered at benches on the cobblestone wharf gathered the remains of their takeout dinners and headed home. A few couples strolled by, oblivious to everything but each other. No one stopped Kevin to wish him well. He doubted anyone noticed him. Many people didn't know about golf tournaments and didn't care one bit about what burned inside him. In the morning, Dads would go out with sons to collect the Sunday paper and fresh morning rolls, families would be off to church, and the fishing boats would make their way out to sea again.

Parked cars crowded the street near the Sea Bird. Kevin noticed the rental wasn't there, Foot still out or parked a distance away.

"Foot?" Kevin called as he ducked under the door frame. "Foot?" he yelled as he walked into the sitting room. "I'd like to talk, buddy," he said. "Got a tournament tomorrow. Where are you?" Kevin went to the bottom of the stairs and called up, "Foot?"

He took a beer over to the window seat in the sitting room. The sea and sky slowing turned dark. Tied for the lead in a major tournament when I've never played in one, he thought, trying not to think about it. Tied for first in the Open. He shifted his focus to the Isle of May just visible on the horizon and tried to imagine the puffins flying about. His mind escaped to Gloria and that last kiss. That led to seeing her waving to him on the first tee which meant he still had to play the last round of the British Open tied for the lead. "Foot!" he yelled, just to hear the sound and the hope of an answer.

As Kevin sat gazing out the window, the vastness of the dark North Sea invaded the tiny cottage and washed his soul far out, away from any sight of land and things he knew. The pull of the tide took him further away. The seas built higher and higher until they were as tall as church steeples and he as small as a cork tossed from wave to wave. He didn't belong leading the British Open. Who did he think he was? What had been a good effort yesterday would become a disaster tomorrow. Kevin didn't even know how to hold a club any more.

I can't do this. I'll make a fool of myself and Gloria will see me collapse. I'll fall apart in front of thousands watching in person, millions more around the world on television, collapsing just like they all expected me to do today which I almost did. Kevin stood up and paced the small room. Four paces and turn. Four paces and turn. Back and forth.

Tied for the lead. But did he have the game to win? No, he did not. Did he have the game to contend? Probably not. Hold off somebody's charge? No way. Everybody wanted this one. Tom Watson had a fist full of Open titles. Old Tom, Young Tom, Watson Tom, Jones, Nicklaus, he had a chance to join them tomorrow. But could he hold together? The weight of the British Open wrapped its golden cord around Kevin's neck and dragged him under the surface. Where was Foot?

"Damn that dumb son-of-a-bitch!" Kevin swung a roundhouse right in the air, twisting to his knees with the force of the swing. He clenched both fists and held them to his chest. He squeezed his eyes closed, trying to maintain control. His arms and legs twitched. He could hardly breathe.

14

When the shower turned cold, Kevin got out. He had waited for Foot until nine, as long as possible before preparing for play. Foot didn't factor in his pre-game routine, but with every step Kevin thought about him and became more upset that his caddie was out doing another one of his stupid business deals on the last day of the Open. They had been a team, but not now.

On sinking ships, Kevin's current state, crew members have to decide when to leave the sailors who can't be found. At some point the ship has to be abandoned and they have to save themselves. Only the Captain has the traditional role of martyrdom. During the heat of the tournament in Las Vegas, Kevin had asked Foot to call him "Captain" as a way to overcome the damage along his water line and finish the round with blazing guns. Kevin didn't want to be Captain any more, to look out for his crew, to go down with the ship.

It's not as bad as that dungeon, he tried to tell himself. Down there in the dark he clenched his fist, got angry and forced his way forward. He had to be brave because of Gloria. She's who pulled them through. He might have stayed in the Bottle Dungeon until Saturday morning, and then if nothing happened, he would have waited until Sunday, then Monday.

Kevin sat brooding at the sitting room table when the phone rang. Great, it's Foot, Kevin thought.

"Hi, son," Mom and Dad said.

"What a surprise. What time is it there anyway?"

"It's either late or early," his dad said. "We haven't been to bed yet. But we wanted to wish you luck before you played today. My son tied for the lead in the British Open. Isn't that fantastic?"

"We love you," his Mom added.

Kevin talked to them for a while, the support they offered as good as being tucked in between fresh sheets, especially when his father told him he had done well by making the cut in his first major. Everybody will expect you to crumble, he said; just don't crumble too much if you do. His mom said she loved him two or three more times. He imagined her wringing one of the old handkerchiefs he always gave her on mother's day. His dad, ever the pragmatist, worried about the wheels falling off. He had plenty of experience with things going wrong with his weekly softball league and knew that you take the bad with the good. Everybody did, eventually.

Kevin did not tell them about the castle and the Bottle Dungeon nor of his lost caddie, or even of Gloria. He said he'd be alert for a camera sometime and wave to them. After six minutes, his father's awareness of the cost of overseas calls abruptly ended the conversation. "Good luck, son. We'll see you on the TV. Don't quit no matter what happens."

"I love you," his mother squeezed in as he hung up.

That last thought stirred a tiny portion of Kevin's mind. Quit? Fold? Collapse? Be the loser the tabloids have already put into self-serving headlines? The blood of all the heroic Turners of generations past began to boil. Richard Turner of Norman, Oklahoma, called into the bank about his overdue payment didn't give up his dream. He fought to keep his house and the land and he did. Harold Turner Owen, of Gloucester, Massachusetts, lost at sea for ten days, surviving on raw fish and the rainwater he captured in his waxed Sou'wester cap. He accepted he would die, but that didn't stop his trying. And Sarah Turner Ferguson Holloway, Kevin's ancestor as unknown to him as the others, endured the torture of the inquisition and went calmly to the pillar professing her love of God and denying being a witch while being burned alive. Kevin's bloodline would not allow him to entertain giving up for long. The Turners and the Owens and the Holloways of his past were not national heroes of any sort, only solid, hard working, simple people who did what was right.

Kevin took a deep breath, nothing else to do now but get ready. The Turner heritage had been taken out of mothballs, dusted off, and he would not let it go to waste. He had to hope Foot would meet him at the clubhouse, if not; he would find somebody else to carry his bag. A call to Gloria for a ride and another shower initiated his final pre-last-round-of-the-Open routine. He sat in the sitting room chair, closed his eyes and imagined each hole and how he would play it. Last, he chose his British Open TV coverage clothes; Foot's cap for luck, matching dark green slacks, dark blue shirt, dark blue sweater vest and dark blue sweater. Dark would absorb more heat, he figured. The afternoon forecast was for low sixty degree temperatures and brisk winds with the possibility of rain, increasing later. Two ball markers went into his right front pocket, one from Torrey Pines in San Diego and one from Pebble Beach, his lucky ones this week. His rain gear and everything else had been stuffed in his bag and his bag now in parts unknown. He had finished getting ready when he heard Gloria honk the horn out front. Kevin smiled. He had told her not to come in or they might never make it to the course. He planned to arrive an hour earlier than normal to give him time to find Foot and his clubs, or, he dreaded to think about it, last minute replacements.

Once near the course, Gloria drove through the crowd at Golf Place and dropped Kevin off near the Royal and Ancient clubhouse entrance. As he walked toward the door, spectators pushed against the fence protecting the walkway, calling out Kevin's name and wishing him luck. He sheepishly waved, not used to fans recognizing him. A few pressed a pen and a pairings sheet at him, which he happily signed. A familiar voice brought him up short.

"Morning, Mr. Turner." Oscar, dressed in his rumpled but best jacket and tie, baggy pants and well-worn brown leather shoes, stood next to Kevin's red and white Titleist staff golf bag, waiting for him outside the club house door. Kevin stared. His bag. Where the hell was Foot? He opened his mouth but nothing came out. He wanted to take a step but the current pulled him out to sea.

"Foot is not well this morning," Oscar continued. He reached into the inside pocket of his jacket and pulled out a crumpled piece of paper. "He gave me this note for you." Oscar stepped away from the bag to give the note to Kevin, who stood transfixed. Finally his hand rose to take it.

Dumbfounded, Kevin concentrated to understand what it

said. Foot sick? Oscar to caddie? What the hell?

Oscar spoke up. "Foot and me'sel were oot drinkin last night. He took sick. Terrible sick. He's in bed. He gave me your clubs and things and asked me to help. Wi all the trouble I've caused, I'd like tae be of service."

"Foot's okay?" Kevin pictured his friend as a pile of body parts lying beside a bloody axe. Foot wouldn't be in bed sick now. Not during the Open. Not unless he was deathly sick.

"Aye, he'll be fine. Said he'd find us oot on the coourse."

"Where is he?"

"He's at my flat. Nearby. He can catch up easy enough."

Kevin needed calm. He didn't need to have questions on his mind like should he call the police to find his caddie, or to find his body.

"Kevin?" Gloria called. Kevin turned to see a shocked look on her face as she spotted Oscar. "Stay here," Kevin told him and hurried to where Gloria waited on the other side of the barrier.

"What's he doing here? Is that your bag? Where's Foot?"

"I don't know, Gloria. I need you to find Foot. Just a second." Kevin dashed back to find out where Oscar lived. He returned to Gloria with the address. "If you find him there, call the tournament office and have them get a message to me. If you don't find him there, call the cops and tell them everything that happened and then get back here as quickly as you can."

"What are you going to do? You can't have that man caddying for you."

"I don't know. I have to stay with him if he knows anything about Foot. I can't leave him to wander off while I play. I don't have time to explain all this to anyone. I don't know what to do."

"Go play," she said. Gloria kissed him and rushed off, wishing him luck and promising she would be back as soon as possible, Kevin lonelier with every step she took. Fans closed around him and pushed papers and pens into his face. He turned and looked again at the old man who had tossed him into the dungeon and who stood waiting, like a ten-year old at the caddie barn, to see if he would be the lucky one chosen to carry the bag. Oscar, old, frail and crazy as a loon. But Kevin saw his eyes sparkle and his local knowledge could be a blessing. Would Oscar reveal more about what happened to Foot? Did he have any choice in all this?

"Oscar, bring the bag over to the transport car. I have balls to hit."

Oscar tipped his hat, hoisted the bag to his frail shoulder, and followed Kevin as obediently as a cocker spaniel. While worried sick about Foot, wondering how Gloria was doing looking for him, and trying to adjust to Oscar as his caddie, Kevin hit a bucket full of high flying draws, knockdowns that stayed down, and for good measure, high hard fades and lower gentle ones.

Oscar snorted at each shot as it climbed high and grunted when it hit the ground. When Kevin caught one a little thin, Oscar remained silent. Both knew what happened and how disastrous that would be on the course.

Players and their caddies walk by the front windows of the Royal and Ancient clubhouse to get to the first tee. The area is cordoned off so ordinary spectators don't block the view. Unlike most tournaments where players walk a gantlet of fans, here it is almost too quiet, with British reserve mandating no unseemly displays of encouragement. The emptiness made Kevin more nervous, naked, exposed, and alone on the first tee.

"Hi, Kev. Pleased to meet you." It was Tom Duggin, the young Britisher and the other surprise of the tournament.

"Hi, Tom. Nice to meet you. Sure is weird going off last isn't it?"

Tom's laugh took up his whole round face. He was a junior sized Santa Claus without the beard. A couple of years younger than Kevin, Tom had similar experience on the European Tour, a solid player, and strong. His strength would be tested today.

"You as nervous as I am?" he asked.

"Tom, I have no words for it. If fact, my throat's so dry I can hardly speak. But let's one of us take it. What do you say?"

"Sounds good. If I can swing at the ball."

They stood on the tee as the group of Cory Pavin and David Duval played their approach shots to the first green.

"Well, would you look at that," Tom said. Duval's ball had hit the green short of the flag and had spun back into the Swilcan Burn.

Kevin looked anxiously toward the crowd around the tee. Gloria should be back by now. Tom Duggin was announced on the tee. "Play well," Kevin told him. Tom powered a beauty down the middle.

"Now on the tee, from San Diego, California, the co-leader of the Open Championship after three rounds, Kevin Turner." The cheers gave him goosebumps. Without being asked, Oscar handed Kevin the three-wood. It was light in his hands, like a child's plastic toy, a sure sign of nerves. The plan was to see Gloria before he swung. He had to follow the plan. He scanned the crowd again, seeing only the faces of thousands of strangers and all of their eyes staring back at him. While standing behind his ball and looking at the old stone bridge, Kevin closed his eyes and pretended he saw Gloria waving her scarf at him from the stands to the right of the tee. Without looking to his right, he took his stance, aimed at the bridge, and smoked a gentle fade to the center of the fairway. The crowd cheers bid the two men "good luck" as they walked down the fairway.

Few golfers experience walking down the first fairway at St. Andrews leading the British Open. The experience is one of contentment, tension, agony, pride, fear, wishing it was tomorrow and feeling like there won't be enough time to do all the things that needed to be done and there is way too much time in which to falter. It's an emotional whirlpool and a mind racing at the speed of light toward an unknown but forbidding disaster. If the golfer in this situation pays attention to all these feelings and tries to keep up with his thought processes, he will fall apart with the first bad shot, which usually occurs somewhere in the first four or five holes. Players successfully endure this mental state only by accepting being emotionally out of control and then ignoring it. This takes a great deal of experience, or courage, for the player is asking himself to disregard messages of impending doom. The mind is walking a tightrope strung over a Grand Canyon of doubt in the gusting and fickle winds of fate. The player has to convince himself that under these conditions, the messages in his brain are not reacting to reality, but only to the imagined fear that one mistake means a mile drop and an eternity of regret.

Kevin stood beside his ball on the first fairway trying to be brainless. He had a hundred and thirty yards to the hole, which was cut close to the Swilcan Burn that caught Duval. Being short was foolhardy. Kevin asked Oscar for a nine-iron. There was little wind and Kevin wanted to hit past the hole and spin back, and still be putting from behind the hole. He did not want to be short and land in the burn like he had just seen Duval do. Oscar handed him the wedge. "Trust me," he said.

"Trust me," Kevin thought. He was trusting Oscar with his best friend's life. Trust me I'm here to help you. Trust me that my judgement is better than yours. Trust me with this round and your chances in the Open. If he trusted what Oscar told him about Foot, he could trust him with club selection. Kevin took the wedge.

"Hit it just left of the hole," Oscar suggested.

Kevin took his stance, exhaled a ton of excess air, imagined Gloria waving that scarf of hers, and swung. The ball arched high and at his target left of the flagstick, hit about ten feet past the hole and spun back to the right, ending up only a foot away. "Shot," Tom called from across the fairway. Kevin gave him a little wave and then a thumb's up. "Thanks, Oscar," he told his caddie as he handed back the club. Ten minutes later, Kevin stood on the second tee with a three stroke lead over Greg Norman and Cory Pavin, a two stroke lead over David Duval, and one over his playing companion Tom Duggin. Kevin Turner from San Diego, California led the Open Championship.

"Lots of jockeying aroond," Oscar counselled on the fifth tee.

A lip out at five, poor chip at six, and hard won pars on

the rest of the front nine gave Kevin an outward half of one over par. Duggin had stumbled and was three over for the nine. Up ahead, on fourteen, Greg Norman led at eleven under matched a hole ahead of Kevin by David Duval. Cory Pavin remained one behind.

"Aye, now we have a championship to win," Oscar said as they waited on the tenth, named after Bobby Jones. The Duval group was still on the green of this short par four so the last group had to wait. Kevin scanned the spectators for Gloria and Foot as he had on every hole. Oscar insisted Foot was sleeping in his room and would be with them at any moment. Kevin hardly thought about golf any more. He took the club Oscar handed him, aimed where he was told, saw Gloria in his mind's eye, and hit. The same mindless golf he had played so well yesterday.

The green cleared and Kevin took the tee with driver in his hands. Kevin's ball bounded and rolled three hundred and thirty yards to the right center of the green, within twenty feet of the cup. Duggin did the same; both had makeable eagle putts to give them a flying start home. Both missed, but had tap in birdies. A nice leap into the homeward holes if not exactly soaring.

Kevin held his breath watching his tee ball on eleven head toward the Strath Bunker, his target against the hook wind. His cut five-iron hit high right and spun back below the hole, just what he wanted. A two putt par was as good as gold. Duggin blasted out of the Hill Bunker and took two more to get in. Nothing went in for either of them for the next four holes.

Couples set the target by finishing at ten under par. Kevin stood at nine under. He needed one birdie to tie, two birdies to win. That's assuming he managed par the Road Hole and no one ahead of him did anything outrageous.

Sixteen, Corner of the Dyke, measured three hundred and seventy yards and played a little downwind. The out of bounds wall lined the right and the Principal's nose and Deacon Sime Bunkers waited down the middle. The smart play was to hit long and left. Kevin looked over to the right, where the spectators stood three deep along the out of bounds wall. There, Gloria waved frantically two hundred yards down the fairway. She was smiling, but he didn't see Foot. He must be okay or she would be running toward him instead of waiting. Or maybe she was afraid to tell him what happened. It was his turn on the tee.

His ball flew right, straight right, directly at her and toward the low stone wall separating the Old Course from the Eden course. Kevin and Oscar and Gloria watched as the ball fell, hit the wall, and rebounded straight up. The ball bounced high on the stones once again before disappearing onto the other course.

He hit a second tee shot, ignored his ball and rushed over to Gloria. The hell with the rules, Kevin thought, and hauled Gloria over the wall before any marshals intervened. He took her by the hand to the middle of the fairway to talk while Duggin played his shot.

"What's happened?" he asked.

"He was there. Real groggy. Like he was high or drugged. I've never seen anything like it. I found Oscar's room easily enough. Foot snored away in the bed. It took forever to wake him and for him to recognize me. He said he had to get back to the cottage. I got him over to the hospital where they kept him. They said he had ingested pills but he'd be fine. Didn't anyone get back to you?"

"No. I've been waiting. Nobody's come."

"That's bad. I told them at the hospital to have someone call. They wanted me to stay with Foot to keep him oriented."

"Kevin?" Oscar called. It was his turn to hit.

Kevin kissed her. "I think I've just given the tournament away. But cheer me on. There's still a chance to make something happen."

Gloria kissed him back, hard. "Full speed ahead, Captain," she smiled. "Foot told me to tell you that. I put in the kiss part." A good natured bobby escorted her back to the spectator area.

"Everything all right?" Oscar asked as Kevin reached his ball.

"Yes. Everything is okay. Now let's do damage control. Looks like I have to put it past the hole."

"Aye. Ye see the ridge. You have to be past the ridge or your ball will come right back off the green."

Kevin's low punch pitching wedge left him twelve feet above the hole. One putt birdie, except for the stroke and distance penalty. Kevin would need to birdie the Road Hole and the last hole to tie Couples.

At the seventeenth tee, Kevin learned that Cory Pavin had finished at ten under too and Norman had a par putt to equal that score. Two were in a playoff, with maybe Faldo making four.

Duggin was up first and hit his tee shot over the third "O" on the shed wall with solid hook spin. Kevin intended to do the same. Oscar whistled to him and shook his head no. "Ye dinna want to hook the ball here lad. Down wind, you'll no stop the ball on the green unless yer able to run it up. Aim for the last "O", but hit it straight. We're aiming for the right rough, a wee bit o' luck, and a nice wee lie in the thick grass. It's no too bad this year."

Kevin looked over to where Gloria waited. She smiled and waved. He looked back to where Oscar wanted him to hit his tee shot. Without hook spin, a ball hit over the last "O" on the facsimile railroad shed would fly close to the back of the hotel and, if hit well enough, over the garden and glass walled first floor dining room to land in the right hand rough. Ninety-five percent of the ball flight would be over hotel property. Only the last two percent of the flight would be back near the golf course, and nowhere near the fairway far to the left.

"Hit it over the "O" and straight," Kevin confirmed the advice from his substitute caddie.

"Aye." Oscar handed him the driver and stepped back.

Out of bounds here, and the newspapers would declare Kevin Turner a choker. Thirty point headlines would read "Turner the Tepid" or "Turner Turned Tail." Another small headline under also rans might be "Kevin Kollapsed." He hated being a cliché, an object of "I told you so, didn't have it in him, pressure got to him." Many of players play for second if first is out of reach, he thought, before realizing that first was not out of reach until he failed to birdie the Road Hole.

A female voice cried out from the crowd, "Full steam, Captain!"

Kevin swung hard. The ball sailed over the last "O" and beyond where they could see. He and Oscar had to wait for the signal to learn if his skill was good enough. The seconds of flight dragged on. Kevin gestured with upraised arms like Tom Watson years before. "Is it out?" Finally, the undulating buzz of the crowd from the green back to the tee answered the question, and finally, too, the fore-caddie gestured with his hands toward the fairway. The ball landed in bounds.

He had a shot to the green of only a hundred and fifty yards. Kevin surprised his canny old caddie. "Five-iron," he told him. Wordlessly, Oscar handed him the club. Kevin practiced a knock down shot while Duggin hit his approach. Duggin's ball looked good, for a while. It hit short of the green, bounced up to the putting surface and rolled, and rolled more, over the green to the road beyond.

"Eh?" Oscar grunted, pointing with his elbow to what happened to the ball. Kevin nodded. He choked down on his five-iron and hit a low punch shot that flew less than a hundred yards and no higher than twenty feet. It bounced a few times before rolling. The ball rolled for forty yards and more along the fairway, up the bank to the green and all the way back to within eight feet of the hole. Eight feet for one of his needed birdies. He could get into the playoff with a birdie here and another at eighteen. At the professional level, an eight-foot putt, under normal circumstances, has a fifty-fifty chance of dropping. This was the Open.

Kevin looked into the crowd for Gloria. Oscar spotted her climbing up the steps of the grandstand. She turned and waved during the polite applause when Duggin's ball plopped onto the green and came to rest inside of Kevin; in five strokes to his two. As he marked his ball, heartbroken to have given so many away here, Duggin smiled bravely and told Kevin, "Make it, mate."

Kevin found Gloria, walking down the steps and waving, took his stance, and tapped the ball. It wobbled, it jerked, it slowed to a crawl, it nearly died, but it dropped. Kevin Turner was three hundred fifty four yards and three swings from tying for the Open Championship.

This is it, Kevin thought as he and Tom reached the last tee. The only decision was whether to go for the green, a possible eagle and an outright win, or play to maximize his chances for a birdie and the tie. Eagle meant hitting straight at the green and putting the Links Road into play. Hitting out of bounds now would be crazy. His best birdie chance was hitting far left to take much of the Valley of Sin out of the picture. The hole played downwind, which made going for it tempting.

"What do you think, Oscar?"

"Ye have to judge your heart, Kevin. It's up tae yer heart."

"What if it's beating too fast to read?"

Oscar handed him the driver and pulled the golf bag out of the way. Members of the Royal and Ancient looked down from the balcony outside the Secretary's office and out the ground floor windows. Those that bought a ticket and paid an extra two pounds waited in the stands behind the last green. Others, paid and not, watched from along the right side of the fairway. Millions saw a close up of his face on television.

Golf is lethal unless the player is decisive. Hitting and hoping is almost always suicide. Did Kevin believe in himself enough to risk his chances in a four-way playoff or was now the time to strike, while he had a chance for the outright win? Par didn't enter his mind. Finishing a stroke behind was not a goal or even a consequence. That outcome didn't exist.

Kevin blanked the right hand out of bounds from his

mind. He was going for it. That would give him two chances for the win and yet a third for the tie. He could reach the green and one putt. If he missed the green, a chip from off the green was more likely to go in the hole than a sixty yard wedge from the safer left side. And if he was close to the green and chipped near enough, he had the birdie he needed.

Oscar could see the decision in Kevin's eyes. "Aye," he said and nodded his approval.

Kevin aimed at the left side of the green over three hundred yards away and swung with his Sunday best swing. As the ball fell, it curved to the right toward the flagstick as Kevin had planned. The collective groan from spectators behind the green told the story. Kevin's mighty tee shot hit into the face of one of the mounds in front of the green and bounced up and not forward. Instead of a putt for eagle, or a flat chip, his ball had rolled just enough to stop on another upslope, leaving a shot that would have to be hit high when he wanted to hit a low running one through the Valley of Sin.

Big, frustrated, despondent Tom Duggin hit the tee ball Kevin wanted; a patented screamer that rolled to the front edge of the green thirty feet from the hole. "Shot," Kevin told him.

"Blommin bad luck," Oscar said as he surveyed the lie. Hit it short and the ball rolls backward to the bottom of the valley, too long leaves a difficult downhill and fast putt; exactly what Oscar said to avoid the first day they talked. Kevin, however, didn't have a choice. His up hill lie wouldn't allow a low runner. He had to nip the ball with his sand wedge and loft it to the hole, hoping to be long enough, but not too long. If he was too careful, it was also possible to hit the ground behind the ball and chunk it short into the valley or bounce into the ball to skull it over the green into the deep rough hillside in back. He would earn his Championship with how he played this shot.

He had to take a nickel sized slice out of the turf under the ball. Dime size and the ball flies over the green, quarter size and he's in the Valley of Sin.

Thousands of voices went silent, thousands of eyes watched, thousands of hands clenched. Kevin swung back and through, nipping the turf perfectly. The ball landed within inches of the hole, bounced twice and stopped ten feet above the hole. Thousands rose as one and clapped and cheered. Ten feet to join Pavin, Couples and Norman.

Poor Tom, out of it now, quickly putted for eagle, missed, tapped in for birdie and got out of the way to leave Kevin center stage. Before lining up his putt, he had glanced over toward the first tee and saw the waiting three competitors looking back. The playoff would start there, and continue on to the second, seventeenth and eighteenth. Unless that ended in a tie, the Championship would be decided over the four holes. But first, Kevin had to make his putt.

15

Of all the skills necessary to play golf, putting is easiest. Putting requires almost no strength. A half-hour of experience is enough to grasp how to read a green. A player has all the time necessary to look every which way to comprehend the simple problem of rolling the ball along the ground to the hole.

Of all the skills necessary to play golf, putting is also by far the most difficult. The target is small. Tiny imperfections in the grass can throw the ball off line. A small error in distance or direction adds one more stroke to the total. However, the hardest part about putting is there are no excuses. You make it or you don't.

Kevin wanted Foot with him. Miss it or make it, what a time for him to be gone. Kevin looked into the stands behind the green. Gloria waved and gave a thumbs up while she walked back down the steps from an imaginary seat. Fortified, he turned back to the putt; long enough to miss, short enough to make. Downhill with a large break to the right. Oscar looked it over and confirmed Kevin's reading. If he lined it up correctly, all he had to do was hit it. The slope of the green would do all the work.

The spectators, in person and watching on TV, were silent as Kevin stood over the ball. Low and through; no thoughts of winning, no thoughts of losing, none of trophies, money, endorsements. Just the simple thought of pulling the putter straight back and following through to the target, a foot left of the hole.

The putter went back and through. With every roll the fans leaned further forward, inhaling as one. They all leaned to the right as the ball neared the hole, wishing the ball in. The ball ran just as Kevin anticipated. After rolling almost ten feet following a curve to the right, the ball slowed as if from an outside force. The grass reached up and grabbed from underneath. The wind changed direction. Gravity doubled. The earth stopped spinning. The ball stayed out.

The crowd gasped, groaned then was silent as Kevin walked up, looked at the ball for a moment, and tapped it into the cup for a par four, a minus nine for the tournament, and a tie for fourth place with David Duval. Kevin didn't hear the crowd's appreciation for a gallant effort. One small turn. One more inch. An ounce more force. Just a tiny bit more.

Gloria and Kevin stood at the side of the bed looking down at the motionless figure. Foot was tucked under tightly drawn white sheets and a tan blanket, his face so calm and relaxed that the gray/white of his hair seemed to melt into the pure white of the pillow. A man asleep without a thought or a care in the world.

"And he walked over here with you?"

"Oh, yeah, and mumbling about having to talk to Pinky

and telling you about the Strath Bunker, the Japanese were happy, all sorts of things."

"He sure looks out of it now."

A young doctor, dressed in a lab coat, entered the room. She held out her hand. "I'm Doctor Russell. I understand you're friends of our patient here."

"Yes," Kevin answered shaking her hand. "He's my caddie."

"He'll be fine," she told them. "Somehow he overdosed on a very potent antipsychotic medication. Do you have any idea where he would get something like that?"

Kevin and Gloria exchanged glances and both said no.

"Has he taken this kind of medicine before?" the doctor continued. Kevin told her he hadn't. She turned to leave. "You can wake him if you wish. We'll discharge him sometime later this evening. Stop by on your way out at the office if you would to fill out our paperwork. The cost will be covered, by the way, by the national health."

"Drugs," Gloria said as the door closed behind the doctor. "Makes sense. Why didn't you tell her about Oscar?"

"I don't know. Why didn't you?"

Gloria smiled. "I don't know either. The man pushed me down into a black pit, which was pretty mean. We were forced to crawl out which was incredibly scary. He kidnaps your caddie and has the audacity of doing a terrific job helping you around the course. He tried to kill me sort of and looks at me with a twinkle in his eye. I guess all in all he's harmless."

"Me too," Kevin said.

"Benedict."

They both turned toward the sound from the bed. Foot's

eyes opened, but focused somewhere in the vicinity of Hawaii. Kevin waved his hands, "Hello, hello. Earth calling Foot. Come in Foot."

Foot saw him. "Kev. How did you do?"

"Shot even par. Tied for fourth," Kevin answered.

"Great job, Captain." Foot tried to get up but was held by the sheets across his chest. He gave up. "Sorry I missed it."

"Well, since you're tied down, I'll describe the round, shot by shot for your entertainment."

"I'll go get coffee for everybody," Gloria told them. She loved the man with all her heart, but listening while he went over every shot was asking way too much.

Kevin, despite his bitter disappointment, described the round for his friend, trying to balance how well he did, with how much he would have liked Foot to be there and how his absence had nothing to do with the outcome. Foot didn't buy any of it.

"Oh Kev, I'm sorry. We were getting better every round. I could've helped. That damned crazy Oscar really screwed us."

"Foot, I hit good shots. I made only two mistakes, my own doing, and they cost me. That and a few putts that didn't drop. No one's fault."

"Who won?"

Kevin shook his head. "Don't know. I got out of there as fast as I could. I didn't want anyone to see me crying. Foot, one inch. That will drive me crazy for quite a while."

"Golf is a game of inches. And it's how you cope. 'If onlies' will kill you."

"Yeah."

Gloria and Kevin sat with Foot in the hospital until they

discharged him around nine that evening. Gloria and Foot sat with Kevin at the cottage until he chased them away around eleven, when it was dark enough to pretend he could sleep. Every time he rolled over in bed he thought about one more roll of the ball. When he closed his eyes, he saw the ball sitting next to the hole. When he looked out the window into the dark space of the North Sea, he saw the darkness of the tunnel and how hard he had fought, how much strength he had then, and how little more it would have taken to hit the ball just a bit harder. When he slept, his dreams played out the last green over and over and over. The three men waiting for him on the first playoff hole drew further and further away until the playoff tee was miles from the last green. One inch.

He slept. Twenty minutes or two hours. It didn't matter. Sleep wouldn't do him any good. He needed another chance. He could make that putt now ten times out of ten. But the stands were being taken down. Tourists had reclaimed the famous Old Course. There was no room there for him any more.

The call from his parents was difficult. They tried so hard to be understanding. Anybody could have missed that putt his mother told him. His father said it was a tough way to lose, then corrected himself and said that Kevin didn't lose it, he just didn't win. They wondered when he would be home.

Kevin sat up in bed. Before the tournament, he would have been happy with fourth place. It meant an automatic invitation for the next British Open, being held in Ireland for the first time in decades. On his flight over, that was something he had dared to dream. Wining would have been beyond a dream. The dream didn't happen. So what? Dreams are dreams. One inch. One inch from a dream. But he could have lost the playoff. Pavin was tough in head to head situations, and Norman and Couples were too. Four holes against that bunch wouldn't have been easy. But to have no chance to compete. He did have a chance. And he missed. Short. One inch.

He wished Gloria was there. No, he didn't. His gloom too deep to put on something so new and fresh. That damn Oscar. What a terrible thing. Thrown down a dungeon for God's sake. Maybe his water phobia was gone. Maybe missing that putt would ruin his nerves next time he had to make one.

She was leaving Tuesday, back to Dornoch. What was he going to do? Foot was leaving Tuesday too, skipping the Loch Ness expedition and going back to the West Coast. What did he want? The answer as immediate and as futile this time as it always will be. Another chance. Doug Sanders had another chance when he missed his two and a half footer on the eighteenth at St. Andrews in 1970. He tied Nicklaus though he lost the playoff the next day. Of course, thought Kevin, how did Sanders handle it the night before the playoff, knowing he would have won it all with that little putt on the last hole? Kevin shook his head. Sanders lost the playoff by only one stroke too. God, golf is a crazy game.

He slept a little, then, unfortunately, he woke. That's when the morning after "if onlies" attacked Kevin like a swarm of African bees. He woke up wondering if only he had pulled his tee shot on two instead of pushing it. If only he would have hit the putt harder on eight. If only the bounce off the stone wall on sixteen had gone left instead of right. If only the putt on eighteen had been hit a little harder. Just one inch.

"Kevin?" Foot called from the bottom of the stairs. "I've made great coffee, the rolls are only an hour old, and I've hidden all the newspapers. The coast is clear to face the morning after."

"Okay," Kevin called down. "Right after I bandage my wrists."

Later in the day, Gloria came over. They sat on opposite sides of the sitting room table by the window. Foot was out souvenir shopping.

"Did you ever really, really want something," he asked her, "and could have had it, but you didn't get it?"

"Sure," she smiled, sadly. "I think everyone's had that experience."

"So close."

"Yes."

They looked out over the North Sea and to the Isle of May. Kevin sighed.

"Does it take a long time to get over this sort of thing?" she asked.

Kevin smiled at her in spite of himself. "No idea. I've never been so close in a major tournament. In fact, this was my first one."

"And you're totally unhappy that you didn't win."

"No, not that. I'm totally unhappy that I left that last putt short."

"Would you feel better if you had hit it so hard that it ran over the hole and didn't go in?"

"No. I don't know. Long is better than short."

"How about a walk to Pittenweem? There's a fish market today."

"The world continues even after I missed that putt?"

It was her turn to laugh. "Kevin, I will bet you anything that no one on the wharf will have any idea who you are or what crimes you have committed or even care."

"I'll bet you at least one would."

"You really want to bet?"

"No. But I like the sound of that anything."

The walk took them past three hundred year old houses, past the spot at the Anstruther Harbor where Oscar sat as a young man on a mission before continuing to the Sea Bird, close to the hundred year old Anstruther golf course, and along ageless rocks at the shoreline. They stood on a small rise and looked at the sea. "Today," he said, "folds into yesterday like waves curl at the shore before returning invisibly to eternity."

"Kevin. I'm impressed."

He blushed. "A friend of mine, the guy who teaches about the mental game told me that one time. He says the most important task in life is getting perspective on things. One wave doesn't mean much, it goes back to where it came. So I missed a putt. I'm here, in wonderful Scotland, holding your hand." He squeezed it a little.

"And I'm here holding yours. Will you come home with me tomorrow? For a little while?"

Go home with you? To Dornoch?"

"Aye. I'd like that very much."

Foot told Oscar he would have to call the police. They perched like two pensioners on the Bow Butts park bench overlooking the West Sands and the golf course. Sounds of hammering and the intermittent clang of dropped steel pipes of dismantled stands filled the background. Gulls surrounded their bench picking at the leftovers of the fish and chips Foot bought at the stand down by the Sea Life Centre. The men sat apart, facing each other in a stand-off. Foot had been playing amateur psychiatrist, with just a touch of detective thrown in.

"I did only what was necessary," Oscar argued. "I hurt naebody. I wouldna hurt a fly."

"Oscar, you dumped the two of them into the dungeon, you drugged me and put me in the hospital. Lucky I have the constitution of an ox. What would you call doing that? I'm trying to understand, here. You have this medicine. Why aren't you taking it?"

"It's too dear to take all the time. And I can talk to Barry when I'm no taken it."

"Ah yes, Barry. He's dead, you said."

"Aye."

"And you say the medicine costs too much?"

"Aye. They changed how much I have to pay. Now it's two pound ten each time. I canna afford that."

"Oscar, did you get what you wanted out of all this?"

"Aye. Kevin's a good lad. We showed them the traditions of the game. Just a wee bit o' bad luck at the finish ended our chances. But Kevin will be back. There's a part of the old Tom in him. I'm no so sure what would have happened if I ha played mesel. Maybe nothin good."

"Oscar, you have to take your medicine. If you don't the police will arrest you and make you go back to the hospital."

"I dinna want to go back there." Oscar shivered as a cool breeze swept up the slope.

"I'll pay for your medicine if you promise you'll take it."

"There's the other reason. I can talk to Barry when I'm no takin it. When I'm takin the medicine, I've no one else to talk to, exepten wee Benedict."

"You're in the bar every night."

"Aye, right enough. Drinkin a pint or two by mysel, then going to the castle or tae hame."

"So, Oscar, you're lonely now, without Barry."

Oscar looked at Foot, man to man, with tears filling his eyes, thin hair ruffled by the breeze. "I didna think my life would be like this. I wanted tae farm like me da. That's all I wanted. Not go to hospital and take all kinds of medicine."

Foot reached to touch Oscar's leathery hand. "Oscar, I want to be your friend. After all, it took us both to caddie for Kevin and we got him to fourth place and I'm damned proud of that."

Oscar looked down where Foot's hand was on his, and put his other hand on top of Foot's.

"I'd buy ye a pint, but that scoundrel Kevin dina pay me for yesterday."

Gloria and Kevin scrambled over the rocks hand in hand to where she said it was possible see down the Firth of Forth all the way to Edinburgh. They had rested on a bench in front of the antique store again licking the ice cream cones sold next door and watching the fishing boats being unloaded. Gloria said she needed to work off the extra calories by going out to the point above the harbor.

"See," she pointed out in the haze. "That hill is just left of

Edinburgh. That gray brown in the distance is the town. On clear days you can see the buildings and the hills beyond. We take the train from there to Glasgow and then up to Inverness. If we're lucky, we'll get one of the old trains, the kind with separate compartments. In the British Rail system, only the Scots seem to get the romantic cars. The English prefer sitting in rows without having to face each other. Either that, or they're dumping all the old cars on the Highland lines while everybody else gets the new ones."

"Like the kind in the movies? With the sliding door? I've never been on one of those."

"They're terrific, unless you have to share with someone obnoxious, but that's rare. It's never happened to me."

"How could anyone be obnoxious to you?"

"You flatterer you," she slapped him on the arm.

"Flattery will get you everything."

"It sure will," she said. "Ready to go back?"

16

Foot left in the rental car taking Kevin's golf clubs with him to Glasgow airport. Gloria's sister-in-law dropped them off at the train station in Leuchars. The Tuesday morning commute was crowded from Leuchars to Edinburgh and more so across the valley to Glasgow. Although they could have gone the eastern route through Perth, by beginning in Glasgow, where the train originated, they found an old car and sprawled over the compartment so no one else would join them. The compartment was paneled in dark pine with wooden shelves above the seat to hold luggage. The two windows on either side of the sliding wooden door had blinds they pulled down. This was their private car swaying and clattering along the rails, shared only to Stirling where the two businessmen who didn't read the symbolic "do not disturb" sign got off. From there, the view of green and yellow rolling hills and farmland was theirs alone.

Gloria noticed the far-away look in Kevin's eyes and guessed where he was. "Did it come up short again, sweetheart?"

Kevin turned back from the window. "Yeah. The worst part is being known for missing a putt. My career will now be defined by what I didn't do rather than what I've accomplished."

Gloria came over and sat by his side. "Honey, forgive me, but, you haven't established a career yet and what you have accomplished is finishing one shot out of the lead in your first major tournament."

"No," he answered, still wanting to wallow in the fecal warmth of self pity. "You saw the newscast, 'Kevin Turner Comes Up Short at the Open.' Bigger than life the ball rolls toward the hole and hits glue. 'Turner misses.' That's what people will remember."

"What about that German guy and that one tournament?"

"Langer at the Ryder Cup?"

"Yes, Langer. He had a putt to win the Ryder Cup and he missed and nobody thinks less of him."

"That's different. He's a big winner and one of Europe's best players. He has a reputation that will overcome any miss."

"Well, you'll just have to build a reputation then."

"I did on Sunday," he said, chin down to his knees.

Gloria had to bring up her news sometime and it may as well be now. She had promised her sister-in-law she wouldn't wait and would tell him at least by the time they reached Aviemore where the deep green of the highland mountains reached into the sky and the streams that rushed by the tracks would wash away all cares. But even that wouldn't work on Kevin. Now was as good a time as any.

"Kevin, I have a bit of news for you. Difficult news, I'm afraid. I haven't been fully honest with you, and we need to talk."

Kevin's heart sank like a water ball at her words. Like all

men since Adam, the phrase "we need to talk," always meant trouble for the stronger sex.

"About what?" he asked, worried that his inability to shake off his putt had soured their relationship.

"About me." Her eyes dropped. She held her hands tight in her lap.

"About you?"

Gloria took a deep breath. "I told you I write children's books for a living and that's true, only it's a small part of what I do." She took another deep breath and looked him square in the eyes. "I have a child. A six-year old daughter."

"You have a kid?" Kevin asked and immediately regretted his obvious astonishment and the look of fear in her eyes.

"Yes."

"I'm sorry I reacted funny." Kevin shook his head. "You caught me by surprise."

"You needn't be sorry. I just want you to understand. She is my life. Nothing else mattered until I met you. I invited you to come with me so you two could meet and you decide what you wanted. I'm the one who's sorry," she emphasized, "that I didn't tell you. Now it doesn't seem fair that I didn't."

"Gloria, having a child is not a horrible thing. I would have understood. I've dated other women with kids. I love kids."

"Kevin," Gloria took a deep breath and let it out slowly. She looked toward the window. "Barbara is different. She's not like other children. She has a disease, something they call Rett Syndrome. It's rare and only girls get it. Nobody knows why. She has it pretty bad. She's not bright and charming like other weans. Just the opposite. She doesn't attend school. She stays at home and I do what I can to make her life worthwhile."

Gloria let the words spill out, like storm water's final breach of an earthen dam. "Oh God," she looked at Kevin, her eyes pleading for him to understand. "She was fine for a while. She was born normal, but then she was slow to walk and started this compulsive moving her hands to her mouth like she was putting food in it all the time. The doctors were concerned. Her head stopped growing but her features haven't. She grimaces all the time and grinds her teeth. A year ago she suffered convulsions." Gloria started to cry, holding her arms out in front of her and shaking her head "no" as he reached for her. "I should have told you. I'm sorry and I won't be surprised if you take the next train back."

Kevin forced his arm around her shoulders. "You've told me now. I would have come no matter what so it's not important when you told me. What about the father? Is he helping any?"

"I don't know the father. I was raped," she said, stone-faced.

Kevin pulled her closer and remained silent.

Gloria cried as Kevin held her. "I'm sorry," she said, lifting her head. Kevin kissed her red nose. "Nothing to be sorry for," he told her.

"What do we do now?" she asked.

"What do you mean, what do we do now? We go to your place and have a nice time. Who's taking care of her?"

"The wonderful Reverend Simpson of the Dornoch Cathedral. You'll like him..."

Kevin interrupted. "I know him. At least I sorta know him. He was in a video tape on Scottish golf courses I watched before coming over. He described Dornoch, while Sean

Connery did St. Andrews and the others. So the golfing Reverend Simpson is taking care of your daughter?"

"Yes. What a coincidence. You'll get to play the course with him if you like. And if you don't mind my playing as well," she added.

As the train chugged up the slopes of the highlands and along the banks of the River Ness into Inverness, the romance of their little compartment returned. Gloria melted into Kevin's arms as they looked over the hills and glens.

Kevin's mind worried more productively now, focused on how he would respond when he first saw the little girl. He had seen pictures and movies of kids with strange mental disabilities, some disfigured and retarded. But those were only pictures and of strangers. This would be Gloria's child. And to be raped. That explained her reluctance to having a physical relationship. But, he thought, holding on to her a little tighter, none of this changes anything. I love her.

From the small train station in Inverness, they carried their suitcases to the Highland Bus line and boarded the single-decker bus for the far north town of Wick at the end of the A9 highway. Part way there, the bus would make the short detour to Dornoch, noted for the eight centuries old cathedral and as the site of the last legal witch burning in Scotland.

The bus pulled into the town square and dropped them off at the combination newsagent, taxi stand and mortuary. Edmond Pitts was a busy man in this small town of seven hundred. He welcomed back one of his own and bid hello to the stranger. "Can I take you somewhere then?" he asked, when their luggage was unloaded and set beside them. Mr. Pitts waved to the driver as the bus continued on its route.

"Aye, to my place," Gloria told him. "I've got a boarder for the next week."

Mr. Pitt's expression didn't change. He, like everyone else in town, knew what had happened to her, and about the child, and how no man from this town or anywhere had been welcomed at her house.

Lifting the bags into the boot of the car, Mr. Pitt made conversation. "Do you play golf, Mr. Turner?"

Kevin smiled. I play golf. I may miss putts but I play golf, he thought. "Yes. I play," he answered. "I'm looking forward to seeing Dornoch. Tom Watson says it's the best."

"Aye, and none better on the East Coast," he replied, well aware his statement included both St. Andrews and Muirfield. "But lucky for us, we're tae far away fra the rest o' the world tae be much bothered. You can still walk on any time of day." He winked. "Ceptin the noo, during the tourist season."

He opened the back door and they piled in. Mr. Pitt turned from the driver's seat. "Would you be wanten to pick up Barbara?"

"No. Take us to my place. We'll come back and get her later," Gloria answered.

They were in the car two minutes. "Here you are then," Mr. Pitt said, pulling in front of a small one story brick house set back fifty yards from the street. The houses on either side were four-story stone structures, very much like small hotels with large lawns and sweeping driveways. Across the street was an open field of knee high grass and gorse and the wide blue expanse of the Dornoch Firth. Half way out the car, Kevin ducked back in as two jets screamed five hundred feet overhead.

Mr. Pitt laughed. "Aye, that was a near one. We've an air base too. They like to watch the golfers."

Kevin paid for the ride and carried the luggage to the door. Gloria was embarrassed as she fumbled with the keys. "I don't normally have guests," she said, opening the glass outer door and entering the alcove to unlock the inner door.

"Is your reputation ruined?" Kevin smiled, and then realized how dumb that was. "I'm sorry. I don't know how small towns are."

Her sitting room was tiny, crammed with a couch, two chairs and a small dining table. It was furnished in Scottish traditional; Scandinavian, Victorian, antique farm, fifties and some unidentifiable. Copies of old Masters hung on the wall as well as some he recognized as Hopper and Picasso. His junior college course in art history finally useful. Off the hallway was the kitchen on one side, bathroom on the other, and down further, a child's bedroom on the left, storage on the right and at the end was her bedroom.

"Very nice place," he said.

"Thank you. Please sit down," she told him motioning to the chair in the sitting room. "I believe I have a bottle or two of beer in the fridge. Would you like some?"

"Yes, I'd love one. When are we going to pick up your daughter?"

She brought him a bottle and a half poured glass. "I thought I'd run down and get her in a few minutes."

"You don't want me to go with you?"

"No. I think it would be better for you to meet her here. In fact," she hesitated. "Would you mind going for a wee walk while I get her settled? It might be better for her to meet you after she comes home."

"Sure," he told her. That sounded reasonable enough. It would be difficult for all of them at first. But Kevin anticipated no problems. He liked kids. "Even monsters?" the voice asked from deep in his mind.

"Finish your beer. I'll talk with Reverend Simpson. We'll be back about five."

"I'll be gone," he confirmed. "I'd like to wander around anyway. How far is the golf course?"

"That's another surprise." She pointed out the window. "See that little rise there? The one with the scrawny bush?"

Kevin looked out the widow. The bush she meant was across the street and fifty yards away. "Yes," he said.

"The fourth hole is just below it. The clubhouse and the Golf Hotel are about half a mile back down the road."

"Any more surprises?"

"No," she kissed him on the lips. "That's the last of them. Unless," she looked thoughtful, "we can think up more later." She kissed him again, slower and softer. "I'll be back. And thanks."

Kevin followed and waved as she drove her tiny yellow Mini down the street.

After finishing his beer, he followed her directions the half mile to the course. As she had described, he walked through the gravel parking lot of the hotel to the golf course clubhouse. For a course of international reputation, the clubhouse was disappointing, until he realized that it was a small version of the one at Carnoustie, a functional reinforced concrete structure designed only as a convenient site for purchasing a ticket and grabbing a quick drink, not a destination by itself like

American clubs. The pro shop was not much larger than Gloria's sitting room; a glass counter, two racks of clothes and a line of putters along the window and that was it.

"Can I help you, sir?" the middle aged man behind the counter asked as he was putting a pair of shoes up on the head high shelf along the wall.

"Yes," Kevin said. "How much..."

The man turned to look at his customer. His startled look stopped Kevin in mid sentence.

"You...you're Kevin Turner. Are you not?"

"Yes," Kevin grinned. This was a first, to be recognized somewhere other than a tournament site. Quite a nice feeling, until he recalled why he would be recognized.

The man vigorously shook his hand. "Well done, Mr. Turner. An excellent tournament. A bit o' bad luck at the end, but we were pulling for you."

"Thanks."

"And there'll be no paying for your golf while yer here. De ye need clubs as well?"

"Yes. I didn't bring any with me."

"Aye. We've no much. But we'll put together a set for you. It's a pleasure to meet you."

Kevin was like a kid again exploring the putting green and watching the players on the first tee for a while and later observing the last green from the enclosed sun room of the hotel. The view from there took in the championship course and the short course, as well as the Dornoch Firth and the rolling farm hills to the south. From where he sat, he saw the clock tower on the clubhouse slowly moving toward five o'clock. He was getting nervous. What if she was a monster?

On the walk back, he imagined the worst faces possible, with eyes pushed wide apart at odd angles, noses shaped like mushrooms and mouths that were open sores instead of pink lips. She would be bald or have an old man's scraggly hair and talk with a guttural man's voice. One ear would hang by a thin strand of skin. Her eyes would roll uncontrollably and she might even drool or spit. And she would hobble hunched over or drag one of her legs instead of walk, grunting each time she moved. Kevin wanted to be ready for the worst. He wanted to smile when they met.

Gloria's car was parked on the street; lights were on in the house. Kevin waited in front of the door. He took a deep breath and knocked. "Me, me," a child's voice yelled. There was the patter of little shuffling feet then the door opened.

Tiny white shoes with a buckle strap, white knee socks covering a little girl's legs, a white and pink dress and a thin body and glorious red hair on a hideous head that was half normal size and shaped like a potato. Her eyes were set almost to the sides. She had to turn her head to look at him.

"Hi," he said, kneeling down to her height. "I'm your mother's friend Kevin Turner."

Barbara screamed and ran to the back bedroom.

Gloria walked down the hall followed by her daughter who was clinging to her legs. Gloria's eyes searched for his reaction. She reached out her hands to invite him in.

The evening was pleasant. Barbara explored this intrusion into her home, eventually sitting in Kevin's lap as they watched television. After her bath, she returned to the sitting room to kiss him goodnight. This left the two adults to sort out their own bed plans. Gloria opened the discussion.

"I have been putting you off. You understand why now, of course."

"I do. I'm sorry."

"I invited you here because I wanted you to meet Barbara. And also, because I have only one bed."

"You have a couch. I could sleep on the couch. I don't mind that. Done it a hundred times."

"Not in my house. I want you to sleep with me. But, Kevin, I'm not fully comfortable with making love to you. I'm not sure I can."

"Gloria. I will sleep with you. I will hold you. I will kiss you. I will not do anything if you don't want me to."

"You can go to bed with me and not expect sex?"

Kevin looked into her eyes. "I love you. Yes. I can sleep with you and not expect sex."

In bed together later, they talked. Kevin admitted it was still hard to get used to, but he would. Gloria answered his questions. Yes, Barbara was getting worse and did not know, could not conceive, that she was abnormal, that she had a terrible disease, and that she would not live to be a teenager. Gloria was happy her child could still communicate and play almost the same as other kids and she didn't have to be back in diapers yet. They didn't have sex that night, but they made love for a long time.

At breakfast they planned the day. Barbara wanted to drive north to John O'Groats, just to be in the car going somewhere. The adults agreed and they all had the most marvelous picnic, looking at the islands and trying to be the first to spot a whale. That night, Kevin wondered about her moods. She has medicine, Gloria told him. She needs medicine for pain and a lot of the other problems her disease caused. Sometimes she needs medicine to counteract the pill's side effects; other times she needs tranquilizers to feel okay. "I don't like the idea of pills to help her mood, but I will do whatever it takes to give her as much quality of life as we can."

The next night he asked her about the rape. "I'd like to understand," he said. "But you don't have to tell me."

"Two men," she said in a monotone. "I was walking back to the house from town, when one of them jumped out from behind a wall and put an old feed bag over my head. They dragged me behind the house. One held me down while the other raped me. They took turns. I couldn't identify them and nobody was ever caught."

He held her after she talked, but it didn't seem to be enough.

On Thursday, Gloria had to take Barbara to the doctor in Tain, the largest town in the area and close by since the Kessock Bridge over the Firth was built. She had arranged a golf match with Reverend Simpson for ten o'clock. He would wait for Kevin in the sun room of the hotel. Gloria kissed him goodbye on one cheek, Barbara on the other.

Reverend Simpson was a grandfather angel. His smile was warm and his white hair splayed over his ears like a rakish halo. His voice, soft, was like a clear Scottish stream with a touch of the essence of heather. Kevin liked him immediately, and reminded him how they first met via video. "Jim" blushed at the compliment, and complained about how much of a disadvantage he had playing with such a golfing star.

Like all Scots, Jim took golf seriously and casually at the same time. They wagered a ball, Kevin giving up twelve strokes. After the front nine, Kevin was down four holes. He had never seen such a course in his life. Every green was up on a mound. Any shot not hit just right would bounce one way or another, never nearer the hole. The bunkers he found reminded him of the Bottle Dungeon. He couldn't figure out where to aim his tee shots and had no clue about breaks on the green. Overall, he was having the best time of his golfing life. Jim had a million stories and a keen putter. Kevin was transported by the course and his opponent to golfing paradise.

The match ended on the sixteenth. Kevin made a few putts to get as close as only three down, but a good drive on sixteen put him on the hill. His blind two-iron was caught by the wind and driven to parts unknown. His lost ball cost him the ball, the hole, the match and the wager of another ball. They played the final two holes on the way in so Kevin enjoyed the finish of the course. "That way," chided the good Reverend, "You'll not have an excuse if I beat you again."

They were relaxing in the sun room when Jim asked if Kevin had met Barbara. "It's a terrible thing that happened to her, to them both," he said.

"Gloria had told me about her daughter. I was a little scared to meet her, actually."

"Aye, I can only imagine. She's a sweet, loveable child. Sometimes quite a handful, but it's not her fault. Terrible things are happening in her wee body."

"What do you think will happen?"

The Reverend shook his head. "She will not live a long time. No one knows how long, of course, but these children rarely become adults. And it will be a difficult life. Gloria is a wonderful mother, but she has a life, too. No one can expect her to give it all to the lassie. But that's what she expects of herself. I was surprised when she told me you were here. As you might expect, she doesn't have much to do with men. You must be very important to her."

"Is she okay?"

"Gloria?"

"Yes. I wonder sometimes, from what she does and what she says."

"I don't know if a woman can ever be right after such an experience," Reverend Simpson told him. "Let me put it to you this way, Kevin. How much has your wee putt affected you?"

"I wondered if that would come up sometime."

"Well?"

"To tell you the truth...of course to tell you the truth," he stammered to the Reverend, "missing the putt was not a super big deal. I put a good stroke on it. The ball just stopped before I figured it would. I didn't like missing out on the playoff, but the big worry I had after was how people would brand me with the choke label. There's nothing I can do about it. You're just stuck with something like that."

"Aye, and poor Gloria is stuck with the reminder every day of what happened to her and how what should be a blessed event can become something horrible, for everyone."

"I wonder where I fit in."

"I wondered that myself. Kevin, I can speak frankly with you. We've played golf together and I saw how you coped with your own moment of disappointment. I assume you two met while you were in St. Andrews for the Open."

"Yeah, we met and things just clicked."

"Do you feel that you love her?"

"Yes. I do. I've never felt this way for anyone in my life. Her having a child, even the child she has doesn't mean anything. I'd like to have a relationship with her."

"Kevin, I don't know you well, but I do her. And perhaps I shouldn't be sticking my nose where it doesn't belong, but I don't think Gloria is ready for what you're suggesting."

"Why not?"

"We've discussed things. I can't tell you about them, but they mean she cannot allow herself a life yet."

"Because of Barbara?"

"That's only part of it."

Kevin protested. "But Jim, I'm in love with her. We can take care of Barbara together."

"Kevin, it may work. I'm not a fortune teller. All I'm saying is that you need to talk with her, straight, no wishes in the by and by. Talk with her about what she wants, what she needs and what you are to her. You may find you don't like the answers."

"Well, thank you for your advice, Reverend," Kevin said getting up. "But I think I can figure out things pretty well on my own."

"Yes, Kevin. I just wanted to give you some advice. It may be good or no."

Kevin politely shook the Reverend's hand and left.

Dinner was strained. Barbara had to endure uncomfortable procedures at the doctor's office and screamed all the way home. Gloria was subdued and Kevin forced a smile so at least one of them looked happy. He talked about losing to Reverend

Simpson and how wonderful the golf course was. Each word fell listlessly and soon he just pushed his food around on the plate. They played Snakes and Ladders, Barbara's favorite game, until bedtime.

After tucking her in, Gloria brought in a small whisky for Kevin and sat with him on the couch.

"You talked to the Reverend, I take it."

"He asked about our relationship. I pretty much told him it was none of his business."

"He's a good man. He cares an awful lot."

"I like him. But he doesn't know us. What we have."

"He knows me very well. What did he tell you?"

"Nothing. Just that he didn't think you were ready for a relationship." They each looked around the other, afraid where the conversation might lead. "Gloria, were you a virgin when it happened?"

"Yes," she said, so softly he almost didn't hear her.

"Have you had a relationship with anyone since?"

"No." She looked at him, her face that of a child, full of innocence and hope, and that of an old woman, etched with despair. Her wisdom was far beyond his and knew good and evil were like reflections in a mirror, and that something as wonderful as their relationship could cause terrible pain. She knew and was ready to flee.

"Why me?"

She smiled that same smile with her eyes he had first fallen in love with. "You were nice, handsome. I felt safe with you. I guess."

"What was Reverend Simpson talking about, you not being ready?"

Gloria's smile faded, replaced by a look of detachment. "I told him I didn't think life is worth living. That my life is only a biological event, and that if self awareness is anything other than an evolutionary accident, it's a terrible trick played on all of us by a cruel God." She looked up at him with a rueful smile. "He didn't like that very much."

"You believe that?"

"Of course I do. I don't like living. I'm alive now only to take care of Barbara."

"We had such a good time together. Doesn't that mean something?"

She stroked his cheek. "Yes it does. It means a lot. I have never been happier in my life."

Relieved, Kevin asked, "So we're okay?"

"I don't know."

17

Near the end of the third week of July, in Northeastern Scotland, at a latitude of 58 degrees north, at noon, on a bright, cloudless day, with not a breath of wind and no rain within a hundred miles, when every other golf course in the northern hemisphere was crowded with six to twenty foursomes wandering behind the first tee, mumbling and complaining about the slow group in the fairway, the Dornoch golf pro standing behind the counter in the tiny shop shrugged his shoulders and suggested that the almost famous golf professional go out by himself. Kevin had chatted with the pro for twenty minutes waiting for man, woman, boy or girl to show up. Royal Dornoch was a course to play with someone, anyone, so you can say, "did you see that?" or "isn't this fantastic?" Playing by himself would also give him time to think. Kevin didn't want that.

When Gloria told him she had to drive Barbara to Inverness and she wanted to take her by herself, he realized that she wouldn't let a man into their tight relationship. She wanted to, maybe. Alone with each other they were perfect. They touched when they were together as smooth and natural as the limbs of a willow in a summer breeze.

Kevin took his driver out of the bag that was lying on the ground like any Sunday player's just to the right of the tee marker. But with studied professionalism not seen here since Chip Beck and Andy North helicoptered in for an exhibition years before, Kevin set up to the ball. The green was in reach of a monster drive and Kevin intended to reach it. He relaxed his forearms and shoulders and took a wider stance. Kevin's intense swing launched his black Titleist into outer space, far into the blue sky. Seconds passed before the ball re-entered the atmosphere and, red hot, smacked down twenty yards short of the elevated green, bounced once, then bounced again before rolling onto the putting surface three hundred and fifty yards away. The pro from behind the shop window tapped on the glass, pointed at the green and clapped. Kevin smiled and waved. At least here, on the golf course, he had an idea of the rules and what worked. Kevin hoisted the borrowed bag of clubs onto his shoulder and traipsed toward the green.

His ball was twenty feet below the hole. He made the putt for eagle and went on to the par three second without changing his expression. He made birdie there and looked as if he was filling out tax forms. On the seventh hole, the four-ball ahead of him waved him through. Kevin waved back indicating that he was in no hurry and was content to play behind them. He hated slow play, but he belonged nowhere else right then. By the turn he was six under.

She hadn't said anything, it was her attitude and little signs that even Kevin noticed. Yesterday after dinner they all went for a walk. Barbara grabbed Kevin's meaty hand in her child sized one, which pleased him. Her reaching for him was a compliment, a gesture of trust, like that of a wild bird that hops closer with each toss of bread eventually to pick crumbs from your fingertips. Gloria let go of his hand and bent to pick up a paper that was blowing along with the wind. She didn't take his hand again. They walked together down the road, step matching step, as intimate as solders.

Kevin birdied two more holes and eagled the par five. He parred the rest except for a bogey on sixteen and matching birdie threes on the final two par fours. Had he turned in his scorecard, he would have owned the course record. Instead, he retired to the hotel sunroom to think.

He loved Gloria. Of that he was sure. She loved him. He was as sure of that as a man can be. The question was whether she had room in her life for him, or if she preferred to take care of Barbara and ignore her own life, and his. Kevin looked out the window over the eighteenth green and saw a familiar figure three-putting from only twenty feet. As Reverend Simpson wheeled his trolley past the clubhouse and up the few steps to the hotel parking lot, Kevin waved from the side window and motioned him to come in. Jim raised his head with a big smile and waved back, then pantomimed putting his clubs in the car first.

"I'm surprised you would want to talk with me again, Kevin," he said sitting down after they exchanged hellos.

"Well," Kevin laughed, "anyone who three putts the last green and can still smile is a man I want as a friend. And, someone as wise as you I want as a friend too. Jim, I was wrong about me and about Gloria. She needs to protect Barbara leaving not much room for me."

Jim sucked in his lips. "Yes," he said. "I fear that too. I've no doubt she loves you as well as she can."

"Jim, what do I do? I love her. She's all I want."

The Reverend Simpson looked down at his hands, and rubbed the palms together before answering. "Patience. Give her time. You're the first man she's been with in her adult life. It's new and threatening. To enjoy a relationship with you would be to abandon wee Barbara. She'll have to learn how to have her own life and to be a good mother to the wee wean at the same time. It's no easy."

"I have to leave in a couple of days. I have a tournament in New Jersey."

"Aye," the reverend nodded his head, but said nothing more.

Kevin was silent for a while too. He sighed. "I guess I have to decide how married I am to golf too, don't I?"

"It's priorities. It is what we want. It is what we decide is right for us."

"You do what's right," Kevin agreed. "How do you know what's right?"

The reverend smiled. "I gave a sermon once, how it is easier to know what is wrong than what is right. Wrong is stronger in the heart most times. Right is in there, but sometimes almost silent. That's okay. It pushes us to look a little harder inside. He is very wise."

"God?"

"Aye."

"What happens when you look and still make a mistake?"

Reverend Simpson rubbed his palms together then

interlocked his fingers and shook his hands up and down between his legs before bringing them up and tapping his chin. He sighed and pursed his lips. He dropped his hands to his lap, opened them up and clapped his hands softly together once and rubbed them back and forth again.

Kevin thought he was never going to answer. Finally he did. "Kevin, you can't make a mistake. Not in the sense of doing something wrong. If you look hard inside and decide based on what you find in your heart, you're doing the best you can do. That's never a mistake. Any good athlete knows that you do your best and adjust. It's when you don't do your best, when you become defensive and obstinate, never listening to a reasonable difference of opinion."

"You're right," Kevin said. "I once played a par three with a seven-iron and the ball fell short into a pond. Rather than admit the seven wasn't enough club, I hit again only harder the second time. Naturally, I went into the pond again. I finally admitted to myself that I was wrong and took a six-iron. So I have to trust what I feel about Gloria."

"Trust it and express your feelings to her. She's a strong girl. She's proved that. Talk to her about what you want."

"And what I think is going on in her?"

Reverend Simpson laughed. "My boy, if I knew what a woman thinks, I'd write a book. Never, never, never talk to a lady as if you know what she's thinking. You'll be wrong every time, even if you're right. Tell them what you assume or your opinion, and then listen. And make sure they know you're listening. It's the only way."

The barman in a stiff white shirt wove between the chairs

scattered through the middle of the room, unlocked the padlock and rolled up the metal screen that closed off the bar. Happy hour was about to begin.

"Can I buy you a drink?" Kevin asked.

"Oh, no. No thank you. I'm off to my supper." Reverend Simpson got up and put his hand on Kevin's shoulder. "Talk to her, Kevin, and listen. Listen to your heart and listen to her. She's a grand woman."

Through dinner and an endless game of Snakes and Ladders, Kevin wondered how to talk with Gloria so she would tell him what he wanted to hear. He wished that she would say she loved him and she was adjusting to having him in her home and her life. He wanted to ask her the right question to get the right answer. She had busied herself with dinner and declined his offer to help, setting the plates, humming to herself and only half listening to his feeble attempts at raising the issues that were so new to his heart.

Barbara was sick during dinner. She so wanted to be like the adults and say things at the table. Tonight, with the adults silent, she tried to fill the empty space, but couldn't eat and talk at the same time. Halfway through she almost choked. Instead, she released a stomach full of soup over the table, which Gloria quickly cleaned up. After dinner, Kevin helped dry the dishes while Barbara set up her favorite game. Gloria looked at him a few times during play, but he couldn't read anything in her eyes.

She put Barbara to bed then went into her bedroom, closing the door behind her. Kevin watched from the sitting room, worried that this was an escalation in the separateness. A few minutes later, the door opened and she came out wearing a thin, dark green silk dressing gown that draped softly over her body and was tied around her waist. It was an outfit for seduction. She sat with him on the couch, legs pulled under her.

"You seemed agitated all evening, so I wore my new dressing gown to see how agitated you can get. I bought it in St. Andrews. I've never worn a dressing gown before," she said, looking more cuddly than was fair for holding a meaningful conversation.

"Yeah, I was kinda agitated," Kevin admitted. "I've had a lot on my mind."

"Barbara?" she asked, turning toward him slightly so the fabric pulled across her breasts.

"Only a little Barbara. Mostly us."

Gloria eyes narrowed. "What about us?"

Kevin took a deep breath. Here we go. "You seem to be pulling away. That since we've gotten here, things between us have worsened."

"I have to take care of Barbara. She's my child. I'm not free like I was in Anstruther, paying attention only to you. And to us," she added belatedly.

"I don't have a problem with that. What bothers me..." Kevin hesitated. What he said now could ruin everything. He loved this woman. She sat, expressionless, like an empty canvas ready for paint. But. He was no painter. Kevin sighed again. He bit on his lips and fiddled with his hands like Reverend Simpson did. He studied the woman he adored who was waiting for him to talk to her. He sighed once more, then began. "Gloria, I'm not sure you have room in your life for me right now."

Gloria looked down at her lap and then back at him. She tilted her head to the side in the way he adored. The hair he loved to touch slid along her shoulder, strands catching on the silk fabric of the gown. He tried to ignore the rise and fall of her breasts. She took a deep breath and smiled, a thin one that faded and made Kevin's heart stop.

"Kevin," she said, "maybe you're right. It may be I don't have room for you." Her eyes lifted to his and darted about looking for his response and found none, his reaction hidden behind his game face.

"Do you want there to be room?" he asked, dreading her answer. He ached for her, would give up everything for her, and yet would leave the house and her right now if she told him to. "Do you want that?" he asked again.

"Yes," she answered. Tears began to fill her eyes and rolled one by one down her cheeks. She looked at up at him and blinked. "I want there to be room for you."

Kevin's heart peeked out from behind his stoic look, like the sun from behind a rain cloud. His face reflected the warmth.

"I love you," she said, reaching to his cheek and touching him as softly as an angel would.

"Is Barbara asleep?" he asked.

Gloria smiled. "She had a big day and a late evening playing games. She was asleep before her head touched the pillow."

Kevin got up and closed the door to the hallway, putting a

chair against it just in case. He stood in front of Gloria and held out his hands. She reached up and he pulled her to her feet. "I love you," he said, savoring the words on his tongue. Gloria waited for him, arms at her sides. Kevin reached for the neckline of her gown. His fingers ran along her smooth skin and prodded at the material, pushing it aside. She focused on his face as his eyes followed the movement of his hands. He felt her warmth and the goosebumps as the cool air reached her skin.

Softly, and slowly, he exposed more of her, the rough dark cloth stretching against the whiteness of her half bare breasts. Her breathing quickened as Kevin eased the gown over her shoulders, letting it drop to her waist. He traced the back of his fingers along the curve of her breast then cupped his callused hand to push and squeeze. Her eyes closed, her nipples hardened and her chest became rosy pink and still her arms remained at her sides, letting him have her. His hands continued downward until both were tugging at the thin ribbon belt. Quickly it was untied and the gown dropped to her feet. Gloria reached her arms around his neck and pushed her naked body against his full length. Kevin reached between them to fondle her breast again as his other arm went behind her to lower her to the floor. Suddenly her body stiffened. She shivered, pulled away and started to sob, deep heaving sobs that filled her nose and choked her throat. Passion fled. Kevin pulled her down onto the couch and into his lap, holding her.

She burrowed her face into his shoulder and moaned. "They hurt me. They really hurt me." Kevin held her tightly, absorbing her pain and suffering the guilt of all men.

They clung together in that small house on a gentle rise a mile from the sea. Behind the door, the clock in the hallway chimed the half hour and then the hour. He rocked her, lulling them both. Rain fell on the roof and pattered against the window. Gloria's desperate breathing slowed. Fingernails she had dug into his skin relaxed. She sagged deeper into his arms.

Gloria took a stuttering breath and leaned away from him. Her face was puffy, her eyes red. She sniffed to clear her stuffed-up nose. "I must look a mess," she coughed.

"I love you," Kevin told her, stoking her hair. She smiled and snuggled back into his chest. Her warm tears wet the front of his shirt. Kevin kissed the back of her head. First just on her hair, then he nuzzled his way through to her skin and kissed her again. She shivered.

"I'm sitting here naked and you have your clothes on," she told him from against his chest.

Kevin reached down to the floor where her gown had dropped and draped it over her shoulders. She kissed the front of his shirt, hesitated a moment, kissed him on the cheek and pushed herself up. Kevin watched as she slipped her arms into the robe and pulled it around her.

"Would you like a hot chocolate?" she asked as she tied the belt.

"Sure," Kevin answered as she moved the chair away from the door and went into the kitchen.

Sitting at opposite ends of the couch a few minutes later, bare feet touching, Gloria told Kevin again about the men who had grabbed her and held her down and took turns while she prayed not to be killed while she so much wanted to die. She told him she was weak and afraid and had emotionally shut her eyes. "I was running," she said, "like a little girl holding her breath and running past a graveyard on her way to school. I didn't know what I was doing until you touched me and you squeezed my breast. One of them did that, the same way. The memory came over me and I was there again, held down, struggling. They were hurting me. I lost you and I lost me and it was just them grabbing me and hurting me. Kevin, this kind of crime never ends."

Kevin listened, his hot chocolate untouched. He had no idea what to say, how to make it better. Was this the end of their relationship? Was she saying what they had didn't exist? Was it fair to ask? Was he being selfish when she was so hurt? Kevin looked at her. She was staring into her empty cup. He pushed his foot against hers. After a moment she pushed back.

"What are you thinking?" he asked.

Gloria looked up from her cup. Her smile answered his question, but she told him anyway. "I was thinking that we have something. Something special." She inhaled and let the air out. "But," she added, "right now I have things I need to do on my own."

"But..."

Gloria held up her hand to stop him. "Kevin. I love you. I have no doubts about that. But, I need to repair myself. No one can do it for me, or even with me. Maybe a professional can help." She laughed. "All I need to do to see a psychiatrist is visit my G.P. in Golspie, get a referral from him to a specialist in Inverness and wait ten months for an appointment." She shook her head in frustration. "What I mean is that I don't, I can't, lean on you right now. I need to come to you complete, whole. And I'm not whole. I believed I had a complete life here taking care of Barbara. Until I met you. Then everything changed. For a week I forgot everything. That was because of you. By myself, I cling to my daughter like she would wither and die if I didn't, pretending I was all she had and she was all I needed. I have to change and I have to find out if I can change and how I go about doing that."

Kevin looked at her, his future evaporating, leaving him alone when he only wanted to be with her.

"Can you understand?" she asked.

He nodded his head and they sat looking at one another with nothing more to say.

The rain stopped. Only a few stragglers plopped one by one on the concrete step. The breeze, fresh from the rainsquall, rushed through the rose bushes outside the window and brushed the long branches against the glass.

They slept together that night, cuddled like spoons, their minds a hundred miles apart.

The three of them played the short course at Dornoch the next morning early enough for Kevin to catch the eleven o'clock bus to Inverness. Gloria had a terrible grip, the worst Kevin had ever seen. Her right hand was so far under the club it pushed her right elbow into her stomach. She explained that her father had taught her to keep her right elbow in and that's how she did it. The grip caused her to lift the club up on the backswing instead of swinging away from the ball; for a downswing she slashed at the ball like she was chopping wood. Barbara griped the club like it had always been part of her and swung like she'd done it a thousand times when this was her first time. She had no desire to hit the ball at anything in particular; she just liked to hit it. In another few months it was likely she would no longer be able to do that.

Kevin chased her ball wherever she hit it and altered Gloria's grip bit by bit over the nine holes and she patiently did what he suggested over eight. On the last hole she went back to the old way and scored her only par.

An hour later, Gloria and Barbara stood with him in the square waiting for the bus. Barbara fiddled with all the zippers and straps on the suitcase. Gloria sometimes fussed with her to leave the case alone and sometimes let her play. Kevin wondered what to say to Gloria who was standing so near, yet so far. As the bus turned into the square, they looked at each other, desperate to connect in the few moments left.

"Hug, hug," cried Barbara, aware of what a bus meant. Kevin bent down and took her in his arms. "Mum, too," she said, reaching for her mother. "Mum, too."

Gloria joined the hug. Kevin wrapped them both in his arms and held tight, fighting the tears that were welling up. Two passengers got off and the driver loaded Kevin's luggage as the three clung together.

"I'll see you soon," Kevin told them, breaking away. He kissed Barbara on the top of her head and Gloria on the lips. "I love you," he told her.

As the bus labored up the hill toward the highway, Gloria and Barbara waved until they couldn't see him waving out the back window anymore. Then they walked home holding each other's hand.

Kevin settled into the last row of the bus. Only a third of the seats were taken, almost all by tiny white-haired ladies in thick coats off to shop in the city. The only other man on board looked like he had retired twenty years ago and had nothing else to do but to go with his wife, to wait in a pub along the high street with a pint and a cigarette while she popped in and out the stores.

Kevin could still feel the wet kiss Barbara had given him on the cheek in return for the one he had given her head and the soft touch on his lips where Gloria had said goodbye.

He looked at the assemblage of heads in the rows of seats in front of him and counted. Half wore hats, small simple felt affairs without adornment, suitable and characteristic of the dour, harsh, simple life of their wind swept country. The other half were bareheaded, all with white hair, some with spots of pink showing through. Those that sat together tilted their heads toward one another and chatted away in lilting highland brogues. Those by themselves chose the aisle seat, and peered forward to help the driver find his way.

Is this what would happen to his Gloria? Old. Alone. The highlight of the week taking a shopping trip into Inverness? And poor little Barbara. What was going to happen to her?

A couple of hours later he sat on one of the circles of metal benches in the waiting area of the Inverness train station. The high glass roof let in plenty of light and provided room for the pigeons and sparrows that made a home there, swooping down from the rafters and strutting along the tiled floor picking at scraps. Kevin envied them their little world; the roof was as high as heaven needed to be.

He observed families struggle toward the trains, wrestling with luggage and bundles and baskets and strollers, dragging overtired children or yelling at the older ones who ran too far ahead and envied the couples who walked by, even the ones who didn't hold hands or look at each other. He envied the young girls in faded blue jeans sitting on the floor or leaning against a post, noses deep in a paperback, alone with their dreams until their trains came in.

Kevin had his own compartment on another old train car, doubling his loneliness. The snack cart had come by early. A cup of coffee, hot, black, and shortbread wrapped in plastic waited for him on the little fold-down table under the window. His feet were propped on the opposite seat. He had all the comforts of home, he smiled wistfully, except who would really make it a home.

The rolling hills raced by as the train swayed and clattered back to civilization. He had known other women, not many compared to a lot of men his age, but he did well enough. He liked women, loved one or two before, but none like he loved Gloria. Kevin smiled at the memories. His initial reaction was always sexual and they seemed to want him as much as he wanted them. The relationship would grow, lovemaking fall into a pattern, then she would want more of him and he could never give. There was always more golf.

Would I have stayed if she asked, he wondered. But she gave him an out. "I'll write to you when I'm ready," she said. Maybe she wouldn't write. Maybe he didn't want her to. A lot ran through his mind on the four hour trip. One thing came to mind he could do something about.

The train pulled into Glasgow at seven. He called the airport to delay his departure one day. By eight-thirty he was in Edinburgh. Kevin was at the train station in Leuchers by eleven and asleep in bed at the Sporting Laird on North Street, St. Andrews, by midnight.

18

I'm sorry," the man inside the starter's hut told him. "I don't think you'll be able to play until at least four this afternoon."

"And I can't put my name down on a waiting list?"

"No, sir. We don't have a waiting list. If a group will let you play with them, you may join them. But I can't set up a game for you and singles cannot reserve a tee time."

"So it's hang around here hoping for a game or coming back at four?"

"Yes, sir. And I can't guarantee four o'clock. That's just my best estimate."

Kevin mulled over his limited options of playing the Old Course one more time. Only the steel bases remained of the spectator stands that had lined the first tee and made that welcoming backdrop for his last drive of the tournament. No official was there to lead him from the green to the scorers' area and there was no quick walk into the Royal and Ancient Club House through the crowd of sympathetic fans. The quiet walkway in front of the clubhouse now teemed with tourists outfitted in plaid slacks and bright red Old Course sweaters. Most were men in pairs or groups of four, describing how each played the first or last or seventeenth or whatever hole made the best story. A few wives stood close by, sighing or discussing what restaurant might be a good place for dinner. The starter interrupted Kevin's sad observations of what had happened to his home away from home.

"You might get right on the New Course or the Jubilee just up the road." The starter pointed toward the Ladies Putting Green. "Or," he added pointing further afield, "you can drive over to the Eden and Strathtyrum by the practice range. I'm sure you could get on those as well."

Kevin thanked him and rethought his plan. It was clear he was not able to dash on the Old Course to put one of his demons to rest and get out of town. He climbed the steps of the Woollen Mill's snack shop and picked up a cup of tea and another one of those ever present packages of shortbread. He sat among the weary and over-loaded shoppers, joining them looking out over the course and the West Sands to the sea. His vision, however, was much different than theirs. He didn't want to wallow, but his thoughts were plodding just above melancholy. Missing by one tiny inch in the grandest tournament in the world of golf could feel a lot worse. But loving a woman who loved back should feel a lot better.

Kevin finished his tea and wandered up the Scores to the castle ruins, paid his fee and took his time going through the exhibits of Kings and Cardinals, of wars and stories of the common citizens of the "auld grey toon." He walked through the door and onto the path he took that night with Gloria and Oscar, then through the castle entrance and into the central courtyard. Kevin waited while a family came out of the Bottle

Dungeon room before joining another family inside. The boy kept saying "cool," as his father explained what happened here over the years. Kevin sensed Gloria's warmth against him and heard the odd echo of Oscar rushing away. He left the castle ruins and walked over a small rise to the cemetery, visiting the grave of Young Tom Morris and paying the pound fee to climb St. Rule's Tower. The view from the top took in all of the ancient town, the golf courses, a patchwork of farms to the east and south and far over the bay to the Leuchars air base and the thick Tentsmuir Forest beyond. This was a home, a pretty, welcoming place. He looked north over the steel gray water of St. Andrews Bay, toward Dornoch. One of the Royal Air Force jets he saw taking off could get there in minutes and land within a couple of miles of her. The noise of two young couples walking up the steps broke his mood and he climbed down as soon as they passed.

Kevin walked to Jim Farmer's shop on St. Mary's Place. Jim had helped him when he was struggling on the European Tour and had made it a point to find him and wish him well before the Open. Jim no longer tried to qualify, but he had a solid game that Kevin wouldn't challenge on a windy day without being given at least one stroke a side. His staff said he was away at a tournament in Gullane. It was only noon. Kevin walked back to the Old Course and to the Golf Museum. That was an interesting hour of studying the old sticks and fooling with the interactive videos that were around every corner. Then he went down the hill to the Sea Life Centre. That was another nice hour. While sitting on a bench on the Bow Butts eating fish and chips bought from the stand outside the Centre,

God's rubber mallet of insight bounced off his skull. He had to find Oscar.

He found him in Ben's, sitting at the same table where he and Foot sat the first time. The glass in front of Oscar was near empty, and the old man was looking desperate. They saw each other at the same time.

"Hello, Kevin, lad," he shouted. It was if Oscar had seen him only yesterday.

Kevin walked over and shook his hand. "Oscar, may I join you?"

"Aye, laddie. Always room at the table for one more. I'd thought ye'd be on yer way by noo."

"Nope. Got one more thing to do before I go and I need your help."

"Kevin," Oscar reached for Kevin's arm and gripped his forearm, his face drawn up in a picture of regret. "I must apologize for what I've done. I've been takin my medicine and it's made me think. I shouldna have thrown ye doon the dungeon and given old Foot some o' the pills. I'm verra sorry."

"Oscar, you're forgiven," Kevin told him with a wave of his hand. "There's something more important I want to tell you. I never paid you for your services for the last round." Kevin pulled out twenty hundred pound notes. They made a wide fan in his hand. "Here, this is the going rate for caddies carrying the last round of the Open when their player makes fourth place because he missed a putt on the last hole."

Oscars eyes opened wide, his jaw dropped, all the wrinkles in his face vanished. He had never seen that much money in his life. "Aye," was all he could say, beaming as he was from ear to ear.

Kevin put the notes in a neat pile and placed them in front of Oscar. "Now, what I want to do," Kevin told him, "is play the Old Course again, this evening, with you as my caddie. I'll pay you if you'll do that. Okay?"

"Oh aye, aye," Oscar said, holding two thousand pounds in his hands, not hearing a word of what Kevin was proposing.

"Oscar."

"Aye?" he said, not taking his eyes from the money, as if it might fly away.

"Oscar."

He looked up, but held more tightly to the hundred pound notes.

"Oscar, I'd like to play the Old Course again, with you as my caddie."

"Aye. That will be fine."

"And I'll pay you a hundred more pounds."

Oscar almost fainted.

The view from behind the windows of the Royal and Ancient Clubhouse at twilight on a summers' eve is a moment of magic, a spectacular meeting of earth, sun, and sky lasting perhaps an hour. Every roll and contour of the Old Course stands out in relief, like waves on a broad green sea and often extraordinarily beautiful as it was this evening, tossing and rolling against a background of pink clouds and darkening sky. Players coming in now are the die-hards, the pilgrims to the Mecca of golf who will never get enough of this hallowed ground and who will remember these moments forever. In these magical sixty minutes, golfers become part of Barry Hardon's eternal circle.

Some members of the R & A like to stand by the windows of the trophy room to watch the players and the lengthening shadows on the far hills. Behind them the sun reflects golden off the glass cases displaying ancient prizes such as the Queen Adelaide Gold Metal, the Silver Cashmire Cup, the Amateur Trophy and most famous of all, the claret jug of the British Open Championship. This prize is ringed with the names of Jacklin, Trevino, Faldo, Watson, Palmer, Cotton, Hogan and Nicklaus, and for now without one Kevin Turner.

If a member standing in that room turned his head left that evening toward the eighteenth green, he would have seen one of the die-hards assessing a ten-foot downhill putt; his venerable caddie by his side, judging together the speed and borrow. If his attention wasn't called elsewhere, he would have seen the player stand over the putt with the grace and confidence of an expert, the putter going back and through, the ball rolling surely to the hole and stopping an inch short of falling in as if held back by the hand of an invisible force.

If the member continued watching, he'd see the player rake back the ball with his putter and try once more, again coming up just short. Then a third try with the same result. By this time any upstanding member of the old club would have glanced down the eighteenth fairway to see if there was a group being held up in their play to the green by this player's repeated attempts. There was none. Looking back to the green, the member would have seen the man's caddie standing over that same putt and waggling the putter around like it was a burning marshmallow on a stick. From somewhere out of this convoluted routine a quick jab at the ball sent it rolling toward the elusive target. The ball rolled toward the cup, and in.

If the member attended carefully, he would have seen and heard the observing player shake his head and mutter, "I'll never understand this game." The player then went over to the old caddie, put his arm over the man's shoulder, and the two walked off the green.

About the author:

Bob Brown has written golf, management and self-improvement books and is a hands-on educator and consultant. He is executive director of Keepers of the Game, a non-profit association dedicated to the core values of golf and president of Collective Wisdom, Inc.

You might also enjoy:

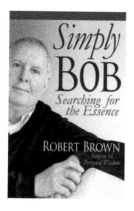

The story of Bob's search for the meaning of life. Bob's life was shattered in under seven seconds. It wasn't illness or accident. It was a documentary movie in high school and it took him forty years to recover.

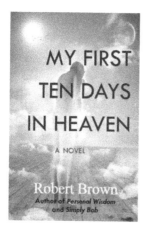

An atheist finds himself in Heaven, and wonders who made the mistake.

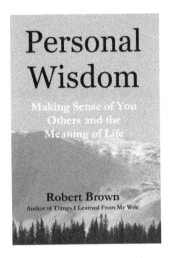

Personal Wisdom

Making Sense of You Others and the Meaning of Life

Robert Brown
Author of Things I Learned From My Wife

Bob's ideas, tips and tools to live an absolutely wonderful life.

Bob learned early and often that a wife has wisdom beyond understanding.

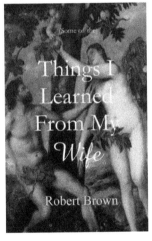

(Some of the)

Things I Learned From My Wife

Robert Brown

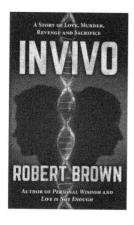

It is spring, 1996 in a small university town on the east coast of Scotland. Harold Spencer, MD, PhD is in the middle of a bold experiment to cure genetic disease. Opponents say he is going too far and too fast; yet he is driven to end the heartbreak of parents and the early end to so many lives. The breakthrough he has sought is within reach. Yet disaster lurks, within the town and within his own lab.

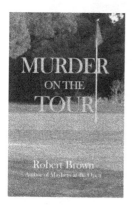

Golf is a gentleman's game, until players turn up dead. Tour rookie Kevin Turner is within one bad bounce of quitting. If he fails to win a check in Las Vegas, he's out of money and down the road. Foot, his semi-retired businessman caddie will let him go, too. He hates quitters. It is Tour golf with a few murders, a beautiful woman, a rich caddie and a desperate rookie.

CPSIA information can be obtained
at www.ICGtesting.com
Printed in the USA
FSHW010621020519
57778FS

9 781537 558127